STANDUP GUY

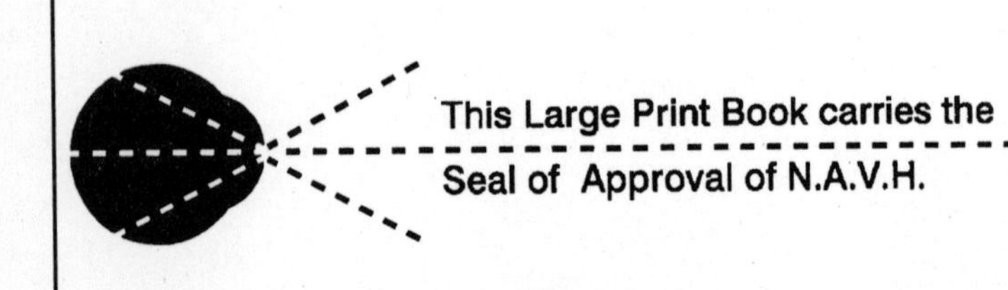
This Large Print Book carries the
Seal of Approval of N.A.V.H.

STANDUP GUY

STUART WOODS

THORNDIKE PRESS
A part of Gale, Cengage Learning

GALE
CENGAGE Learning

Detroit • New York • San Francisco • New Haven, Conn • Waterville, Maine • London

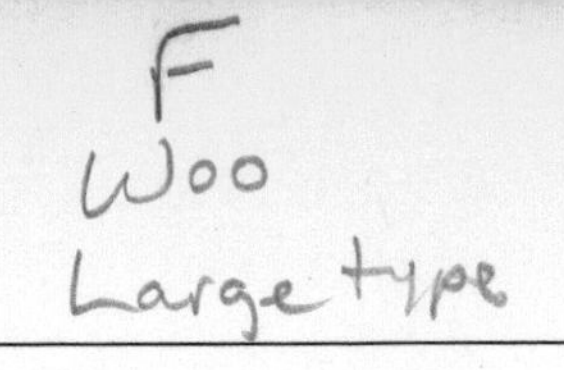

Thorndike Press, a part of Gale, Cengage Learning.

Thorndike Press® Large Print Basic.
The text of this Large Print edition is unabridged.
Other aspects of the book may vary from the original edition.
Set in 16 pt. Plantin.

LIBRARY OF CONGRESS CATALOGING-IN-PUBLICATION DATA

Woods, Stuart.
Standup guy / by Stuart Woods. — Large print edition.
pages ; cm. — (Thorndike Press large print basic)
ISBN 978-1-4104-6388-3 (hardcover) — ISBN 1-4104-6388-5 (hardcover)
1. Barrington, Stone (Fictitious character)—Fiction. 2. Private investigators—Fiction. 3. Large type books. I. Title.
PS3573.O642S73 2014b
813'.54—dc23 2013040436

Published in 2014 by arrangement with G. P. Putnam's Sons, a member of Penguin Group (USA) LLC, a Penguin Random House Company

Printed in the United States of America
1 2 3 4 5 6 7 18 17 16 15 14

STANDUP GUY

1

Stone Barrington made it from his bed to his desk by ten AM, after something of a struggle with jet lag. Granted, the three-hour time change between Los Angeles and New York was not a killer, but it mattered. As soon as he sat down his intercom buzzed.

"Yes?" he said to his secretary, Joan Robertson.

"You have a visitor," she said, "name of John Fratelli. Says he's a friend of Eduardo."

"Send him in," Stone said. Any friend of Eduardo Bianci's was a friend of his.

A vision of the mid-to-late twentieth century appeared in the doorway.

"Mr. Barrington? May I come in?"

"Of course," Stone said, rising to greet his visitor, who was wearing a boxy, light gray flannel suit, a starched white shirt, and what appeared to be a clip-on bow tie. He was carrying a salesman's suitcase and a porkpie hat and had a haircut that had probably been accomplished entirely with electric clippers — short sides and a Brylcreemed top. "Come in and have a seat, Mr. Fratelli."

"Thank you," the man replied. "It's nice of you to see me." This was delivered in what appeared to be an old-fashioned Brooklyn accent, the likes of which had not been heard for many years from a man as young as Fratelli, who appeared to be no older than fifty. He came in and took the proffered chair across the desk and set down the suitcase.

"How may I help you?" Stone said, hoping the man was not a salesman.

Fratelli stood again, reached into a pocket, and pulled out a wad of bills; he peeled off five hundreds and placed them carefully on Stone's desk.

"All right," Stone said, "you've paid for a consultation and bought yourself some attorney-client confidentiality."

"Good," Fratelli said, sitting down again.

"I should inform you, though, that if you confess to a crime and I end up representing you in court, I will not be able to call you to the stand to testify on your own behalf."

"Why not?" Fratelli inquired.

"Because I cannot call a witness to the stand who I know will lie under oath."

"I understand," Fratelli said. "That's reasonable, I guess."

"How is Mr. Bianci?" Stone asked, by way of getting the man to relax.

"Who?"

"Did you not tell my secretary that Eduardo had sent you to me?"

"Oh, I meant Eduardo Buono."

"Not Bianci?"

"No, Buono."

"I don't know anyone by that name," Stone said.

"Well, he knows you."

"How does he know me?"

"He read an article about you in a magazine — *Vanity Fair.*"

That magazine had published an excerpt from a book about Stone's late wife, Arrington. "I'm afraid I —"

"Eduardo says you're a standup guy."

"Well, as kind a characterization as that may be —"

"Eduardo and I shared a living space for twenty-two years."

"I'm happy for you both, but that still doesn't —"

"Eduardo was a very smart man, even if he did get caught."

"Ahhhh," Stone said. Now he understood. "Where did you do your time, Mr. Fratelli?"

"Sing Sing."

"And when did you get out?"

"Yesterday afternoon."

"How long were you away?"

"Twenty-five years, to the day. I did my whole sentence, no parole."

"What was the rap?"

"Armed robbery. I did it, no excuses. That's why I didn't apply for parole."

"Then you, not I, are the standup guy, Mr. Fratelli."

Fratelli actually blushed. "Thank you," he said softly.

"Now, please tell me, how can I help you?"

"Eduardo left me two million dollars," he said. "And change."

"Congratulations, but if you're looking for investment advice, I'm not —"

"I'm looking for advice on how not to go back to prison," Fratelli said.

"That's fairly simple, Mr. Fratelli — don't commit another crime."

"Oh, sure, but —"

"Oh, I think I see. Did Mr. Buono acquire your inheritance by extralegal means?"

"Exactly."

"Did he rob somebody?"

"Exactly, but Eduardo said the statue was done."

That stopped Stone in his tracks for a moment, then he figured it out. "Do you mean the statute? The statute of limitations?"

"That's it!"

"Well, the statute of limitations for robbery is five years, so if you and Mr. Buono were cellmates for twenty-two years . . ."

"So it's mine, then?"

"I wouldn't go as far as that," Stone said. "It's problematical."

"I was afraid you'd say something like that."

"Mr. Fratelli, let me put this hypothetically, since you and I do not want to discuss a real crime."

"Okay, I get that."

"If prisoner A committed a crime, and the statute of limitations has run out, then he can mention prisoner B in his will."

"It wasn't exactly like that," Fratelli said. "There wasn't — I mean, in this story prisoner A didn't have a will, he had a safe-deposit box. He, hypothetically speaking, had a bank account, and every quarter for twenty-five years, the bank deducted the rental of the safe-deposit box from his account. From time to time, his lawyer deposited funds."

"And prisoner B has access to the box?"

"Prisoner A told me — ah, him — where to find the key."

"And has prisoner B visited the box?"
"You could say that."
"And he emptied the box?"
"About an hour ago," Fratelli said. "Just as soon as the bank opened, prisoner B was there with the key."
"Did anyone see what he removed from the box?"
"No, he was in a little closet, and he had brought a suitcase. He just walked out with the money."
"I see."
"His question is, what's he going to do with it?"
"Whatever he likes," Stone said. "As long as no one knows he has it."
"Does prisoner B have the money legally?"
"A better question might be, is anyone going to be looking for the money? A widow? A nephew? A bookie?"
"He didn't have any of those, and nobody knows about the money. Hypothetically."
"How about the lawyer who made the bank deposits?"
"He died three weeks ago."
"Then, Mr. Fratelli, prisoner B is laughing."
Fratelli laughed.
"His first move should be to go to a bank — a different bank — open a checking ac-

count with less than ten thousand dollars, then rent another safe-deposit box. After that, he could remove enough money periodically to support himself. Lashing out with large amounts could get him into trouble, as you might imagine. People will steal, after all."

"Yes, they will," Fratelli said.

"Ten thousand dollars is the magic number. If prisoner B banks that much, a form reporting it goes to the Internal Revenue Service, and, although they are said to have stacks of those forms, which they never read, it's not a good idea to generate such a form. After all, they may start reading faster, or they may teach a computer how to read them."

"That's good advice," Fratelli said.

"One other thing: if you should seek legal advice again, it might be in your interests to go to an attorney who has not heard this hypothetical story."

Fratelli stood up. "Thank you, Mr. Barrington," he said, offering his hand.

They shook, Fratelli left, and Stone opened a desk drawer and raked the little stack of hundreds into it.

Joan came in a moment later. "While you were talking to Mr. Fratelli, a secretary to the president of the United States called.

You're invited to dinner tomorrow evening with President and Mrs. Lee at their apartment in the Carlyle."

Stone had not heard from the Lees in months. "Call back and say that I accept, with pleasure."

"You may bring a date."

Stone's current squeeze, the fashion designer Emma Tweed, had returned to her native London for a few weeks. "Say that I will come alone."

2

Stone wore a dark suit and a tie, because he didn't know who else was invited. He entered the Carlyle Hotel and got off the elevator at the penthouse level, where he was greeted by two Secret Service agents to whom he identified himself. That wasn't good enough; they went over him with the wand.

Katherine Rule Lee, now retired as director of Central Intelligence, answered the door. She was wearing tight jeans and a sweater, and she looked good in both. "Oh, Stone," she said, offering both cheeks to be kissed and giving him a hug, "nobody told you to dress down?"

"I didn't get that part of the message," Stone said, "but I'm not in the least uncomfortable."

"Will's watching the news. Knob Creek?"

"Perfect."

She pointed him at the living room, then

went to the bar, while he continued.

Will Lee stood up and offered his hand. "Good to see you, Stone."

"And you, Mr. President."

"It's still Will."

"Good to see you, Will."

The president waved him to a chair, and Kate brought him his drink.

"They're showing excerpts from last night's Democratic campaign debate," Will said.

The three of them watched in silence until the program ended, then Will turned off the TV. "What did you think?" he asked Stone.

"I think there are at least three guys and one woman in that field who would make a good president."

"And?"

"And not one who could win against Taft Duncan," Stone said, referring to the Speaker of the House and presumptive Republican nominee.

"I'm afraid I agree," Will said. "What have you been up to Stone?"

"I've just come back from Los Angeles, where my son, Peter, who recently graduated from Yale, has established himself on the Centurion Studios lot as a director. Dino's son, Ben, is his partner, and Peter's girlfriend, Hattie Patrick, writes the music for their films."

"I've met them all, last year at the opening of The Arrington," Will said. "Remember?"

"How could I forget?" Stone said.

They all shared a laugh.

"And what does the next year hold for you?"

"My year seems oddly empty, with Peter on the other side of the country, so I guess I'll have to think about practicing some law. Bill Eggers is making broad hints about my absences from the firm."

"Ah, yes, the partners won't want to share income with one of their number who is an absentee."

"Well, I have made a lot of rain," Stone said, "so I don't think I have to worry about them ganging up on me. What brings you to town?"

"Well, Kate is supposed to have an informal meeting with the board of Strategic Services tomorrow evening."

"Yes, I know, I'll be at the dinner." Kate had been invited to join the board of directors after Will left office.

"Our other reason for being here is to see you," Will said.

That puzzled Stone. "Oh?"

A man in a white jacket appeared and announced dinner, so they all went to a table with a spectacular view of the New York City skyline. Stone took a sip of his wine and waited for the president to finish his thought.

"Stone," Will said, "the day before yesterday I received a bundle of twenty letters, each of them written by a Democratic Party bigwig or a major campaign contributor, all individually composed but with the same subject. Can you guess what that subject was?"

"Well, it seems a little late in the game to get a constitutional amendment passed that would allow you to run for a third term."

"Thank God for that," Will said. "What they wanted was what they see as the next best thing." He sat silently and waited for the penny to drop.

It took Stone a moment. "Kate," he said finally. "They want Kate to run."

"Terrible idea, isn't it?" Kate said. She had been quiet until now.

"I think it's a terrific idea," Stone said. "But we're halfway through the primaries."

"My very point," Kate said, "but Will doesn't think that is an impediment."

"And I think Stone can figure out why," Will said.

"Because it looks like none of the candidates is going to have anything like a majority of the delegates going into the first ballot at the convention."

"Right you are."

"So, for the first time in I-don't-know-how-long, we'd have a brokered convention?"

"Since 1952," Will said, "when Adlai Stevenson got the nomination. We've had some close brushes since, but not the real thing. The primary process usually works to nominate a candidate."

Stone thought about that. "I was just thinking about Gore Vidal's play *The Best Man,* which dealt with that subject."

"Do you remember what each candidate needed to get the nomination?"

"Yes, the support of an earlier president, a Trumanesque figure."

"Right."

"Well, I don't think Kate would have any trouble getting the support of the sitting president, would she?"

"I'm trying to get him to withhold that support," Kate said.

"Actually, she doesn't have to try," Will said. "It would be politically impossible for me to support her."

"The Republicans would say you're trying to create a dynasty," Stone said.

"Not just the Republicans," Will replied. "A lot of Democrats, too, especially the three or four leading candidates."

"So, you'd have to sit back, clam up, and wait for the convention to sort it out — after the first ballot."

"Exactly," Will said.

"You don't really think anybody's going to buy that, do you?" Stone asked.

"Of course not. All the commentators and not a few of the delegates will say I'm pulling all the strings."

"And how would you handle that?"

"By not pulling any strings."

"You mean you'd actually sit out the nomination without showing the slightest support for Kate?"

"Not so much as a nod or a wink," Will replied. "And not a word of advice to her or any of her supporters on obtaining the nomination. If she gets it, then I'll shoot my mouth off at every opportunity, of course, but after tonight, I won't say a word to her or anyone else on the subject, except 'no comment.' "

"You see how crazy this is?" Kate said.

"Kate," Stone said, "let me ask you a question: do you think you'd make a good president?"

"I think I'd make a sensational president,"

Kate said.

Stone turned to Will. "And, Will, do you think she can beat Taft Duncan?"

"In my last word on the subject, yes," Will said. He looked at his watch. "I'd better hurry," he said. "I'm sneaking into the Blue Note to hear Chris Botti's last set."

"Can I come with you?" Stone asked. "I'm a big Chris Botti fan."

"No, you have a meeting to attend."

"What meeting is that?"

"In about an hour the twenty people who wrote me those letters are arriving here for a drink with Kate, so I can't be here. But you can."

Will got up and shook Stone's hand. "Hope to see you soon, Stone, but when I do, I don't want to hear a word about Kate's plans."

"Gotcha, Will." He and Kate watched him disappear out the door, two Secret Service agents close behind him.

"Well," Kate said, heaving a sigh. "Now I have only you to help me greet the throng."

"What are you going to say to them?" Stone asked.

"I think it's better if you hear it at the same time they do," she said. "Now, if you'll excuse me, I have to get into something more presidential." She got up and left Stone to contemplate his dessert.

3

Kate came back at five minutes before the hour and handed Stone a sheet of paper. "Here's the list of the invitees. The good news is, every one of them accepted."

Stone scanned the list quickly. "This is a great tribute to you," he said. He knew half a dozen of them, at least slightly; Bill Eggers, the managing partner of Stone's law firm, Woodman & Weld, and Mike Freeman, CEO of the world's second-largest security firm, Strategic Services, were close friends. Half of them were women, either politicians or businesspeople.

Kate took back the list and shoved it into the pocket of her jacket.

"Your suit looks great, perfect for the occasion," Stone said.

"I won't be wearing Chanel suits often after tonight," she said. "I'll have to expand my J. Crew wardrobe, though. They're bringing some things for me to look at tomorrow."

"Are you nervous about this meeting?"

"I am. It's the first time I've ever asked for anyone's support, except for Will. Will you introduce me when everyone's here?"

"Of course. Is there anything in particular you'd like me to say?"

"Just say what Will would say, if he were here. Thank them for their letters, which Will turned over to me, and explain his hands-off position."

"He's serious about it, then?"

"Dead serious. He says he won't even discuss it with me. And explain to them that they shouldn't try to discuss it with him."

"You know this is going to be in the papers tomorrow, don't you?"

"I wouldn't be shocked," she replied. "Someone will blab, it's human nature, I suppose."

The doorbell rang, and Kate led Stone into the living room to await the guests while the butler answered the door.

Half an hour later, all of the invitees had arrived and were at least halfway through their first drink. Kate nodded at Stone; he stood and tapped his signet ring loudly against his glass, then set down his drink. Silence fell.

"Good evening to all of you," Stone said.

"My name is Stone Barrington. I know some of you and look forward to getting to know you all over the next few months. The president was unable to join us, as he has an extremely important appointment to hear some jazz down in the Village."

That got a good laugh.

"And, I should tell you, that wasn't a joke. The president won't be joining us at any of our meetings or speaking to any of us or anyone else about the subject of this meeting. He recognizes that this is the beginning of an unusual — no, a *unique* political campaign, and he believes he can best serve the interests of his party and his country by staying the hell out of it. So, please, when you next see him, make no reference to Kate and her campaign. He did want you to know, however, that after the convention has made its choice, he will have a great deal to say about his wife's campaign to you and to anybody else who will listen. Now, Kate wants to talk to us and tell us how we can help." He turned and extended a hand toward the first lady.

"Ladies, gentlemen, you know why you are all here, because you started this. You were kind enough to get together and write individually to Will, suggesting a course of action. Will immediately turned your letters over to me, and told me to get on with it, if that's what I wanted to do. That *is* what I want to do, and I am going to need your continuing help and advice. Since this is all your fault, you are now the steering committee for my campaign."

"How much is it going to cost us, Kate?" someone called from the back of the room.

"All I want from you is your friendship, your affection, your wisdom . . . and a check for a million dollars payable to a superPAC that's being set up as we speak." Loud laughter. "And that's just for starters, because I am going to ask each of you — at the moment we secure the nomination — to get on the phone and start raising twenty-five million dollars each, and the smaller the contributions, the better. That will give us half a billion dollars to run on — about half of what we'll need for the whole campaign.

"Now, I know it will be difficult for all of us not to discuss this with anyone else — spouses, lovers, business associates, barbers, bookies — but every day you can keep your mouth shut about this evening and our mutual intentions, the stronger the move we make will be when we make it. I'm doing half a dozen exit interviews while I'm in New York, and I don't want to have to face questions about my political intentions. At this moment, you are the only people who know of my intentions. Now, everybody grab a seat, if you can find one, and start asking me questions."

Stone sat quietly and marveled at how knowledgeable, fluent, concise, and witty Kate was when fielding the questions. She was going to be great on the road and in town hall meetings. The questions went on for an hour, then there was another half hour of chatting, exchanging of business cards, and congratulating Kate. Stone was the last to leave.

"I thought that went just perfectly," he said to Kate at the door.

"I thought so, too, Stone, and thank you for being here and helping me in Will's absence."

"I'm very glad to be here, and I'll be very glad to help in any way I can. Let me know when you need my check."

They hugged and kissed, and Stone left the apartment feeling that he had been part of something historic. As he waited for the elevator, the doors opened and Will Lee stepped out. "How did it go?" he asked, then threw up a hand. "No, I don't want to know."

"How was Chris Botti?"

"Brilliant."

"So was Kate."

Will clapped his hands over his ears, and Stone got onto the elevator, laughing.

When he got home, he found a pocket recorder and dictated an account — everything he could remember about the evening.

He went to bed excited.

4

Stone took his breakfast tray off the dumbwaiter, along with the two morning papers, the *New York Times* and the *Daily News.*

As he ate his eggs and bacon he went over the lead stories of both papers: not a word about last night's event. He switched on the TV and was greeted by the sight of the president leaving the Blue Note. A local reporter stuck a microphone in his face.

"Mr. President, where's the first lady? Couldn't you get a date?"

Will laughed. "She had a dinner date with somebody else," he said.

"And who was that?"

"She wouldn't tell me." He got into the waiting SUV and drove away.

Immediately after Stone reached his desk, Joan buzzed. "John Fratelli to see you."

"Again?"

"He says it's urgent."

"All right, send him in."

Fratelli appeared in the doorway, still carrying his suitcase.

Stone waved him in. "So, Mr. Fratelli, why aren't you at a bank opening an account?"

"I tried," Fratelli said, holding up his suitcase to display three bullet holes.

"Are you hurt?"

"The money stopped the rounds," he said. "I wasn't heeled, so all I could do was hide behind my bag."

"Did you call the police?"

"I didn't think that was such a good idea."

"I see your point," Stone said. "What bank did you go to?"

"One on the corner of Forty-second and Third. I forget the name."

"And you never got inside?"

"No."

"Any idea who shot at you?"

"We're still under lawyer confidentiality?"

"Yep."

"I don't know if you're old enough to remember," Fratelli said, "but a long time ago, some guys stuck up a freight terminal at JFK and walked away with a big crate full of money that was being shipped to a foreign bank."

"I'm old enough to remember," Stone said. "And I suppose your friend Buono was one of them?"

"He was their leader," Fratelli said, "and some of them were unhappy with their cut. Eddie took half, something like seven million, and the others split the rest. They got away clean, and Eddie told them all to lie low for eighteen months, not to buy anything expensive or showy, just to live regular, you know?"

"I know," Stone said.

"Well, all of a sudden half a dozen bookies in Brooklyn got paid what they were owed, so right away, the street knew who pulled the job. Then one of them bought a red Cadillac convertible, and all of a sudden there were cops everywhere."

"As I recall, the busts came only a couple of weeks after the robbery," Stone said.

"That's right."

"Mr. Fratelli, it sounds like what you're telling me is that Eddie didn't spend any of his half of the money — what was it? Seven million?"

Fratelli nodded solemnly.

"But you only got the two million in the safe-deposit box?"

Fratelli nodded again.

"Arithmetic tells me there's another five million out there somewhere."

Fratelli nodded.

"How many guys did the job?"

"Five."

"How many are still alive?"

"Two."

"And where are they?"

"Out," Fratelli said.

Stone held up a hand. "Don't tell me who they are."

"One of them was at Sing Sing when Eddie and me were. He made a couple of attempts to get Eddie to tell what he had done with his money, but I . . ."

"You were watching Eddie's back," Stone said.

Fratelli nodded. "For twenty-two years."

"Did you recognize the man who shot at you?"

"Two of them: one driving, one shooting. Young guys. I don't know any young guys."

"Mr. Fratelli," Stone said, "I think you need to get out of town."

"But I've still gotta —"

"The rest of the money, wherever it is, has been safe all these years — a few months more isn't going to hurt."

"I guess I'd better get on a plane, then."

"No, Mr. Fratelli, not a plane. These days everything gets X-rayed."

"Train?"

"A better idea, but your shooters might

be watching. Same with the bus station."

"Then how'm I going to get out of town?"

"I don't suppose you have a driver's license?"

"Not anymore."

Stone thought about it. "Do you know what a livery service is?"

"No. Uniforms?"

"Cars — black Lincolns, mostly, with drivers. They're an expensive way to travel, but you can afford it." Stone rummaged in his desk drawer, came up with a card, and handed it to Fratelli. "This is a big one, a chain. You don't want to deal with a small, neighborhood outfit — no telling who owns it. What you do is, you pick a place you want to go, say Pittsburgh."

"Why Pittsburgh?"

"It's just an example. You call this service and tell them you want a car to drive you there. They'll be happy to take cash. Then, after you're under way, you change your mind and tell the driver you want to go somewhere else, like Boston or Washington, D.C. Anyplace with train service. When you get there, have him drive you to the station and take a train to anywhere you like, except back to New York."

"Okay, that makes sense."

"Something else."

"What else?"

"You need a change in your clothing, to blend in better."

"What kind of clothing should I get?"

"Go to Brooks Brothers. You know it?"

"Yeah, it used to be on Madison."

"It still is. Buy a couple of suits, some shirts and ties, the works — a wardrobe. They sell luggage there, too. Buy a couple of pieces, insist that they fit your suits while you wait. Buy a new hat, and when you get a chance, grow some hair, maybe a mustache. Next time you get a haircut, don't let the barber use electric clippers. You getting the picture?"

"Yeah, I want to look like a regular businessman. But I don't know where to go after that."

"Pick someplace nice, take a vacation, enjoy yourself."

"Maybe Florida," Fratelli said, smiling a little.

"Don't tell me," Stone said. "Another thing, on your way to Brooks Brothers, tell the cabdriver to find a Radio Shack."

"They still got those?"

"They still got those. Buy something called a throwaway cell phone — you'll find it useful, and don't forget to recharge it every night when you go to bed."

"Who am I going to call?"

"Use it to make hotel reservations on your trip. Another thing, when you open your bank account, ask them to give you something called a debit card. You can use it like a credit card, and they'll take your charges out of your account."

"This is all very good advice, Mr. Barrington."

"Don't mention it." Stone picked up the phone and buzzed Joan. "Please hail a cab for Mr. Fratelli," he said. "I don't want him standing on the street, looking for one." He hung up. "Good luck, Mr. Fratelli. I don't suppose we'll be meeting again." Stone leaned a little on that.

"Yeah, right," Fratelli said. He put some more hundreds on Stone's desk and left.

Stone's private line rang, and he picked it up. "Hello?"

"It's Dino. You up for dinner tonight?"

"Sure."

"Eight at Patroon?"

"See you there."

5

Stone arrived at Patroon as Dino was getting out of his car, a large black SUV. He clapped his friend on the back. "No more town car?"

"They stopped making them, and the department got these tanks to replace them."

A moment later, after a warm greeting from Patroon's owner, Ken Aretzky, they were seated at their usual table. There was really no replacement for Elaine's, without Elaine, but Patroon was serving pretty well.

Drinks arrived without being ordered.

"So where's Viv?" Stone said, asking after Dino's wife.

"Working, where else? Mike Freeman keeps her busy." Viv was a retired detective sergeant, now working for Strategic Services.

"Oh, shit," Stone said, "I forgot, I was supposed to be at Strategic Services an hour ago. Kate Lee is stopping by to get acquainted with the board."

"You want to leave?"

"No, it's too late, it was just for drinks." Stone looked around to see if anyone was close enough to overhear them. "Can you keep a secret?"

"You ask me that after all these years?"

"You have a wife, now."

"So I can't tell Viv whatever this is?"

"Not a word — not until you see it in the papers, if you do."

"Okay, okay, unburden yourself, or you'll explode."

"K. is going to run for president."

"President of what?"

"Not so loud. The U.S."

"Can she do that?"

"She's a natural-born American citizen."

"But, I mean . . ."

"I know what you mean, and the answer is yes, she can do that."

"But the primaries?"

"She's going to wait until the convention."

Dino gave that some thought. "Oh, I see, Will doesn't think anybody will get a majority?"

"Not on the first ballot."

"Sounds tricky."

"Only if someone pulls way ahead during

the primaries, and the polls don't show that happening."

Dino thought some more. "She'd make a terrific president."

"That's what she said."

"Stone, can this work? Can she raise the money?"

"She's already raised twenty-one million: twenty other people and me."

"She can't run on that."

"And each of the twenty-one has agreed to raise another twenty-five million."

Dino flinched. "Don't look at *me.*"

Menus arrived, and they ordered.

"So," Dino said, "what are you going to get?"

"Get?"

"For raising all this money. Ambassador to the Court of Saint James's? Or will you have to settle for some banana republic?"

"Nothing but the satisfaction of seeing Will Lee's policies continued, and I expect Kate will have a lot of her own."

"What about the other twenty guys?"

"Men and women. They can fend for themselves."

"Yeah, I guess they can."

"Something else came up."

"Is it a secret?"

Stone thought about that. "Yes, I guess so.

Attorney-client privilege is involved."

"Oh, the shyster's seal of the confession."

"More or less. You remember that big heist at Kennedy, what, twenty-five years ago?"

"Buono," Dino said. "Eduardo Buono."

"What a memory!"

"Who could forget a fifteen-million-dollar heist? And less than half of it recovered." Dino took a swig of his scotch. "Hey, you didn't find the money, did you?"

"No, and I don't know where it is, but someone with whom I have recently become acquainted has, ah, stumbled across some of it."

"Wait a minute," Dino said, screwing up his forehead. "John Fratelli."

Stone gaped at him. "I didn't say that," he said, looking furtively around.

"He got sprung a couple of days ago."

"How could you know that?"

"I had a drink with Sean Donnelly last night. He was the lead detective on the case, retired fifteen years ago."

"I thought he was dead."

"He looks kind of dead, but I ran into him at P.J. Clarke's, so unless he's pulled off a resurrection, I guess he didn't die, quite."

"I guess."

"So, what sort of shape is Fratelli in after twenty-five years inside?"

"Oh, he's in remarkably . . . Wait a minute, I never mentioned that name."

"So the shyster's seal is still intact. Relax. Is Fratelli walking and talking?"

"Both."

"So Eddie Buono told him where the loot was."

"Maybe. Maybe some of it."

"How much?"

"Don't be so fucking nosy."

"I'm just curious."

"I know you're curious, but I can't have you whispering in Donnelly's shell-like ear."

"Why would I give a shit if John Fratelli has dipped into Buono's honeypot?"

"I seem to recall that you are a highly placed police official, chief of detectives, namely."

"I'm off duty," Dino said.

"You haven't been off duty since the day you graduated from the academy. And you would just love to bust this case wide open."

"I wouldn't mind seeing Donnelly get the credit for that."

"Not going to happen," Stone said.

"So where's Fratelli?"

"On vacation."

"Florida, huh?"

"Stop doing that! I didn't mention Florida!"

"You're a mine of non-information," Dino said.

"Dino, you can't act on any of this. You said you could keep a secret."

"No, I didn't. I said I wouldn't tell Viv."

"That was about the Kate thing, not the . . . client thing."

"I'll have to review our conversation in my mind, to see if that's true."

"Don't review, take my word for it. I'm not having a client of mine who's done his time getting sent up again for, ah, accepting an inheritance."

"Oh, well, the statute's expired, hasn't it?"

"Right."

"Unless 'inheriting' this sum is a new crime? Like receiving stolen goods?"

"Let it go, Dino."

"Okay, okay, I'm just busting your balls."

"It's what you do best, isn't it?"

They ate their dinner and talked about other things.

6

Stone's ass had barely touched his office chair the following morning, when Joan buzzed. "Mike Freeman on one."

Stone heaved a rueful sigh and picked up the phone. "I know, Mike, and I'm sorry."

"I hope something terrible happened to you that prevented your being there," Mike said.

"You're beginning to sound like Dino."

"I'm beginning to understand Dino's attitude," Mike said.

"I got embroiled in a discussion about a client and didn't realize that I'd missed the event until it was too late. I offer my abject apologies."

"Kate asked for you. A lot."

"I'll write her a note," Stone said. "Maybe if I include a check for a million dollars, that will mollify her."

"A very good idea."

"What's the name of the superPAC?"

"The Best Woman."
"Won't people guess whom it's for?"
"We're hoping most people will think it's for Hillary Clinton."
"Good luck with that."
"Look, this is going to get out anyway. I was amazed that it didn't make yesterday's papers."
"So was I. The event is already a day and a half old, and nothing's out there. Is it possible this could last awhile?"
"I don't think so," Mike said. "Frankly, I'll be relieved when it breaks."
"When it does, everybody will accuse Kate of being a spoiler for the other candidates. I'll bet she starts getting write-in votes in primary states."
"You go write her a note, now," Mike said. "I'll see you later."
Stone hung up, got out a sheet of his best stationery, and wrote his apology. He buzzed Joan. "Please make out a check to something called 'The Best Woman.' "
"For how much?"
"A million dollars."
"Good God, for that kind of money she'd *better* be the best!"
"And bring it to me for my signature with no further comments or questions, please."
"Yes, boss."

A moment later, she appeared with the check. Stone signed it, stuffed it into an envelope, and addressed it to the White House box number where Kate got her personal mail. "Post this, please. No, FedEx it."

"FedEx won't ship to a P.O. box."

"All right, make it 1600 Pennsylvania Avenue, D.C., plus the box number."

"Are you bribing the president?"

"Out."

"And by the way, you have a visitor." Joan walked out of the office.

"Who?" Stone asked, but she was already gone. Then John Fratelli filled his doorway — at least he thought it must be Fratelli, because the haircut was still the same. Stone waved him to a chair. Fratelli was wearing a double-breasted, pin-striped suit, a crisp white shirt, and a gold necktie. A pearl-gray fedora was in his free hand, and his shoes were new and elegant. He was pulling the largest, most beautifully burnished leather duffel Stone had ever seen — on wheels, yet. It seemed very heavy.

"Good morning," Fratelli said.

"Mr. Fratelli," Stone said, "you are a vision of loveliness."

"I took your advice," Fratelli said. "They were great at Brooks Brothers. Turns out

I'm a perfect forty-four extra long. All they had to do was fix the trouser bottoms." He sat down and turned the duffel on end, where it remained. "All I got to do now is grow some hair."

"And I see you got a larger piece of luggage," Stone said, then held up a hand. "I don't want to know why you needed it."

"I've got a smaller one for my new clothes," Fratelli said. "It's in the car."

"What car?"

"The livery Lincoln, remember?"

"Yes, but I thought you were getting out of town yesterday."

"I thought I might enjoy a night at the Plaza Hotel before I left," Fratelli said, looking pleased with himself. "I had a couple of drinks and a steak in the Oak Bar, but I had this bag with me at all times."

"I think you're going to have to find a safe place to leave the contents," Stone said. "You can't go everywhere with a bag that size and that heavy without people wondering, especially if you're paying cash for everything."

"You're right, I know, but when I saw me in the mirror in my new suit, I thought I deserved a night in a fine hotel. Oh, and I paid for it with my new debit card. That was very insightful of you, Mr. Barrington.

Carrying enough cash to do business does get to be a burden."

"Has anyone taken a shot at you today?"

"Not yet," Fratelli answered.

"Then your disguise must be working."

"So far."

"Then you should get on the road, before someone from your past recognizes you."

"You know," Fratelli said, "I would have thought that getting recognized by somebody from my past would have been impossible — until yesterday." He stood up, reached into an inside pocket, withdrew an envelope, and laid it on Stone's desk. "I don't think we'll be meeting again," he said, "and I didn't want you to think I didn't appreciate your advice." He put on his fedora, gave it a tap to settle it, and wheeled his money out of Stone's office.

"Good luck!" Stone called after him, and he answered with a little wave. Stone picked up the envelope and counted the money, then inspected it. The picture of Benjamin Franklin was different from that on the current bills, and the Treasury seal and serial numbers were in red ink.

Stone buzzed Joan and asked her to come in. He counted all the hundreds that Fratelli had given him and handed them to her. "Please deposit this three thousand dollars into my main account, but do it at a different branch, where you're not known."

Joan looked at the money, then back at him. "Am I going to get arrested?"

"Probably not," Stone said. "Now get out of here."

"If I'm busted, I'm going to tell them everything." Joan shrugged.

"You don't know anything," Stone pointed out. "You're just making a bank deposit."

"Hah!" she cried as she left.

7

Less than an hour had passed, and Joan had returned from making her bank deposit. She buzzed Stone. "A Detective Donnelly to see you," she said.

"Tell him, since he doesn't have an appointment, he'll have to wait."

"Gotcha."

Stone read the *New York Times* and did the crossword puzzle, then he picked up the phone. "You may send in Detective Donnelly," he said.

Sean Donnelly, always a big guy, had gained weight since Stone had last seen him.

"Sean," he said. "Long time." They shook hands, and Stone waved him to a chair. "What's up?"

"I believe you have a client named Johnny Fratelli," Sean said.

"Well, Sean, if I did have such a client I would be unable to either confirm or deny it, because my client list is confidential."

"You know he's your client, I know he's your client. Why?"

"Sean, after all these years in the department, do I have to explain the concept of client-attorney confidentiality to you?"

"He was seen coming out of this office yesterday."

"Was he? Maybe he just came in to ask directions. People do that sort of thing all the time."

"He was carrying a heavy suitcase with bullet holes in it. Somebody shot at him."

"Well, Sean, shouldn't you be looking for a shooter at this time, instead of harassing an attorney for information you know he couldn't give you, even if he wanted to?"

"I remember when you were a smart-ass detective third grade," Sean said.

"I remember that, too," Stone replied. "Why don't we talk about that instead of . . . What was that name again?"

"Johnny Fratelli, and you're still a smart-ass."

"I expect you could gather a large body of opinion behind that statement, Sean, especially at the NYPD, but discussing it at length would be a waste of our time. Instead, why don't you tell me what this is all about? I'm dying to know."

"It's about seven million dollars," Sean said.

"And to whom do those funds belong?"

Sean sputtered a little. "There's some question about that."

"If you're looking for it, then I suppose it must be stolen money."

"It is."

"And when was it stolen?"

"Roughly twenty-five years ago."

"Then that theft has been erased by the statute of limitations. You've heard of that, haven't you?"

"Sure, I've heard of it," Sean said. He was turning a little red now.

"Then on what legal grounds are you pursuing this money?"

"Grounds?"

"Sean, think back to the Police Academy. One day there was a lecture on the legal grounds for charging a person with a crime. Were you out sick that day?"

"I know about grounds."

"And I should also point out that you have not been a police officer for what, fifteen years? What is this, some sort of citizen's investigation?"

"I don't care about the crime, and I don't care about Fratelli. I just want the money back."

"Back? Did you ever have the money?"

"I want to give it back to its owner."

"And who might that be? Let's see." Stone turned to his laptop and did some Googling. "Ah, the Acme International Transfer Corporation, now defunct. Sean, I'm afraid the owner no longer exists, not since 1989. And the money? Well, I'm very much afraid that belongs to whoever possesses it, under the long-standing and universally accepted legal principle known as 'Finders, Keepers.' See the Magna Carta, Article Four, Section Three."

"Now, listen —"

"You can't argue with the Magna Carta, Sean."

"You're about to get yourself in some very big trouble, Stone."

"Come off it, Sean. You blew this case a quarter of a century ago, and now you've heard that this guy . . ."

"Fratelli."

". . . Fratelli got himself recently sprung — on parole?"

"Nah."

"Sprung after doing all his time like a standup guy, and now you and your friends want to rob him?"

"What friends?" Sean asked, looking alarmed.

"Well, I'm assuming that a graduate of the New York City Police Academy and a veteran trained marksman of the NYPD, if he took a shot at a guy, would hit him and not put three rounds into a suitcase, so therefore he must have had some less talented and inexperienced help."

"There could be a cut in this for you."

"Sean, I don't need your cut, I'm awash in dough. Don't you read the gutter press anymore?"

"Yeah, I read about that," Sean said disconsolately. "All right, I asked you nice, I offered you a cut, you gave me nothing."

"Nicely summed up, Sean."

"But the next guys that ask ain't going to be so friendly about it."

"Now, now, Sean, threats are against the law."

"Okay, I tried," Sean said. He got up and shuffled out of the office.

"Have a good day, Sean, and don't shoot at anybody!" Stone called out. He heard the outside door slam.

Joan came into his office. "You know," she said, "things are going downhill around here. These last two guys are the kind of people you used to see before you became an upscale, corporate lawyer. Should I be worried?"

"Joan," Stone said, "it's you who keeps sending these people in to see me — it's not like I'm soliciting their business."

"Well," she said over her shoulder as she stalked out, "you must be doing *something* to attract them."

8

Stone had a sandwich at his desk, then Joan came in with the *New York Post,* which he subscribed to but rarely read. Today would be an exception.

RUSSIAN MOGUL DIES
ON PRIVATE JET

Yuri Majorov found dead of
"heart attack" at Moscow airport

Stone's heart leapt. He turned quickly to the inside pages for the story.

> Russian zillionaire Yuri Majorov arrived aboard his private Gulfstream jet airplane at a Moscow airport a few days ago, dead. Crew members aboard his airplane said that he had gone to sleep before the aircraft left Santa Monica Airport, in California, for Moscow, with a planned refueling stop in Gander, Newfoundland, where he

seemed to be still asleep. But after landing in Moscow, when a flight attendant attempted to awaken him, he was stone-cold dead.

Majorov's body was taken by Russian police to the Moscow morgue, where an autopsy was performed, but no cause of death could be determined. Authorities await the results of tox screening, to see if any drugs were present in his body, but these tests can take weeks or even months in Russia.

Majorov, the son of a KGB general, was educated at Moscow University and trained as an intelligence agent for the KGB. After the collapse of the Soviet Union he made a major fortune, forming cartels to buy state-owned businesses. He used the proceeds of this wealth to establish himself as a European businessman, but the smell of corruption lingered around him for the rest of his life, and he was rumored to be an important figure in the Russian Mafia.

Stone didn't know exactly how Majorov had died, but he knew who had effected his death, and he was immensely grateful to that person. His phone buzzed.

"Mike Freeman on one."

"Hello, Mike."

"Have you seen the *Post*?"

"I've just read it, and I feel a warm glow all over."

"You know who did that, don't you?"

"I do: he whose name shall not be spoken."

"I don't know if you saw the reports in the Los Angeles papers of the death of Vladimir Chernensky at the Bel-Air Hotel."

"I didn't, but I didn't need to."

"I hope that, since this business is all cleared up, our friend might soon be coming to work for us at Strategic Services."

"Have you spoken to him?"

"Not since leaving L.A., but I expect he'll be spending some more time out there. After all, he's teaching your son to fly."

"Peter already knows how to fly, now he's working on his instrument rating, and so are Ben and Hattie. In a few months, they'll all be flying the Mustang."

"Right."

"Have you thought of hiring him to work in L.A.? He seems to like it there."

"It crossed my mind, but that hasn't come up in our conversations."

"I'll be interested to know how it turns out."

"I'll let you know."

The two men hung up, and Stone leafed through the rest of the paper, finding nothing of interest. Then his phone buzzed again. "The first lady on line one," Joan said.

"Hello, Kate. I'm so sorry to have missed the event last night."

"Thank you, Stone, I got your very kind note. And your very nice check. Are you free for dinner this evening?"

"I am."

"Come and have it with me at the Carlyle. I'm on my own, and we can't go out together without causing talk."

"Love to."

"Seven?"

"See you then."

"Dress down this time."

"Will do."

Stone arrived on time, finding Kate in her usual jeans and a sweater. Somebody brought him bourbon in a glass and they sat down before the fireplace.

"How is your time in New York going?" he asked.

"Busy. Apart from my political ambitions, we're faced with dozens of requests for end-of-term interviews. Will is having me do as many of these as possible."

"I should think those interviews could be

very important to your ambitions," Stone said. "After all, they won't be hostile, they'll be warm and admiring, and they'll get the country accustomed to seeing your face and hearing you talk."

"Yes, well, I tried to do a minimum of those things when I was still DCI, so I guess I'm making up for lost time. Stone, I'm curious about something."

"What's that?"

"You've been close to Will and me for a long time, now, and you've never asked us for anything. Do you know how rare that is? Everybody, even among our closest friends, seems to want something — help with a bill in Congress, funding for some pet local project, something."

"It never crossed my mind," Stone said. "At least, not until this afternoon."

"Is there something we — Will — can do for you?"

"Since you ask, yes. But my request is an odd one, and one you and Will might not wish to grant, for all sorts of reasons."

"Tell me about it. If we can't do it, then nothing will go farther than this conversation, but maybe we can help."

"You recall the saga of Teddy Fay?"

Kate laughed. "How could I forget it? I knew him when he was still at the Agency, you know, and I liked him."

"He's surfaced," Stone said.

"Oh, God, where this time?"

"First, in New Mexico, where he saved my son's life."

Kate's jaw dropped. "How on earth did he do that?"

"You may remember a Russian mobster by the name of Majorov."

"Of course, you had all that trouble with him in Paris."

"Today's front page of the *New York Post* is devoted to him. He was flying from L.A. to Moscow in his private jet, and when he arrived in Moscow, he was dead, ostensibly of a heart attack."

"But?"

"Teddy did that. Majorov had been trying to take over The Arrington, and I wouldn't deal with him, so he went after Peter. Teddy took two assassins off Peter's trail when he, Ben Bacchetti, and Hattie Patrick drove across the country; then he turned up in L.A. and was helpful again. I owe him Peter's life."

"And you want what for Teddy?"

"A presidential pardon."

Kate's jaw dropped again. "I don't see —"

"Hear me out," Stone said. "Every president, at the end of his term, hands out pardons — sometimes few, sometimes many. Would it be possible for Will to issue a sealed pardon — say, at the request of the intelligence services — so that Teddy's name and the pardon's contents would never be disclosed?"

"I don't know if that's ever been done before," Kate said.

"Kate, I know what Teddy has done — or may have done, but he's never been convicted of anything in a court of law, and no notice has ever been given by the FBI that he's wanted for anything."

"You have a point," she said. "Let me talk with Will about it. I'm sure he'll want to get some advice, and I'll ask him to limit who he asks for it. I wish I could give you an answer now, but it will have to wait, maybe until near the end of Will's term."

"Thank you, Kate. It's an unusual request, and I'll understand if it can't be granted."

The butler called them to dinner, and they went in.

9

Stone was having his usual breakfast in bed when his private line rang. Caller ID said the U.K. was calling. "Hello?"

"Stone, it's Emma."

"Good morning, or rather, good afternoon." It was five hours later in London. "I hope you're well."

"Sort of well."

"That sounds like not great."

"Personally, I'm fine, but not business-wise."

"What's the problem? Not that I know a hell of a lot about business, but I'll help if I can."

"Somebody is copying our designs, stitch for stitch, and selling them at less than what it costs us to make them."

"Do you know who it is?"

"No, and I don't know how to find out."

"Have you called the police?"

"Yes, days ago, but they don't seem to take

this sort of thing seriously. They say I'd have more luck bringing a civil action, but I don't know who to sue."

Stone thought for a moment. "Maybe a private investigator would be the best thing."

"I don't know any private investigators."

"Neither do I, but I know a recently retired policeman, one Detective Chief Inspector Evelyn Throckmorton, who might be able to help."

"Throckmorton? You must be joking — it's like a name out of Sherlock Holmes."

"Yes, it is, isn't it. But he knows policemen all over Europe, so he could be useful to you."

"I don't see how."

"Tell me, how soon after you introduce something do the knockoffs appear?"

"Simultaneously. Once, a couple of days before."

"Then it sounds like an inside job."

"I know that term from film noir, but I don't know what it means."

"It means that somebody working for you — or for someone with access to your designs, like your manufacturer — is selling them to someone else."

"Ah, yes, I suppose I should have thought of that."

"I'd give it some thought. It's the first

thing Throckmorton would want to investigate. Is there someone who works for you that you don't entirely trust? A disgruntled ex-employee? Think along those lines. Would you like Throckmorton's number?"

"Yes, please."

Stone looked it up and gave it to her. "How are you coming along on moving some operations to Los Angeles?" He had an ulterior motive for wanting to know.

"Surprisingly well," she replied.

"It might be harder for people to steal your designs in Europe if you were working out of the United States."

"Oh, you just want me back in your bed!"

"Guilty!"

"If it's any consolation, I miss being there. Soon, I'm going to have to start picking up lads in pubs to quench my fires."

"Quenching fires is one of the things I do best," Stone said, "but it's hard on a transoceanic call. We could have phone sex, but all sorts of people might be listening."

"I'll see what I can do to move things along," she said. "We can't have the intelligence services eavesdropping on our sex lives."

"Then get your ass in gear!"

"Let me speak to your DCI Throckmorton. The sooner I get this resolved, the sooner I can be back in New York."

"Then why are you wasting time talking to me?"

"You're right! Goodbye!"

They both hung up.

Stone got up, shaved, showered, and dressed and went to his office. He had not even gotten through the mail when Joan buzzed. "There's a teddibly, teddibly British chap named Throckmorton on line one."

Stone pressed the button. "Evelyn?"

"Barrington."

"I don't suppose I can call you Detective Chief Inspector since you're retired, and Former Detective Chief Inspector seems a bit much. May we be on a first-name basis?"

"Stone," Throckmorton said.

"I trust you're enjoying your retirement."

"I was, until I heard from this woman, Tweed, to whom you gave my private number."

"It occurred to me that a DCI's pension might do with an occasional bolstering."

"Are you trying to sound British, old chap?"

"Hearing your voice brings it out in me. Are you taking the job, or did you tell her to get stuffed?"

"Who is this woman?"

"She's one of Britain's most famous

fashion designers, actually — just the sort of person you would never have heard of."

"Is she mad?"

"In the British sense of the word? No. But she is angry — her business is being attacked."

"So she said. Probably some disaffected clerk making a few quid on the side."

"That was my first thought, too."

"Can she pay?"

"In addition to being very famous, she is very successful."

"Ah, then it might not be entirely a waste of my time if I went to see her."

"It might not."

"What are you doing with yourself? I haven't seen you since you somehow poked your nose into that explosion at the American Embassy last year."

"I'm trying not to poke my nose into things like that," Stone said. "I'm just a quiet-living, respectable attorney-at-law these days, dabbling in my clients' businesses from time to time."

"I'm sure you're making ungodly amounts of money. That's what Americans do, isn't it?"

"Every chance we get. Now here's your chance to stuff your bank account by putting all those recently unused police skills to work in the private sector."

"Ah, yes, the private sector — never had much to do with that."

"Try it, you'll like it."

"What should I charge her?"

"To make that sort of suggestion would be a conflict of interest for me, since I have an interest in the lady. Let's just say that good businesspeople understand that people with skills must be reasonably well paid, and they expect to get what they pay for."

"Mmm, as much as that, eh?"

"Negotiate," Stone said.

"All right, I'll give her a go."

" 'It,' not 'her.' "

"Quite. Good day." Throckmorton hung up.

So did Stone.

10

Shortly before lunch, Joan buzzed. "Two gentlemen with badges to see you," she said.

Stone sighed. "Send them in."

They were not cops; that was obvious from their neatly cut and pressed suits and regimental-stripe neckties. The larger of the two men held up a wallet with a badge pinned to it. "United States Secret Service," he said. "I'm Special Agent Willard, this is Special Agent Griggs."

Stone thought Griggs looked familiar, but he couldn't place him. "Have a seat, gentlemen."

Willard removed a plastic envelope containing a bank note from his jacket pocket and handed it to Stone. "Do you recognize this?" he asked.

Stone looked at the money and handed it back. "Yes," he said. "It's a United States hundred-dollar bill."

Griggs laughed; Willard didn't.

"Do you recognize this particular bill?" he asked, handing it back to Stone.

"Well, I don't recognize the serial number, if that's what you mean. Otherwise, it looks just like every other hundred-dollar bill I've ever seen."

Willard handed him another hundred-dollar bill. "Compare it to this one, and tell me what you see."

Stone looked at the second bill, then again at the one in the plastic bag. "Slightly different portraits," he said, "but they're both Benjamin Franklin."

"Do you see the red seal on the one in the bag?" Willard asked.

Stone looked again. "Hard to miss," he said, "since it's red. Aren't you fellows trained in currency recognition? Why do you need my help?"

"Of course we're trained in currency recognition."

"Is it counterfeit?" Stone asked.

"No, it's perfectly genuine, it's just old."

"Agent Willis —"

"Willard."

"Willard. Is it legal tender?"

"Yes."

"Then what is it you want? I'm trying to help, but so far, I'm at a loss."

"This bill," Willard said, holding up the

plastic bag, "was deposited in your bank account the day before yesterday, by a woman I suspect is your secretary."

Stone buzzed Joan. "Can you come in for a moment, please?"

Joan came and leaned on the doorjamb. "Yes, Mr. Barrington?"

"These gentlemen work for the United States Treasury Department, and they would like to know if you deposited this" — he took the bag from Willard and handed it to her — "in my bank account the day before yesterday."

"Well," Joan said, "I did make a cash deposit the day before yesterday, but I don't recognize this particular bill. I hardly knew the ones I deposited."

"Thank you, Joan." She left, and Stone handed back the bill to Willard. "Anything else?" he asked.

"Mr. Barrington, where did you get the bill?"

"I expect I received it as payment for legal services," he said, "which is what we offer around here."

"Who paid you with this bill?"

"Neither I nor my secretary recognize this particular bill," Stone said. "I thought we both made that clear."

It was Willard's turn to sigh. "Mr. Barrington, can you recall receiving cash for payment during the last week or so?"

Stone stared at the ceiling for a moment and pretended to think. He was thinking about having Dover sole for lunch.

"Yes," he said, finally.

"And who made that payment?"

"Gentlemen," Stone said, sounding as patient as he could, "I am under the impression that, in addition to currency recognition, agents of your service receive some training in the law?"

"That is correct."

"Then you are aware of something called 'client-attorney confidentiality'?"

"So you decline to tell us who paid you with this note?"

"I decline to disclose the name or names of my clients," Stone said.

"We believe this bill to have been stolen," Willard said.

Stone frowned. "How recently? You did say it was old."

"Yes, it was part of the 1966 series of hundred-dollar bills, and we believe it was part of the loot in a robbery committed twenty-five years ago."

"And are you investigating that event?"

"We are."

"Sadly, gentlemen, you are wasting your

time. The statute of limitations would have expired five years after the robbery; therefore, the money you hold in that plastic bag is an innocent hundred-dollar bill."

"Mr. Barrington, there is no such thing as an innocent hundred-dollar bill."

"Well, I suppose you presume it to be guilty, since you have arrested it, but that hundred-dollar bill is entitled to the presumption of innocence. If it was once guilty, it has been pardoned by the statute of limitations. Now, if you took it from my bank account, please put it back, and leave it alone. I have bills to pay."

Griggs was having a hard time suppressing laughter, but Willard plowed on. "Mr. Barrington —"

Stone stood up. "Gentlemen, it has been a pleasure meeting you, but I don't see how I can be of further help. I wish you and that poor hundred-dollar bill a good day."

The agents got to their feet.

"Agent Griggs," Stone said, "you look familiar. Have we met?"

"In a manner of speaking," Griggs replied. "I was on the presidential detail last year when you visited the White House."

"Of course, that would be it. Good to see you again."

The two men filed out of the office, and

Stone heard the front door close behind them. Joan came in. “You knew that was going to happen, didn’t you? When you sent me to the bank?”

“I said you probably wouldn’t be arrested,” Stone said, “and I have probably kept my word.”

11

Stone polished off his Dover sole and took another sip of the Far Niente Chardonnay. "That was a delicious lunch, Bill," he said to the managing partner of Woodman & Weld. "I dreamed about it at my desk this morning." They were having lunch at Eggers's regular table in the Grill Room of the Four Seasons, which was downstairs in the Seagram Building, where the Woodman & Weld offices were located on four floors.

"I'm glad you enjoyed it," Eggers said.

"And I'm still enjoying the wine."

"Coffee?"

"Thank you, no, it keeps me awake in the afternoon."

Eggers chuckled. "I believe you had something of a wake-up call this morning,"

"I believe you have remarkable contacts in federal law enforcement."

"Why are you being investigated by the Department of the Treasury?"

"Something about an ancient hundred-dollar bill," Stone said, "going back to the sixties."

"A *stolen* hundred-dollar bill, I'm told."

"Possibly. I didn't ask it about its criminal record."

"Stone, you haven't developed a sideline in money laundering, have you?"

"Accepting cash for payment of services is not a sideline," Stone said. "Those funds have been duly recorded in my books and will, in due course, be disclosed on my tax return."

"You want to tell me what's going on here?"

"I believe I just explained that."

"I thought you had given up representing felonious clients when you became a partner of Woodman & Weld."

"Bill, if we gave up representing felonious clients, how would anybody at Woodman & Weld make a living?"

"You seem to have a low opinion of us."

"Certainly not! I have only the highest regard for my law firm and my partners."

"But you think our clients are felons?"

"Do you doubt that some of them are? Not that they ask us to represent them in such cases, but after all, that used to be what I spent a good part of my time doing for the firm, before I became a partner."

"Where do you find these people?"

"They seem to find me," Stone said. "This one got into my office by saying that Eduardo had recommended me."

"Eduardo Bianci is sending you criminal cases?"

"Turned out it was a different Eduardo, and it wasn't exactly a case. Not yet, anyway. The person in question merely wanted some advice, for which he paid me in cash."

"I hope you haven't explained to him how to open an offshore bank account, et cetera, et cetera."

"No, I have not."

"I'm relieved to hear that, because —"

"Actually, I recommended a safe-deposit box in a respectable bank."

"That's still advising a client on how to hide his income."

"I suggested a safe-deposit box as a security measure, not a means of tax evasion. If he had asked me for tax advice I would have been obliged to advise him to list all his income on his return."

"Do you think he will do that?"

"I have no reason to think he won't, but as I say, he didn't ask me for that sort of advice."

"You're bandying words. You do realize

this could come back to bite you on the ass?"

"The feds have already had a free snap at my ass and missed by a mile. And, to answer your next question, I told them nothing but the truth."

"But not the whole truth."

"I had not taken an oath to tell them that, but I did not tell them anything that could be characterized as a breach of attorney-client confidentiality. I told them what I believe you, yourself, would have, in the circumstances."

"Those circumstances are extremely unlikely to arise in my practice of the law."

"Oh, really? Have you seen this morning's *Wall Street Journal*? A front-page story reported that a prominent banker client of yours, who shall remain nameless for purposes of this conversation, has agreed to pay the Justice Department a settlement of one-point-three billion dollars, in order to avoid criminal prosecution for mortgage fraud. Did you not negotiate that settlement?"

Eggers looked uncomfortable. "The man is not a felon, he made a business mistake."

"Now who's bandying words? There, but for one-point-three billion dollars, goes a felon."

"The difference is, my client is a banker — yours is a bank robber."

"I beg to differ: in my client's case, no bank was robbed, and when the non–bank robbery took place, he was tucked away in a cell at Sing Sing, made safe from prosecution by an earlier, ah, 'business mistake.' Your client, on the other hand, packaged thousands of mortgages, many of which he had good reason to believe had been obtained by fraudulent means, and sold them to unsuspecting investors, who then lost a great deal of money. By comparison, my client is an upstanding citizen, never mind that he is traveling about the country with a piece of luggage large enough to hold several million dollars of what was, long ago, someone else's money."

"He's traveling with millions of dollars in cash?"

"I didn't say that. I said he had luggage large enough to accommodate that much. I have no evidence of what he packed into it." Stone polished off his wine. "However, assuming, for the purposes of discussion, that what you suggested is true, how is that different from your client's secreting large sums in offshore bank accounts?"

Eggers threw up his hands. "You're right," he said. "We should, both of us, surrender our law licenses."

"You first," Stone replied.

12

The president of the United States finished his scrambled eggs and sausages and started on his coffee. He could eat sausages for breakfast because the first lady was in New York. The phone on the breakfast table rang, and he answered it immediately, but not before reaching for a toothpick.

"This is the president of the United States speaking," he said. "If you have dialed this number in error, please hang up and try again."

"This is the first lady of the United States speaking, and I did not dial this number in error. You're eating sausages, aren't you?"

"Strictly speaking, no."

"You mean you have already finished eating the sausages?"

"I'm sorry, I don't have any clear recollection of anything I might have eaten at an earlier time. My mind is crowded with details of foreign and domestic policy."

"If you didn't have sausages, why are you using that toothpick?"

Will spat out a bit of gristle. "Excuse me, are we on Skype?"

"No, but if I didn't already know you well enough not to need it, I'd order Skype immediately. Why are you not in the middle of a prep session for our live appearance on *60 Minutes* tonight, instead of luxuriating in sausages?"

"Because it's Sunday morning, and —"

"Aha! Got you!"

"Oh, all right, I was eating sausages, but they were chicken and apple."

"But you hate anything but pork sausages."

"That's why I had only two of them. I'm sure it will make you feel better to know they were awful."

"That does make me feel a little better."

"I'm not in the middle of a prep session for *60 Minutes* because I intend to refer all questions to you, so I don't need to prepare."

"But that wouldn't be a joint interview, which is what they're paying for."

"May I remind you that the president does not accept payment for television interviews? If I did, we'd be doing this on Faux News."

"*That* would be a very short interview."

"Not if they paid me enough."

"Do you mean to tell me that you are really not doing any prep for this interview?"

"Not so's you'd notice it. But on the other hand, neither are you."

"Well, I'm in New York, and I don't have all the support facilities that you have in the White House."

"Would you like me to scramble a team of preppers and chopper them up there? I can do that, you know, I'm the president, and as one of my predecessors once said, 'If the president does it, it's not illegal.' "

"And look what happened to him."

"You have a point."

"I think it would be more fun just to wing it."

"So do I, that's why I'm not prepping."

"You have to watch out for Lesley Stahl, though, she's sneaky."

"I well know it."

"She comes on all sweet and charming, then suddenly she's asking about your Swiss bank account, and somehow, she knows your balance."

"I am fortunate in not having a Swiss bank account, so Ms. Stahl can do her worst."

"God, I hope not."

"I hope not, too. What time can I expect you?"

"Why? Would I be interrupting something if I got there unexpectedly early?"

"I just want time to lower the girls from the bedroom window and kick the champagne bottles under the bed."

"Just a typical Sunday morning when the wife's away, huh?"

"I have to run now, the Chris Matthews show is about to start, and he's having that hot Katty Kay on. You know what a British accent does to me."

"Yes, I do. Isn't she one of the girls you have to lower out the window?"

"Unfortunately not."

"See you in a couple of hours."

"Bye."

They both hung up.

13

Sunday morning, and Stone's phone was ringing. He opened an eye and glanced at the clock. Nearly ten. "Hello?"

"It's Holly."

"Well, spymaster, long time. What's up with you?" He pressed the remote and the bed sat him up.

"At the moment, I'm hungry. Buy me brunch?"

"How soon can you be here?"

"Twenty minutes."

"I'll order now. Hurry!"

But Holly had hung up.

Stone buzzed the kitchen and got Helene, then he ordered eggs Benedict, asparagus, freshly squeezed orange juice, and his usual, Medaglia d'Oro Italian coffee, made strong. He got out of bed, went to the dumbwaiter, and retrieved the Sunday *New York Times,* which weighed almost more than he could lift. He got back in bed and began reading the front page. No mention of Kate's fund-raiser. How long could this last?

Nineteen minutes later, Holly walked into the room, undressing as she came. "I've still got my key," she said. "Hope that's okay." She dived into bed and kissed him.

"It's more than okay."

"The *Times* is going to have to wait," she said, climbing on top of him and kissing him wetly.

"We can always read the *Times,*" Stone said. "We can't always do this."

She eased him inside her. "It's the nation's fault," she said, then sucked in a breath.

"That's it," Stone replied, sucking in his own breath as he went deep. "Blame the country for your absences."

They both stopped talking and concentrated on the activity at hand. They both went off at exactly the same time as the bell on the dumbwaiter.

"I'll play waitress," Holly said, hopping off him and running for the tray.

Stone put her bed up to match his, and they dug in.

"Helene makes the most heavenly hollandaise sauce," Holly said. "I'd ask her for the recipe, but I don't intend to cook ever again. We have a very decent restaurant at the New

York station, you know." Holly was CIA station chief in New York. "You must come to lunch sometime."

"Well, I do have the security clearance for it," Stone replied. "Someday when neither Mike Freeman nor Bill Eggers is inviting me to his table at the Four Seasons, I'll take you up on it. Do they serve Dover sole?"

"On occasion," Holly said. "I never make requests, because I'd get blamed for ordering expensive food. It's more like comfort food."

"Dover sole is comfort food for me."

"Yeah, but you're a multi-zillionaire these days."

"Not my fault," Stone said. "I didn't lift a finger to earn a penny of it."

"What's it like being that rich?"

"It's a combination of a joy and a heavy burden. I'm Peter's trustee, too, so I have to spend quite a bit of time husbanding money and getting it to reproduce."

"What have you bought that you didn't already have?"

"Let's see. A car . . ."

"What kind of car?"

"I'll show you later. And a house."

"Where?"

Stone pointed to his right.

"How far?"

"Less than a stone's throw."

"You mean the house next door?"

"Right. Joan found out the people were selling. She had a look at it, found it newly renovated and decorated, and suggested I buy it and turn it into staff quarters."

"Which means Joan is living next door?"

"Right. And Helene, and Frederic."

"Who the hell is Frederic?"

"The butler."

"You have a butler? Ye gods!"

"He was a gift, actually."

"Somebody *gave* you a butler?"

"My French friend, Marcel duBois. For a year. After that, Fred and I negotiate, if we're both happy. He's a wonder, and he and Helene have formed an attachment and are sharing an apartment. Then there's Joan's apartment and a very nice guest duplex. Plus, we broke through the wall and enlarged the garage and the wine cellar."

"So that's all you bought?"

"Well, there is the new jet."

Holly howled with laughter. "I knew it. I knew you'd go nuts!"

"I didn't go nuts. I would have ordered the airplane anyway. It's a new model from Cessna, a Citation M2, and a nice step up from the Mustang — faster, better range, a little larger. I gave the Mustang to Peter."

"When do you take delivery?"

"End of September. I have to go to school for two weeks. Say, I get two training slots. You want to spend two weeks in Wichita with me, learning to fly it?" Holly already had an airplane of her own and a couple of thousand hours.

"God knows, I've got vacation time coming. Give me the dates and I'll see what I can do. What girl could resist two weeks in Wichita?"

"I warn you, it's going to be hard work. The simulator isn't an airplane, it's more like a computer game, I'm told."

"It would be a vacation for me."

Stone got up and put the tray back on the dumbwaiter and sent it downstairs, then he jumped back into bed. "This is a vacation for me," he said, burying his face in her lap.

"Happy vacation," she said, lying back.

14

Stone sucked in a breath and clenched his teeth as Holly took a curve on the Sawmill River Parkway. "Jeez, Holly, you hit a hundred and twenty for a second there, and I don't think a CIA ID is going to get you out of being arrested by a state trooper."

"What is this thing?" Holly asked, slowing down slightly.

"It's a Blaise, a new French car made by my Parisian friend."

"It's like flying," she said.

Stone wished for dual controls.

"I think I read about this in the *Times,* didn't I? Doesn't it cost something like four hundred grand?"

"Something like that, but I got a deal, less than two hundred and fifty thousand."

"I've never driven anything like it. What's the horsepower?"

"Six hundred," Stone said, "and you're using every one of them at the moment."

He was pressed back into his seat as she accelerated again. He put a hand on her arm. "Please, I don't think my heart can take any more."

"Oh, all right," she said, touching the brakes and bringing it down to eighty. "What's the speed limit out here, anyway?"

"Fifty-five."

"That's a crime, a beautiful drive like this!"

"Here's an idea," Stone said. "Why don't you call a security alert and get the road closed for a couple of hours? Then you can come out here — without me — and become part of a large tree."

"You're such a wuss, Stone."

"What's a wuss? I'm confused."

"Something between a nerd and a 1955 square."

"I'm still confused."

"Of course you are, that's why you're a wuss."

They got back into Stone's garage without killing anybody, but Stone still felt a little queasy.

"You want to watch the Lees on *60 Minutes*?" Holly asked, handing him back the keys.

"Just as soon as I've had a bourbon and

Alka-Seltzer."

They ordered a pizza and ate it in bed, naked. Stone switched on the program and was surprised to see the Lees in comfortable armchairs, wearing sweaters and jeans. A fire crackled in the fireplace behind them. Lesley Stahl was doing the interviewing.

"First question," Stahl said: "Why did you two want to do this live, instead of on tape?"

"Because this way we get to edit ourselves, instead of having you do it for us," Will said, getting a laugh from Kate.

"I want the camera to pan around and give our viewers a look at the family quarters of the White House," Stahl said, "because it's so rarely seen." The camera followed her orders, revealing cozy furniture, bookcases, and even a bar. "Does the bar get used often?" she asked.

"Not as often as Will would like," Kate said, "but now that I'm a lady of leisure, I let him make me a martini before dinner."

"I envy her out-of-workness," Will said, "and I'm looking forward to experiencing that myself."

"So that you can drink more martinis?" Stahl asked.

"I'm a Southerner, a bourbon drinker."

"What's your brand?"

"I won't answer that until I'm a free man and can get paid for it. Let's just say that I enjoy giving the state of Kentucky a little business now and then."

"Let's go back a couple of weeks and look at a bit of videotape from our New York affiliate," Stahl said.

The shot was of Will leaving the Blue Note, claiming ignorance of whom Kate was dining with.

"Mrs. Lee, can you enlighten us? With whom were you dining?"

"If I told you, then *he* would know," she said, pointing at Will.

"I've heard that it was a gathering of twenty prominent Americans," Stahl said. "Come on, tell us who?"

"I can't remember that many names," Kate said. "Can't a lady throw a party now and then?"

"Is that what it was? A party?"

"And a pretty good one, too."

"My sources tell me that a ticket to that party cost a million dollars."

"I don't think there's that much caviar in the world," Kate said. "And no caviar was served."

"You're not going to tell me, are you?" Stahl said.

"You're very perceptive, Lesley. But now

that I'm not pulling down a government salary I can throw a party without publishing the guest list in the White House daily schedule. It's very liberating."

Holly turned toward Stone. "I'll bet you know something about this."

"Maybe."

"Come on, give!"

"Didn't you hear the lady? It'll cost you a million dollars to find out."

"Who do I make the check to?"

"That would tell you more than Kate wants you to know."

"Mr. President," Stahl said, "can you shed some light on this?"

"I wasn't there," Will said, "and I've got your videotape to prove it. And I haven't seen the guest list, either."

"All right, then let me ask you a substantive question: How much advice have you received from your wife over the past eight years, and how good was it?"

"First of all," Will said, "since she was director of Central Intelligence for all that time, I got regular office-hours briefings from her, and they were superb."

"How about after office hours?"

"I got advice from Kate then, too, and it

may surprise you to learn that it was very often about domestic affairs. She has an abiding interest in what goes on inside this country and inside the government, and the advice I got from her about those things was always right on the mark. In fact, I would put her in the top two or three among my advisers on domestic matters."

"That sounds to me like an endorsement," Holly said.

"And I think that's as close as Will will come to one."

"Now that *60 Minutes* has asked about that party," Holly said, "everybody in the media is going to be all over this."

"I'm afraid you're right," Stone said.

"And you were at the party, weren't you?"

"Yes, I was."

"And it cost you a million dollars?"

"It did."

"That can mean only one thing," Holly said, poking him in the ribs. "She's going to run for office."

"Kate can do whatever she wants now, what with Will finishing his second term."

"Well, with the convention looming, it's too late for her to run for president," Holly said, "so it would have to be for the senate in Georgia, wouldn't it?"

"I don't know if there's an open seat down there," Stone replied.

"Then she must be going to —"

Stone kissed her. "Shhhhhh," he said, then switched off the TV.

15

When Stone awoke the following morning, Holly was gone, and her side of the bed had been neatly made up. When he sat down at his desk after breakfast, there was an e-mail from Holly's personal account.

Check this link, it said, and an address was spelled out. He clicked on it. The site was called *Crazy Rumors and Wild Speculation.*

> Last night on *60 Minutes,* the top was peeled off a new political can of worms, namely the "party" thrown by First Lady Katherine Rule Lee last week at the Lees' Carlyle Hotel penthouse for twenty very rich Americans, each of whom allegedly contributed a million dollars to be there. But contributed to what? That's serious political money, and only a run for one of three offices would attract such a sum: a senate seat or the presidency or the vice presidency. Kate Lee is a Georgia resident,

and the incumbent is a Democrat well positioned for reelection, so that's out; it's too late to run for president, what with the primaries nearly over and the convention looming, so that's out. That leaves the vice presidency, and nobody stages a campaign for that. But if Kate wants to be president someday, such a campaign might be a smart move. She's young enough to wait eight years before going for the big job, so we might be seeing something new in national politics. The names of the Big Twenty shouldn't be hard to figure out (see below), and by the way, we hear there were twenty-one guests. Who's the extra man or woman?

Stone checked the list below and found it to be substantially accurate, but his name was not there. He replied to the e-mail: *Sounds like a pretty good guess to me.* He clicked send.

Joan appeared at the door. "There's a political reporter from the *Times* on the phone, named Josh Altman. Do you want to speak to him?"

Stone thought for a moment, then picked up the phone. "This is Stone Barrington."

"Josh Altman at the *Times,* Mr. Barrington."

"Good morning."

"Did you see the interview with the president and first lady on *60 Minutes* last night?"

"Yes, I did."

"A source is telling me that you were the twenty-first person on the guest list of that party. Is that true?"

"I had dinner with the president and the first lady last week," he said.

"And what was discussed at that dinner?"

"It was a private dinner and a private conversation."

"Were you then invited to the big party?"

"As I said, it was a private dinner and a private conversation. I don't know what else I can tell you."

"Somebody posted a made-up guest list on a website this morning. Was it accurate?"

"Good morning to you, Mr. Altman." Stone hung up.

Joan was back; she turned on Stone's office TV and changed the channel to Fox News. A very blonde woman and three men occupied a sofa facing the camera.

"Who knows anything about this party the first lady gave last week at the Carlyle?" the blonde asked.

A young man spoke up. "I've talked to one person who may have been at the party, he won't say. But while I didn't get any names, he hinted that at least one of them was a big-time New York attorney, and several of the guests were prominent Republicans who may have voted for Will Lee last time."

"We all know there were a few of those," the blonde said, then moved the conversation to another subject.

Joan switched off the set. "Looks like the guy from the *Times* isn't the only one on your trail," she said, then she went back to her desk.

Stone's private line rang, and he picked it up. "Hello?"

"It's Dino. I hear Fox News is calling you a big-time New York attorney."

"That sounds more like Bill Eggers," Stone said. "And what are you doing watching TV at this time of the morning? You should be ashamed of yourself, wasting the city's money that way."

"Somebody told me about it," Dino said defensively.

"Nah, you were watching Faux News. Bad Dino!"

"All right, I turned it on to what was said about a police shooting last night, and I just happened to hear."

"What police shooting?"

"Sean Donnelly got popped coming out of P.J. Clarke's in the middle of the night.

He had apparently closed the place."

"Is Sean dead?"

"No, it was a chest wound, caught a lung instead of his heart. He'll live."

"Who the hell would shoot a cop who's been retired for fifteen years?"

"Good question. We're looking at his old cases. Maybe somebody Sean put away got sprung and is holding a grudge."

"I think I'll send him a dozen roses," Stone said, "just to piss him off."

Dino laughed hard. "And don't include a card, it will drive him nuts!"

"Where have they got him?"

"New York Hospital."

"Consider it done."

"You want dinner this evening? Viv's back, and she's always happy to see you."

"Sure."

"Clarke's at eight?"

"You're on." Stone hung up and buzzed Joan. "Sean Donnelly caught a bullet last night. He's at New York Hospital. Send him a dozen red roses, no card, and book me a table for three at Clarke's, please, eight o'clock."

"Done," she said.

Stone picked up a stack of mail and leafed through it. An envelope with a Palm Beach, Florida, postmark caught his eye, and he opened it: a twenties-style cartoon of a man under a beach umbrella, a cocktail in one hand and a cigar in the other. Scrawled at the bottom: *Good advice, thanks! J.F.*

Well, Stone thought, *John Fratelli can afford Palm Beach.*

16

Dino Bacchetti attended a meeting at an uptown precinct, and among the subjects discussed was the shooting of Sean Donnelly.

"What's happening with that?" Dino asked the group.

A detective spoke up. "We're doing the obvious — checking his old cases for somebody newly out of the joint who has a grudge, but nothing yet. Donnelly's being a bastard, won't give us anything."

"Why do you think he's holding out on us?" Dino asked.

"I think he's scared the perp will have another shot at him if he talks," the detective replied.

The meeting broke up, and Dino got into his car and headed back downtown. Then they were passing New York Hospital, and he said to his driver, "Pull into the hospital. I want to visit somebody."

Sean Donnelly was sitting up in bed, his left arm in a sling, disconsolately watching Fox News. He turned and saw Dino standing in the doorway, then turned back to the TV without speaking. A large vase of red roses rested on the windowsill.

"So, Sean," Dino said, pulling up a chair to Donnelly's bedside. "Tell me who shot you last night."

"No idea," Donnelly replied. "The blonde's not bad, is she? I wouldn't kick her out of the sack."

"How come you're stiffing the detectives on your case, Sean?"

"Spectacular tits, huh? Where do they find these women? You don't see them on MSNBC — they've all gotta be so fucking smart over there. Either that or they're dykes, like whatshername."

"Sean, look at me," Dino said.

Donnelly glanced at him, then turned back to the TV. "I'd rather look at the blonde's tits, if it's all the same to you, Dino."

"I guess you retired before the department stopped us from talking like that," Dino said. "I don't give a shit about the blonde, I want to know who put a bullet in you."

"Yeah? Why do you care?"

"Because I don't want the local hit men

running around taking potshots at retired police officers. The best way to stop 'em is to catch 'em. Why do I have to explain that to you?"

"What do you want, Dino? I already finished my Jell-O, so you can't have that."

"I told you what I want, give it to me."

Donnelly sighed. "I was looking into an old case of mine, and I guess I got too close to somebody. Funny thing, the only guy I've talked to about it is your old buddy Stone-fuckingBarrington. Then somebody takes a shot at me. Go figure, huh?"

"Stone had nothing to do with this," Dino said, "so don't try and fob it off on him. Whose toes did you step on?"

"Eddie Buono's, I guess."

"Buono's dead."

"His pal Johnny Fratelli ain't, and he just got out."

"I hear somebody took a shot at Fratelli, too," Dino said. "Would that be you?"

"Me? Why would I want Fratelli dead? He never did nothing to me."

"Maybe he wants the same thing you do, and he got there first."

"I want to solve a cold case — you think Fratelli wants that?"

"Why do you, all of a sudden, want to solve your cold case? You didn't do anything about it for the fifteen years you've been retired."

"Personal satisfaction," Donnelly said.

"You think the money's still out there, don't you?"

Donnelly turned a little red in the face. "I fucking *know* the money's still out there! We got Buono's crew and most of their money, but Eddie never spent a dime of his cut, and he got half! He got busted and sentenced, less than a year after the airport job, for offing Paddy Riley, who ratted him out on an earlier gig. He weaseled out of that one, but not the Riley beef. He went up for Riley."

"And you think Johnny Fratelli knows where the money is?"

"Look, Dino, Eddie Buono was scared shitless about getting raped in the joint. He was a pretty boy, and he just knew somebody was going to climb on him, so he hired Fratelli, who's a big, tough guy, to keep the fags off his back. And he did, too — I talked to one of the guards on their cell block. They were cellmates for twenty-two years! Everybody was too afraid of Fratelli to make a pass at Eddie."

"So, for that, Buono passed on the money to Fratelli?"

"He knew he was dying, what's he gonna

do, give it to the Salvation Army, in the hope of cracking the pearly gates? Them wops stuck together, or at least they did in the old days."

Dino ignored the Italian slur. "So, where's Fratelli? We'll have a word with him."

"He was in town, now I hear he's out of town, nobody knows where. Except, maybe, StonefuckingBarrington. Fratelli was seen in his neighborhood. I guess he needed legal advice, and StonefuckingBarrington had a street rep as a standup guy, who wouldn't rat him out."

"And that's why you went to see Stone? To get him to do something you knew he wasn't going to do?"

"I thought maybe he'd do it for a cut."

"Stone's up to his ass in money. He had a rich wife who lost an argument with a shotgun from an old lover."

"So he told me," Donnelly said. "Who knew?"

"I thought everybody did," Dino said. "I guess you lead a sheltered life."

"I guess."

"Sean, who shot you?"

"Somebody who wants the same thing I do."

"And who might that be?"

"I hadn't gotten that far in my investigation before I got plugged."

"No idea at all?"

"None. Hey . . ." He pointed at the windowsill. "Find out who sent me them flowers — maybe that's the guy."

Dino suppressed a laugh. "What, there was no card?"

"Dino, if I could get outta this bed, I'd kick your ass. Maybe when I do, I will, just for the fun of it."

Dino stood up to go. "Not on your best day, Sean."

"Go see some of your guinea pals — that's who did this. They'll tell you all about it, I'll bet. Maybe give *you* a cut."

Dino walked over, took the remote control from the bedside table, switched off the TV, and tossed the remote out the window. "You'll enjoy the day more without tits, Sean." He walked out of the room and slammed the door. Behind him he could hear Donnelly yelling for a nurse.

17

Stone got to P.J. Clarke's early, so he bellied up to the bar to wait for the others. Charlie, the longest-serving of the bartenders, handed him a Knob Creek on the rocks without asking. "How you doing, Stone?"

"Not too bad," Stone replied.

"How's Dino? We don't see him much since they moved him downtown."

"He's good, be here in a few minutes. You knew he got married?"

"I heard it, but I didn't believe it."

"Believe it." Stone saw two guys in construction clothes and hard hats come through the door, take a look around at all the twenty-somethings in their designer clothes, and leave in disgust.

Charlie laughed. "Not our trade, I guess."

"Charlie, I hear somebody took a shot at Sean Donnelly when he left here last night."

"Yeah, when Sean's here he doesn't leave until we throw him out. I heard the shots and went out there and found him in the gutter, called nine-one-one. I thought he was going to croak."

"I hear he didn't."

"Tell you the truth, t'wouldna been a loss, far as I'm concerned. I wish he'd drink somewheres else. He's got a mouth on him, annoys the ladies."

"You see anybody when you went outside?"

"I heard some rubber burn on Third Avenue, but Sean left by the side door, so I didn't see anything." Charlie took somebody else's order and moved away.

"Did you say something about somebody getting shot here last night?" A woman's voice from behind him.

Stone turned to find a tall woman in designer casual, pale red hair, freckled skin, handsome nose, big green eyes. "I did," Stone said. "In the wee small hours of the morning, right out there." He nodded in the direction of East Fifty-fifth.

"You a cop?" she asked. "You're not dressed like one."

"Used to be, in my extreme youth. Now I practice the law, instead of enforcing it."

"I'm Hank Cromwell," she said, offering a hand.

Stone shook it. "Hank?"

"My mother named me Henrietta. It didn't take."

"I'm Stone Barrington."

"Sounds like a lawyer's name."

"You have something against lawyers?"

"Not a thing. Maybe that's because I've never had to hire one."

"You've led a blameless life, then?"

"I wouldn't go as far as that. Let's just say I never got caught."

"What do you do?"

"I'm an illustrator — books, magazines, advertising — wherever the work is."

Stone handed her a cocktail napkin and his pen. "Illustrate something."

She took the pen, made a few quick strokes, and handed back the napkin.

He found a recognizable sketch of himself, sparely drawn. "Okay, you're an illustrator."

"You thought I was lying?"

"I wanted to see if you're any good. You are." He looked up to see Dino and Viv getting out of Dino's departmental black SUV on Third. "I'm meeting a couple for dinner. Would you like to join us?"

She shrugged. "Why not? I'm hungry."

The couple came through the doors, and Stone introduced them to Hank, then they went to the back room and found their table.

"I'll bet you two just met," Dino said.

"Why do you say that?" Hank asked.

"Because no woman who already knows Stone would have dinner with him."

"Calumny," Stone said.

"I'm on Stone's side," Viv said to her. "Dino just likes to needle him."

"I thought," Hank replied.

"I went to see Sean Donnelly this afternoon," Dino said.

"I hope he was in terrible pain and getting worse," Stone replied.

"You were right about the roses, they were driving him nuts."

"Did he tell you anything?"

"He doesn't know anything," Dino said.

"Somebody thinks he does."

Hank broke in. "Is this the guy who got shot last night?"

"Right," Dino said. "How'd you know?"

"I heard Stone talking to the bartender about it."

"Charlie called nine-one-one, but he wasn't too upset about it," Stone said.

"Sean has that effect on people. By the way, he hates your guts, calls you Stone-fuckingBarrington."

Stone laughed. "I choose my enemies well."

"What about you, pal?" Dino asked.

"Me? What about me?"

"You had any . . . repercussions?"

"A couple of Secret Service agents showed up with a hundred-dollar bill that Joan deposited in my account."

"Payment for legal advice?"

"You could say that. They felt that the bill was too old to be in my possession. It was printed sometime after 1966."

"One of those with the red seal on them?"

"That's it."

"Should I mention that to Sean Donnelly?"

"You do, and I'll shoot you in a painful place."

Dino laughed.

"You guys lead interesting lives," Hank said. "What do you do, Viv?"

"I used to be a cop, too, but these days I'm a security executive."

"What's that?"

"I work for a large security company called Strategic Services."

"And you do what?"

"We secure things and people. How about you?"

"Illustrator."

"She's not kidding," Stone said, producing the cocktail napkin with his portrait.

"Not bad," Viv said.

"You missed the shifty eyes," Dino pointed out.

Hank laughed. "Next time, I'll make them shiftier."

They ordered dinner and a bottle of wine. Four steaks and a lot of fries later, Stone invited them all back to his place for a nightcap. They rode in Dino's car.

"Listen," Dino said, as they got out at Stone's house, "you should watch your ass for a while. Sean knows you're mixed up with Fratelli, and if he knows, other people know."

"I'll keep that in mind," Stone said.

"I know you're not used to it these days, but you should start carrying."

"I guess so," Stone said.

18

Stone let them into the house, entered the alarm code, and took their coats.

"Very nice," Hank said, looking around the well-lit living room. "You must spend a fortune on lightbulbs."

"The new lightbulbs cost a fortune," Stone said, "but they're supposed to outlive me." He herded them toward the study, where the lights were already on, too. "Actually, the lights come on when the alarm code is entered. If it's entered incorrectly, they flash on and off, the cops are called, and the surveillance cameras come on. What can I get you?"

"A cognac, if you have it."

"I have it. Do you have a preference?"

"The costliest," Hank replied.

Stone laughed and poured them all a vintage cognac.

"You seem a little on the paranoid side, Stone," Hank said, settling into the leather sofa. "Security system, flashing lights, surveillance cameras."

"He's not paranoid enough," Dino said, "and if I were you I wouldn't get too near him, until a certain matter is resolved, or you could become collaterally damaged."

Stone pressed a button and a panel slid silently up, revealing a safe. He opened it, retrieved a small handgun and a holster, and clipped it to his belt, then he joined Hank on the sofa.

"There," he said. "Feel better?"

"Only slightly," she said. "There's always the chance that you'll shoot me."

"If it helps," Viv said, "all of us here are armed, with the possible exception of yourself."

Hank reached into her thick hair and produced an old-fashioned hatpin, about six inches long. "Only this," she said, "for incipient rapists."

"I'll keep that in mind," Stone said.

"Why, were you planning to rape me?"

"Not while that pig-sticker is in your hand."

She returned the pin to her hair. "There," she said, "out of the way."

Everybody laughed. Then the doorbell rang, and the laughter stopped.

"Who the hell is that, this time of night?"

Dino asked.

Stone pressed a button on the phone on his desk and a small screen lit up, revealing a well-lit person wearing a blue shirt and a blue baseball cap, standing with his back to the door. "Yes?" he asked into the phone.

The man didn't turn around but waved something that looked like a FedEx envelope. "Mr. Barrington? Delivery."

"Just put it through the slot in the door," Stone replied.

"Sorry, I need a signature."

"Be right with you." Stone stood up.

"Watch yourself, pal," Dino said, standing himself. He unholstered a handgun.

"Be right back," Stone said, unholstering his own weapon.

Viv walked to the door and stood where she could see them.

Stone went to the door, put the chain on, and opened it a crack, standing well away from it. "Okay," he said, "hand it through."

An envelope came through the door and, simultaneously, there came two rapid booms from the other side of the door, and it moved inward, yanking the chain tight. Then there was the sound of running footsteps, the slamming of a car door, and the noise of rubber burning.

Stone unhooked the chain, but Dino

grabbed him by the collar and pulled him back. "This is a police matter," he said, stepping onto the front stoop, his gun held before him.

Stone pulled the door open and looked over his shoulder. Taillights turned right on Second Avenue. "You see anything?"

"Just the taillights," Dino replied. He pointed at the front door, where pockmarks had been left and paint burned away.

"Looks like buckshot," he said. "You're going to need a painter."

"Guess so," Stone said. "You going to call this in?"

"Yeah, but it won't help much. I'll put a squad car out front for the night, though, so you can get some sleep." He produced a cell phone and barked some orders.

When they returned to the study, Hank had not moved from the sofa. "What was that noise?" she asked.

"A shotgun," Dino replied. "There was an attempt on Stone's life. The front door took the damage."

"Won't a shotgun shoot through a door?"

"Not a heavy-gauge steel door," Stone said, picking up his cognac and joining her on the sofa.

"Why do you have a heavy-gauge steel front door, instead of an oak one, like everybody else?" Hank asked.

"Oh, a thick oak door would have probably withstood the blast," he said, "but it would have needed replacing. The steel door will just need a little filler and paint."

"Suppose someone had fired through a window?"

"The windows are armored glass," Stone replied. "I once had a guest important to the government for some days, and they replaced the door and all the windows, as a security precaution."

"So your house is an impregnable fortress?"

"It probably wouldn't stand up to a rocket-propelled grenade," he said, "but those are in short supply in New York City."

"You live in a different world from mine," Hank said.

"Not really, mine just has harder surfaces."

"How did you come to own this house?"

"Back when I was still a serving police detective, with Dino as a partner, my great-aunt — my maternal grandmother's sister — died and left it to me. She and her husband had built it during the 1920s. I renovated it over a period of a year and a half, doing all the work myself that didn't require a plumber's or an electrician's license. My father was a cabinet and furniture maker — an artist, really. He made all the shelves, all the doors, and much of the furniture, like the dining table and chairs. I refinished those, updated the kitchen and the electrical supply, air-conditioned it and, voilà, a home."

"And a free one."

"Hardly. It took all the money I had and all I could borrow, and thousands of hours of labor, most of it mine. I had to use my old law degree to pay the money back."

"Was your mother Matilda Stone?"

"Yes."

"I recognized these pictures," Hank said, indicating the ones on the wall of the study. "I saw them in an exhibition of American painting at the Met some years ago."

"I loaned them."

"How many of her works do you have?"

"She left me four. Over the years I've managed to acquire another dozen."

"I'd love to see them all."

"They're scattered around the house," Stone said, "most of them in my bedroom."

Dino laughed. "Here we go," he said.

Everybody laughed.

"It's late," Hank said, "and I have work due in the morning. Another time?"

"Another time," Stone said.

"We'll send her home in my car," Dino said.

19

John Fratelli sat in a deck chair on a terrace of the Breakers, the monumental, turn-of-the-twentieth-century hotel built by Henry Flagler, the partner of John D. Rockefeller in Standard Oil.

Fratelli was an honored guest in a small suite overlooking the Atlantic, and he had spent his time in Palm Beach well. He had obtained a birth certificate by visiting a Palm Beach cemetery and checking the birth and death dates. His name was now John Latimer Coulter. He had Googled the name and found nothing, so he had applied for and received a Florida driver's license in that name and, through a visa expediter, a United States passport, both with the address of One South County Road, the address of the Breakers. He was also considering buying the suite that he occupied. It would put a dent in his capital, but he thought it a good investment.

An elderly man sat down next to him and snagged a passing waiter. "A piña colada," he said, then he turned to Fratelli. "Can I buy you a drink, my friend?"

"Thank you, I'll have the same."

The waiter trotted off to the bar, and the elderly gentleman extended a hand. "I am Winston Carnagy," he said.

"Like Andrew?"

"With an 'a' instead of an 'e' and a 'y' instead of an 'ie.' No relation."

"I'm Jack Coulter."

"What brings you to Palm Beach, Jack?"

"What brings anybody to Palm Beach?" Fratelli asked with a shrug.

The man laughed heartily. "You're quite right. Where are you from?"

"I was actually born in Palm Beach," Fratelli said, "but for many years my home was in upstate New York. I'm considering buying an apartment here in the hotel."

"I have already done so," Carnagy replied. "It's a wise move, if you can afford it."

"You live here during the season?"

"The year 'round," Carnagy replied. "I'm a retired investment banker, but I still trade a little to keep myself entertained."

The two chatted for a while, then repaired to the outdoor restaurant for lunch, where Carnagy's wife joined them. Tall and elegant, perfectly coiffed and dressed in fashionable beachwear, Elizabeth Carnagy enchanted Fratelli. She revealed that they had two daughters and three grandchildren and pointed them out on the beach below. It occurred to Fratelli that these were the first civilians he had met since leaving Sing Sing.

Soon, Fratelli began to feel that the Carnagys were old friends. Elizabeth finished her salad and went to join her daughters and grandchildren on the beach.

"What business are you in?" Winston Carnagy asked.

"I'm a retired entrepreneur," Fratelli replied. "Tell me, Winston, have you any experience of offshore banking?" Fratelli, having always had an imitative ear, had already begun to adopt Carnagy's manner of speech and some of his accent.

Carnagy looked around furtively, as if there might be an Internal Revenue agent behind a potted palm. "I do," he said. "Are you contemplating such an arrangement?"

"I am, but I know nothing about it."

"Have you greenback dollar bills to lodge somewhere?"

"Possibly."

"Here's how you do it," Carnagy said. "You look in the yellow pages under 'aviation' and charter a light airplane — a small twin-engine job will do — to fly you to Nassau, where you check into a previously booked hotel. The following morning, without checking out of your hotel, you do the same at the Nassau airport, and you fly to Georgetown in the Cayman Islands — just the other side of Cuba. Once there, ask the immigration official you deal with not to stamp your passport. Have your pilot wait, and take a taxi into Georgetown." He produced a business card and wrote something on the back. "Go to this bank and ask for this gentleman, who is the officer in charge of foreign accounts. Open an account with him and deposit your cash."

"As easy as that?"

"Quite. You needn't give him your name, as the account will be identified only by a number, which you must memorize. You may check your statement on the bank's Internet website, using a password of your own invention. Also, they will furnish you with a debit card that may be used anywhere in the world to charge anything, or to obtain cash from any ATM."

"That sounds very handy," Fratelli said. "Does the IRS have any sort of access to the bank's records?"

"No, but don't count on that continuing.

However, since your only connection with the bank is a number, and since they do not have your name and address, you needn't worry about that. You can also ring them up at will and order a cashier's check FedExed to you, should you wish to make a large purchase, like a car or even an apartment in this hotel."

"Winston, you are a mine of information," Fratelli said.

"And should you wish to make investments, I can recommend a local stockbroker."

"Thank you, Winston, but I have other investments in mind."

In fact, Fratelli had already looked up an old "school" acquaintance, now operating as a bookie and loan shark around South Florida. He had lodged a million dollars cash with him, in return for a weekly delivery of fifty thousand dollars cash, or five percent. The man would loan it at ten percent a week and would take care of any necessary leg-breaking out of his cut. But Fratelli would not share that information with Carnagy, who would no doubt be shocked.

That was a million dollars in out-of-date hundreds laundered. A Cayman Islands bank would launder the rest of the contents of his luggage, which now resided in the hotel's vault.

"Do you have a wife?" Carnagy asked.

"No, I have lived the life of a bachelor, though perhaps it's time for me to shop around for more permanent companionship."

"My wife has a very attractive niece," Carnagy said. "Divorced, childless, and with her own money. You might enjoy meeting her."

"I am sure I would," Fratelli replied, "just as soon as I get back from, ah, the Bahamas."

The two gentlemen shared a chuckle.

Down the coast, in Fort Lauderdale, Fratelli's old "school" friend sat in his boss's office, sweating lightly. His boss held up a hundred-dollar bill that sported a red seal.

"Do you know what this is, Manny?" the boss asked.

"Sure, Vinnie, it's a C-note."

"Where did you get it?"

"Get it? Me?"

"One of our handlers spotted it, said it came from you."

"It looks just like any other C-note," Manny said. "Is it bogus? If it is, I've never seen better."

"No, it's not bogus," the boss said, "it's just old."

"Still legal tender?"

"It is. But if you come across another one, bring it to me, and we'll talk."

"Sure thing," Manny said. "Anything else?"

"That's it. Keep up the good work."

Manny left the office flapping his open jacket to cool himself down. He hoped his boss hadn't noticed the sweat.

20

Secret Service special agent Alvin Griggs rapped on his boss's door and was invited in and offered a chair and coffee. He accepted the chair, declined the coffee.

"What's up, Al?" his boss, Agent in Charge Dick Fine, asked.

"You remember the handful of 1966 hundreds that turned up in New York recently?"

"I do."

"Well, we've had something of an outbreak of them in South Florida, the area between Fort Lauderdale and Miami."

"What sorts of places did they turn up in?"

"Everything — convenience stores, bars, gun shops, check-cashing services, laundries, used-car lots, Hialeah racetrack, you name it."

"Any in expensive restaurants or hotels?"

"No, now that you mention it."

"Any in cheaper motels and hotels?"
"No."
"So we're not dealing with tourists, the bills are being spread by locals, and low-end locals, at that, given the places they spend money."
"Good point."
"What does that say to you?"
"Maybe that the source of the bills could be a loan shark lending the hundreds or a bookie paying off bets?"
"I think you're right," Fine said. "Start there."
"Loan sharks and bookies aren't the sort of people we ordinarily deal with," Griggs said. "I don't know any, do you?"
"I suggest you visit some police stations in the area and get some names from the detectives who know these guys."
"Okay, good idea." Griggs made to go.
"And, Al?"
"Yessir?"
"You understand that we can't arrest anybody for possessing or passing these bills? Nothing illegal about that."
"I understand, sir. We just want to know the origin of the notes."
"Why, Al?"
"Because we think they might have come from the proceeds of a twenty-five-year-old

robbery."

"We're not in the robbery business, Al, that's the cops and the FBI."

"Then you tell me why we're interested at all, sir."

"Because we're curious and, at the moment, a little underworked. And we get points with Justice for alerting the FBI to these things."

"Well, if the regional AIC gets wind of this, I'll refer him to you," Griggs said.

"You do that, Al."

The engines of the Beech Baron stopped, and John Fratelli stepped out of the airplane onto the wing, then down to the ground. The pilot followed him and retrieved his large duffel from the rear of the airplane.

"I'll be two or three hours," Fratelli told the young man. "You might want to get some lunch somewhere." He wheeled his duffel into the terminal and out the front door and got into one of the waiting taxis. He gave the driver the name of the bank, then sat back and enjoyed the ride.

His business at the bank took less than an hour, and he left with a thick envelope filled with crisp, new hundred-dollar bills, an account number, a bank statement, a debit card with only a number on it, and an empty duffel. He took a stroll down the main street of Georgetown and found an elegant men's shop, where he bought some Bermuda shorts, some short-sleeved shirts, and other resort wear. He packed them into his duffel, just in case some customs agent got curious about why he was traveling with an empty bag.

Late in the afternoon, he returned to his Nassau hotel, then booked a charter flight back to Palm Beach the following morning. He did a little shopping in the town, getting a good deal on a gold Rolex and paying with his debit card, just to try it out. No problem. Back in his room he threw away the leather box the Rolex came in, along with the warranty and instruction book, after he had read it. He would travel with the watch in his pocket, not on his wrist, and not bother to declare it with U.S. Customs.

The following day he arrived at Palm Beach International and walked into customs.

"Did you buy anything while you were out of the country?" the agent asked him.

"Yes, ma'am, I bought some Cuban cigars, which I smoked, and a few clothes." He paid duty on the clothes, then took a cab back to the Breakers. A note had been slid under the door.

John, it read, *Elizabeth and I would be delighted if you could join us for dinner tomorrow evening. Her niece, Hillary Foote, will also join us.* It was signed *Winston.* Fratelli phoned Carnagy and accepted.

The following morning he went into the sales office at the Breakers and made an offer for his suite. After a little haggling the deal was done, and he called the Cayman bank and ordered the funds wired to the hotel's account.

Now, for the first time in more than twenty years, Fratelli had a home that didn't have bars on the windows. And with a view that didn't include a wall or barbed wire.

21

Onofrio "Bats" Buono, whose sobriquet arose from his wanton use of that instrument when collecting debts, took the call in the little office behind the chop shop he ran in Red Hook, Brooklyn. "Hey, Vinnie," he said. "What's the temperature down there?"

"Eighty degrees, Bats. The tempachur is always eighty degrees down here. I hope you're freezing your ass off up there."

"It's pretty good here, Vinnie."

"Bats, I heard something on the grapevine about the lost proceeds of your uncle Eddie's job out at JFK, and I thought you might want to hear it."

Bats's blood pressure spiked for just a moment, and his breathing got short. "Yeah, sure, Vinnie."

"Let's be straight about this, Bats — if I do something that would help you recover that jack, I would expect to be generously compensated for my assistance."

"That goes without saying," Bats replied.

"No, it *needed* saying, and I said it."

"Whatcha got, Vinnie?"

"I got a series 1966 C-note, the one with the red seal, that's what I got."

"Well, I'm real happy for you, Vinnie. Let me know when you find the other eight million, and we'll talk."

"You don't seem to entirely get what I'm saying to you, Bats."

"You got a C-note, right?"

"There's more where this one came from."

"Which is where?"

"I'm working on that. My theory is that we took it in payment for vigorish or a lost bet."

"From who did you take it?"

"I'm working on that, too."

"Did you hear that Johnny Fratelli is out there somewhere?"

"No shit? Did he bust out?"

"Nah, he served his sentence. Him and Uncle Eddie were tight, you know, for all that time in the joint."

"You said he's out there 'somewhere.' Can you tighten that up for me?"

"Well, if you were just out of the joint, and you had got your hands on big money, and people were shooting at you in New York, where would you go?"

"Vegas?"

"People in Vegas got a different set of bookies, Vinnie. How about Miami?"

"That makes sense."

"Then get something going down there, will you? Fratelli knows a lot of people from the old days."

"I'll look into it," Vinnie said.

"Call me." Bats hung up.

Vinnie dialed a cell phone number.

"Yeah?"

"Where are you, Manny?"

"At Hialeah, where I'm supposed to be."

"I got a call."

"I get calls all the time, Vinnie, so do you."

"This one was from New York, concerning one Johnny Fratelli. Know him?"

"I knew him in the joint fifteen years ago. He's dead, isn't he?"

"That's not what my caller said. He's likely down here somewhere, and I want to talk to him."

"What about?"

"Business."

"Oh."

"Put the word out with your people — I want Fratelli in my office, and there's ten grand for anybody who can bring him here, unbruised."

"Sure, Vinnie, I'll spread the word."

Manny hung up. This was interesting, he thought. Nobody alive could remember the last time Vinnie paid anybody ten grand for doing anything, including murder. He called his own office.

"Consolidated Digital," a voice said.

"It's me. You know that weekly fifty grand we're paying out?"

"Yeah."

"When's the next delivery?"

"Next Tuesday, but we're not delivering, we're wiring from offshore to offshore."

"Where was the last delivery made?"

"At a Burger King up on I-95, around Delray, last Tuesday."

"What's this about wiring?"

"The guy handed the delivery boy an envelope with wiring instructions. It had to be from one of our offshore accounts."

"Where's the receiving account?"

"Hard to say. The nearest would be the Caymans."

"So we've lost touch with the guy?"

"Looks that way. We don't have any more appointments to keep, just wires to send."

"Don't send the next one," Manny said. "Not until you get the go-ahead from me, personally."

"Whatever you say, Manny."

Both men hung up.

■ ■ ■ ■

Not twenty miles from Hialeah, an FBI agent took off his headphones and made a phone call to his boss in the Miami field office of the Federal Bureau of Investigation.

"Bob Alberts."

"Sir, I picked up something interesting on the Vinnie Caputo wire. I thought you might like to hear it."

"How long is it?"

"Five minutes, tops — two calls, both outgoing, one to a Brooklyn number, the other to a South Florida cell phone."

"Okay, play it."

The agent backed up the digital recorder and pressed the PLAY button. The recording played. "Get all that?"

"Yeah, I got it all. Send the recording to my in-box."

"Yes, sir."

Bob Alberts hung up the phone and spent a couple of minutes tapping his nails on his desk while he thought. Then he got a stack of his old notebooks from a desk drawer and started flipping through them. It took ten minutes to find the number, then he dialed.

"Harry Moss," an elderly voice said.

"Hello, Harry, it's Bob Alberts. How are you doing?"

"Well, Bobbie. Long time."

"How's the world treating you?"

"I'm eating a corned beef sandwich out by the pool, that's how it's treating me."

"Life is sweet, huh?"

"You bet your ass, Bob. Why the hell are you wasting your time calling me when you should be out solving crimes?"

"Something came up about an old case of yours."

"How cold?"

"Twenty-five years, give or take. The JFK robbery?"

"What the hell came up about that?"

"How much was stolen?"

"Fifteen million. We got about half of it back, but the brains behind it, a guy named Eddie Buono, died in prison recently, and we never saw a dime of it. What have you heard?"

"We picked up something on a wiretap about a series 1966 hundred-dollar bill, and the guy we're tapping connected it to that robbery. He called somebody in Brooklyn about it. Was there a guy named Fratelli involved?"

"Doesn't ring a bell. I mean, I remember something about a guy named Fratelli, but he was never connected to the robbery."

"I don't know about that, but on our wiretap it was said that a John Fratelli was in Sing Sing with Buono for a long time, and that he recently got out. The Italian gentlemen in New York are looking for him. What do you remember about Fratelli?"

"Let's see: six-four, two-fifty, a real ox. Had a fearsome rep as an enforcer. People were so scared of him they nearly always did what he said or answered what he asked. He hardly ever had to use force."

"How old would he be?"

"Jeez, fifty, fifty-five, maybe."

"Can you think of anything about him that would help us find him?"

"Come on, Bob, what's going on?"

"I think he might have the money, or some of it, that you never recovered."

"Where do you think he might be?"

"Maybe South Florida. Where might he hang out?"

"Jeez, I don't know. Where those guys always hang out: the track, some bar somewhere."

"That's it, huh? Nothing else?"

"I been retired ten years, Bob. You must have somebody fresher than me to ask."

"Okay, Harry, go back to your corned beef sandwich."

"Let me know if there's anything I can do."

"Bye, Harry."

"Bye, Bob."

Harry Moss hung up the phone in a sweat. He had seen Johnny Fratelli in a Burger King less than a week ago, wearing shorts, a Hawaiian shirt, a straw hat, and dark glasses, but he had recognized him. He hadn't put a name to the guy until now.

22

Jack Coulter, née John Fratelli, checked his image in the mirror before leaving his apartment. He had lost twenty pounds since leaving prison, ten of them since buying his Brooks Brothers suits. He was going to need a tailor. His hair was growing out nicely, now merely short, not skin on the sides, and he had started a mustache, which was not a problem for a man who had to shave twice a day to avoid a five o'clock shadow. A few days before, he had noticed a difficulty with reading the newspaper, so he had visited an optometrist and had been prescribed glasses. They gave him a whole new look, he thought, and the advantage of clear vision.

Fratelli met his dinner hosts at the entrance to the Breakers, where he was introduced to Hillary Foote, who was much more attractive than he had envisioned. She was tall, slim, and shapely in the right places, mid-forties. The Carnagys' antique

Rolls-Royce from the fifties collected them and drove them to the Brazilian Court Hotel and its restaurant, Boulud.

Hillary turned out to be smart and funny. She had been divorced a year before and also lived at the Breakers.

"I assume you're retired, Jack," she said. "What did you do when you had to work for a living?"

"I was an entrepreneur," Fratelli replied, "until about ten years ago, when I sold a number of small businesses and became an investor. Now I just loaf. I'm thinking of taking up golf, in fact, as I understand that's what loafers do."

"In that case, I'm the biggest loafer you know. I play to an eight handicap."

Fratelli had no idea what an eight handicap was, but he made a mental note to find out.

"How was your trip to the Bahamas?" Winston Carnagy asked him.

"Very nice indeed," Fratelli replied, adding a small wink for emphasis.

"I'm glad to hear it," Carnagy said, smiling.

"Hillary," Fratelli said, "would you teach me to play golf?"

She laughed. "If I tried to do that, we'd hate each other in no time. What you need is a golf pro. Ask the concierge at the Breakers to set up some lessons for you at their course. Then, after you feel comfortable with the way you're hitting the ball, we'll play together."

"Playing with you is a worthy goal."

They chatted on through their excellent dinner; Winston and Elizabeth hardly got a word in, except to give Fratelli the name of Winston's local tailor.

That night, having delivered Hillary to her door, Fratelli got into bed and reflected on his circumstances. He had traveled to a state he had never before visited, dressed in the sort of clothes he had never worn; he had bought an apartment in the kind of hotel he had seen only from the outside; he had an offshore bank account and a substantial weekly income from his investment with the loan shark. Thinking about that brought him up short.

Manny Millman was the only person from his past who knew he was in Florida, though he knew not where and under what circumstances. Manny and his deliveryman, whom he had met at the Burger King, were the only people who had laid eyes on him and who thus might become a problem for him. But neither knew he was in Palm Beach, so they should not be difficult to avoid. He would have to stay away from the tracks, though, and other places where he might run into them.

He had good friends in the Carnagys, and Winston had become his model for speech and behavior in this new world. And Hillary Foote showed much promise as a pleasing companion.

He needed more social gifts, though, and golf might be one of them. He would have to look into tennis, too. He had been athletic in high school, playing football and basketball. It would be interesting to see how the athletic gift would translate into more sociable sports.

Harry Moss got in line at the Burger King off I-95 and had a look around. The place was only a couple of miles from where he lived, in Delray Beach, and this was his third day running having lunch here, hoping for sight of Johnny Fratelli.

He had used everything at his disposal — the Internet, a search of Florida phone books for the name, he had even tried Facebook — but no Johnny Fratelli had turned up. His only hope had been the Burger King. Who knew? Maybe Fratelli was addicted to the double bacon cheeseburger. He ate his own cheeseburger and searched the restaurant over and over. He saw one man of the right size, but he was Hispanic.

John Fratelli presented himself at the Breakers golf club and was introduced to a kid of about twenty-two, who was supposed to teach him golf. What could a kid of that age teach anybody?

Quite a lot, as it turned out. The boy had a beautiful, liquid swing, and by the end of their first hour together, he had Fratelli hitting his irons nicely. He asked for another lesson after lunch, then got himself a sandwich in the clubhouse.

He liked the atmosphere; the players, mostly men, chatted amiably with one another, and he picked up snippets of golf lore as he listened.

During his second lesson, they started on the woods, and Fratelli found the driver challenging. Still, he had a good teacher.

When they were done, the boy — Terry — complimented him on his swing. "You know," Terry said, "most of the people I instruct have played the game for a while, and I have to straighten out their bad habits. You don't have any bad habits, and you're a natural athlete, with a natural swing. If we can do two hours a day together, I'll have you playing pretty good duffer golf in a couple of weeks."

"I've got the time, Terry, schedule me now."

"Tomorrow morning we'll play nine holes and start to work on club selection and strategy."

"I place myself in your hands," Fratelli said.

Alvin Griggs walked into the clubhouse at Hialeah and asked for Manny Millman. He was directed to a man dressed in a seersucker suit and a golf shirt, with a large pair of binoculars, sitting at a table with a good view of the track, eating a club sandwich. He walked over and, uninvited, sat down.

"Hi, Manny," Griggs said.

"We know each other?" Manny replied, wariness in his voice.

"No, and if we have a successful conversation, we are unlikely to meet again."

"You're a cop."

"Federal," Griggs said, "My name is Al Griggs, but I won't flash a badge. It wouldn't be good for your reputation in this setting."

"I appreciate the courtesy," Manny said. "What can I do for you?"

"I want to have a chat with John Fratelli."

Manny was stunned to hear that name again, but he did a good job of screwing up his face and seeming ignorant. "Fratelli? I knew a guy by that name in the joint, but that was a long time ago. Last time I heard anything about him, he was dead."

Griggs smiled. "Nice try, Manny," he said. "But you're not a good enough actor." Griggs had no idea if Manny knew anything, but he had decided to treat him as if he did and was holding out.

"I got no reason to hold out on you, Mr. Griggs," Manny said.

Griggs reached into a pocket and pulled out a page he had printed from the Internet, in color. "This is a series 1966 hundred-dollar bill," he said. "Note the red seal. Seen anything like that lately?"

Manny took a close look at the page, then shook his head. "It's just a C-note," he said. "I see them all the time."

"Yes, but not with the red seal." Griggs produced a business card and slid it across the table. "If you come across a note like this, and especially if you see Johnny Fratelli again, I'd like to hear about it. There could be a substantial reward in it for you."

"Mr. Griggs, I think you're chasing a dead guy, but if I see any money like that, I'll give you a call."

Griggs thanked him and left.

Manny sat and watched him go. This Fratelli thing was beginning to be annoying. He got out his cell phone and called his bookkeeper.

"Yes?"

"It's Manny."

"Hey, Manny."

"You remember I gave you a million a short while ago?"

"A fella remembers a thing like that."

"How did you distribute it?"

"I shipped all of it to the Singapore bank."

"Did you retain any of the money I gave you?"

"A payout on a long shot came across my desk, twenty grand. I may have used some of it for that."

"But the rest went to Singapore?"

"It did, and I can prove it if I have to. Go online and look at the bank statement. You'll see the deposit."

"I'll do that. What was the name of the big winner?"

"Hang on a sec, I'll see." He came back after a pause. "Howard Silver. He's a regular at Hialeah."

"Thanks." So there was twenty grand in

hot hundreds floating around out there, and Howard Silver, whom he knew by sight, had it.

23

John Fratelli awoke the following morning, and something was nagging at him in the back of his mind. It came to him: IRS. He showered and dressed and had his first shave of the day, then he called New York on his throwaway cell phone.

"Woodman & Weld, Mr. Barrington's office."

"Good morning, this is John Fratelli. May I speak to Mr. Barrington, please?"

"One moment, I'll see if he's free."

"Stone Barrington."

"Mr. Barrington, it's John Fratelli. How are you?"

"Mr. Fratelli, I'm fine. You sound different."

"Perhaps so. I have a legal question for you, a hypothetical one: how would a person recently out of sight for many years avoid having the Internal Revenue Service made aware of his presence?"

"Does this hypothetical person have a Social Security number or has he filed returns in the past?"

"He has never had an SSN, nor has he ever filed."

"Then he should not apply for one, unless he seeks employment, in which case he might want to give some thought to a new identity."

"I see. What else should he avoid?"

"Any sort of transaction requiring a Social Security number: opening a bank account, for instance, or applying for a loan, opening a department store or gas credit card. All sorts of businesses these days require a Social Security number. Of course, he could decline to divulge that number, because it's technically private information. That might work with opening a bank account, but not when applying for credit. A lender would deny his application."

"What about income?"

"Everyone is required to file an annual tax return, Mr. Fratelli, listing income from any source."

"And if one doesn't file?"

"Then they would have no reason to come after him, unless someone had reported his status to them. If this person had, for instance, not filed a tax return during his, ah, absence from society, the IRS would have no knowledge of him. Once he filed, though, they would know him forever."

"Then perhaps he should avoid coming to the attention of the IRS."

"That would be my advice, hypothetically."

"Thank you. I'll send payment for your services."

"Please, no more hundred-dollar bills."

"You object to cash?"

"I object to out-of-date cash. I had a visit from the Secret Service after I deposited those hundreds. They're series 1966 and out of circulation. You can tell by the red seal on the bills."

"What did you tell the Secret Service?"

"Substantially nothing: attorney-client confidentiality."

"That was the right thing to do. I'll send you a cashier's check."

"Mr. Fratelli, please don't bother. You've more than compensated me for my time already. By the way, you should know that the Secret Service are not the only people interested in your existence and whereabouts. I had a visit from a retired police detective named Sean Donnelly, who investigated a crime committed at JFK airport some years ago."

"But you told him nothing?"

"Correct. You should also know that, shortly after visiting me, Donnelly was shot while leaving P.J. Clarke's in the wee hours of the morning."

"Killed?"

"No, just winged. He'll be up and around soon, and as far as I know, he remains interested in your whereabouts."

"Any word on who shot Donnelly?"

"No, but my assumption is it's probably whoever ventilated your suitcase. If I were you I would find a way to exchange your funds for new funds."

"I have already done so."

"Have you spent any more of the hundred-dollar bills?"

"Yes, I've paid my living expenses, but I've made an investment which brings me a weekly return, so I won't be needing to do that anymore."

"How much of a return, out of curiosity?" Barrington asked.

"Five percent a week."

"Did you say *a week*?"

"Yes."

"So, you have loaned to . . . a lender. How much?"

"One very large bill."

Barrington made a sucking sound through

his teeth. "Mr. Fratelli, this is not good. Those hundred-dollar bills will not go unnoticed by the organization employing your lender, and I fear that you may have more to fear from them than from the IRS."

"That's good advice, but I believe things are under control. I've settled in a comfortable spot, and they are not aware of my location or my new name."

"Yes, I noticed the postmark on your card. You'll want to watch that sort of thing."

"You're quite right, I was careless, and I won't be again. Thank you for your advice, Mr. Barrington."

"Did you take my advice on acquiring a throwaway cell phone?"

"Yes, I did. I'm speaking on it."

"You might want to give me that number, in case I hear from any of your old acquaintances. Somebody has already fired a shotgun at my front door."

"I'm extremely sorry to hear that. Here's my number." Fratelli dictated it to him.

"I won't call unless I fear that you are in jeopardy."

"Thank you, and goodbye."

"Goodbye and good luck."

Both men hung up

Fratelli thought about this for a few minutes, then he took up his throwaway cell phone and called Manny Millman.

"This is Manny."

"This is John Fratelli."

"Hey, Johnny, how's it going?"

"I'm getting feedback about some certain C-notes."

"Ah, yes, I've heard something about that."

"How did you dispose of the cash I gave you?"

"It was shipped to an offshore bank account the day after you gave it to me."

"All of it? Don't lie to me, Manny."

"Apparently, twenty thousand of it was paid to a punter who had a long shot come in. I just heard, and I'm going to recover whatever he has left and send it out of the country."

"A very good idea," Fratelli said.

"But at least some of it is floating around out there. And, Johnny, I had a visit from a Secret Service guy."

"Asking about the C-notes?"

"Asking about you. I told him I thought you were dead."

"Stick with that story," Fratelli said.

"I will, and, Johnny, your request is being honored to transfer your weekly vigorish from offshore account to offshore account."

"Very good."

"How can I get in touch with you, Johnny, if anything else should come up?"

"You can't. I've left the state and made myself at home elsewhere."

"You're sure there's not a number?"

"Okay, I'll give you a throwaway cell phone." He dictated the number. "Memorize that, Manny, then burn it."

"Johnny, like I told you before, I'm grateful to you for your help when I was in the joint with you. I won't rat you out."

"Thank you, Manny." Fratelli hung up.

Manny got up from his table and started walking the Hialeah clubhouse, looking for Howard Silver.

24

Howard Silver stood at the hundred-dollar window at Hialeah and took one last look at the odds board. He was about to turn back to the window when he found himself abruptly pushed out of line.

"Come with me, Howard," Manny Mill-man said, taking a firm grip of Silver's elbow and propelling him toward a door marked "Employees Only."

"What the hell, Manny? I don't owe you anything."

"I know, Howard, and I'm grateful for your business." Manny opened a door and shoved him into a conference room. "Have a seat," Manny said. "We're going to have a little conference."

"What's the beef, Manny? I don't under-stand."

"Howard, when your long shot came in, we gave you twenty grand in hundreds, that correct?"

"Well, yeah, that's how much I won."

"I'm sorry, but through an administrative oversight you were given the wrong hundred-dollar bills."

"No," Howard said, shaking his head vehemently, "the ones you gave me are working just fine, everywhere I go."

"How much have you spent, Howard?"

"I don't know exactly."

"All right, let's do it this way: how much you got left?"

Howard made a little involuntary jerking motion that moved his left arm across his chest. "I'll go home and count it and let you know," he said.

Manny removed Howard's arm from its frozen position, stuck his hand into Howard's inside pocket and came out with a thick bundle of bills, bound by a rubber band. "Looks like ten grand here," he said. "Give me the rest."

"Manny, I won it fair and square," Howard protested.

"I know you did, Howard, and I'm going to replace your money with other money that won't get you killed."

"What do you mean, get me killed?"

Manny put a finger to Howard's head, pulled an imaginary trigger, and said, "Bang. Like that, killed."

"I don't understand."

"Let me explain it to you. A long time ago some money was stolen. In hundred-dollar bills." He picked one from the stack and held it up. "Like this one. See the red stamp?"

"Yes."

"They don't put that on hundreds anymore. They look different nowadays."

Howard picked up the note and held it up to the light. "Looks okay to me."

"Well, Howard, I know it doesn't have the word 'stolen' stamped on it, but believe me, it is. Empty your pockets, Howard. All of them."

Howard began pulling a handkerchief, a comb, some car keys, and a wallet from his pockets, then he produced a money clip holding a thick wad of hundreds.

"Is that all of it, Howard?"

Howard nodded.

"None of it at home?"

Howard shook his head.

"Did you deposit any of it in your bank account?"

"Of course not, my wife sees the statements."

"I want to know every single place you left one of these hundreds," Manny said, shoving a legal pad from the table in front of him toward Howard and placing his pen on it. "Start from where the nice man gave you the twenty grand, and go from there." Manny picked up the bound wad of hundreds and began expertly counting them. His fingers were a blur.

Howard began to make a list.

"Write how many hundreds you left in each place," Manny said, pulling the stack from Howard's money clip and counting that.

"There," Howard said, shoving the legal pad toward Manny.

Manny looked at the list. "Howard, no normal human being could read this handwriting. Take me through it, slowly."

Howard took the pad back. "Okay, I picked up the money from the man out in the trailer, then I left and came up to the clubhouse, to the bar, and I bought everybody there a round. That came to five hundred and change, so six hundreds."

Manny wrote down six. Howard continued with his day — lunch, more drinks, then a series of bets at the hundred-dollar window. "I didn't lose it all," he said. "I won some back."

"I'm not interested in what you won back, Howard, just the hundreds with the little red stamp on them."

Howard worked his way through the list. He had bought a couple of suits at a Lauderdale shop that Manny knew; he had given a hundred to a beggar on the street because he liked the beggar's dog. Manny knew the beggar; Manny knew the dog. He had sent some flowers to his girlfriend, as distinguished from his wife. Manny knew the flower shop. This continued to the end of the list.

Manny toted up a total. "Okay, you spread around about three grand on the street, and another five hundred in the clubhouse. You bet another four grand. We got a total of twelve thousand, one hundred dollars on the table here." Manny went through his pockets and produced wads of cash, much of it in hundreds. He counted out the money, then made Howard count it again, then gave him newer hundreds and took all the old ones and stuffed them into his pockets.

"Now listen, Howard," Manny said. "I've made you whole, right?"

"Right."

"And I've saved you from going to prison or getting a hole in your head, if you keep your mouth shut. You going to keep your mouth shut, Howard?"

"Yes, Manny, I certainly am. And I very

much appreciate your help in all this."

"Not a word to another soul, Howard, or people will come after you. If anybody asks you about a hundred with a red stamp, you don't know nothing, you never heard of such a thing, got it?"

"Got it."

Manny walked Howard back into the club, then he took the elevator down to the parking lot and walked a hundred yards, where he came to a parked Cadillac with an Airstream trailer attached to it. He hammered a code knock on the door, which was opened by the bookkeeper.

"I got twelve thousand, one hundred bucks in hundred-dollar bills," he said. "You shipping today?"

"I ship every day," the bookkeeper said.

"Give me eleven thousand one hundred from your shipment and replace it with this."

The man counted out the money and accepted the stack from Manny. "What's this about, Manny?"

"Accounting," Manny said. "Now send your shipment, and we never had this conversation."

The man nodded, and Manny left the trailer and went back to the clubhouse.

Meanwhile there were seventy-nine series

1966 hundred-dollar bills in the wind in and around Lauderdale and points north, south, east, and west, for all he knew. Since they weren't bundled, there was a good chance they'd just disappear, until some scanner in some bank somewhere picked them up. It was pretty near untraceable, and it was the best he could do. He put it out of his mind and went back to handicapping.

25

Stone's day was closing, and he called Holly Barker.

"Yes?"

"It's Stone. Dinner tonight?"

"You poor dear, did last weekend make you think I was available for a social life again?"

"It gave me hope."

"Stone, I had a little break in work, and I was randy, just like you."

"You certainly know how to sweet-talk a guy."

"I am once again submerged in work, and there's no time for sweet talk. I'll call you if I can ever breathe again, all right?"

"All right."

"I do love you, baby, but my country needs me more than you do right now."

"Okay." They both hung up. That had been a little depressing, but that was the way Holly was. In the meantime, he had no plans for the evening, and Dino wasn't pretty enough. It occurred to him that he had not called Hank Cromwell, who had drawn such a nice portrait of him. He did so.

"Well, I wasn't sure you would call," she said.

"O ye of little faith."

"You didn't say you would."

"That was implicit in my request for your phone number."

"I guess it was, at that."

"I know it's late to call, but would you like to have dinner tonight?"

"I would," she replied. "Where and what time?"

"Where do you live?"

"Murray Hill."

"In that case, may we meet at Patroon at eight?" He gave her the address.

"Sounds good. I don't know the restaurant. How dressy is it?"

"I'll wear a necktie."

"Ooookay. See you then."

Stone hung up, and Joan came to the door. "Anything else? I thought I'd get out of here at a decent hour."

"Good idea. I just have to sort out what's on my desk, so I'll remember tomorrow what I was doing today, then I'm out of here, too."

"Good night, then." She vanished.

Five minutes later, the phone rang. "Hello?"

"It's Emma. How are you, darling?"

"Just thinking I would never hear from you again. And you?"

"Feeling guilty for not having called since you gave me the name of that sweet DCI Throckmorton."

"Sweet? Are we talking about the same grizzled curmudgeon?"

"Oh, his mustache and eyebrows could use a trim, and he's a little grouchy, but he responds well to gentle treatment and a smile."

"I'm relieved to hear that. I thought he was some sort of android invented by the Metropolitan Police."

"Well, he knows what he's doing, I'll give him that. It took him three days to sort out my problem."

"And how did he do that?"

"He began questioning everybody with access to my designs, and he can be a very intimidating questioner. He just asks and sits there like he's daring them to lie to him. Very effective."

"I must remember that technique."

"Anyway, it was the art director on our

account at our ad agency. He started asking questions in that way of his, and she crumbled like a biscuit. She'd been color faxing somebody in Paris every design of ours that crossed her desk, which was about ten percent of our output, just the things we were using in our advertising."

"I congratulate you."

"I gave Throckmorton a check for ten thousand pounds. Do you think that was fair?"

"Fair? I'm surprised he didn't clutch his chest and turn blue."

"It wasn't enough?"

"It was more than enough. I doubt he's seen that much cash in one place in his whole life, unless it was the proceeds of a bank robbery he was investigating. Are you sending your design thief to prison?"

"I declined to bring charges against the poor woman, but she got fired."

"That was wise of you. I doubt if she'll do it again, if she can find another job in the ad business. Does this happy turn of events mean you'll be coming to New York now?"

"I will be, but not now. It's very, very busy here, and we're planning the bigger office in L.A."

"Oh."

"Don't be sad, my dear. We'll see each

other soon. Sooner, if you'd like to turn up in London for a few days."

"Now, that's an interesting thought. Do I have to stay at the Connaught?"

"Certainly not, you're not allowed to stay anywhere but with me."

"You're sure you have room?"

"It's a king-sized bed, or as I like to think of it, playing field."

"Let me see when I can carve a few days out of my busy schedule. Maybe I'll surprise you."

"Promise?"

"Sort of. Joan has already gone home, and she's the only person who can give me permission to leave town."

"Then I will look forward to hearing from you. Good night."

Stone hung up. Ah, London: it had been a while, and he loved London.

26

Alvin Griggs was called into his boss's office during what would ordinarily have been his coffee break, and told to sit down. He did.

"Al, we've taken in six more series 1966 hundred-dollar bills," the AIC said. "Two of them at Fort Lauderdale International Airport, where somebody, we don't know who, yet, paid cash for an airline ticket, we don't know where to, yet."

"And the others?"

"Two at the Greyhound bus station ticket office in Miami — again from whom and to where remain to be determined. Then there was one given to a livery driver in Miami and deposited into his bank account, and one — this will amuse you — taken from a high-end hooker who got busted."

Griggs was not amused. "So, the money is being used for the purposes of travel and entertainment? Sounds like tourists to me

— two of whom were on their way home to wherever. It occurs to me, too, that since we have found so few of these notes, not very much of the money is in circulation — certainly not seven million dollars of it."

"I'm entertaining the notion that what we've found is like the fuse to a bomb."

"You mean, if we follow the trail, it will blow up in our faces? I tend to agree."

"Very funny, Al."

"I wasn't trying to be funny. I believe one person has all the money, and that he's spent it rather sparingly while he figures out how to launder it. What we're picking up didn't come directly from that person's hands. We're getting it two or three generations of spenders away from him. One guy wouldn't be taking both an airplane and a Greyhound bus out of South Florida."

"You have a low opinion of this case, don't you, Al?"

"It's just that we seem to be in a lose-lose situation. The best we can hope for is to identify the guy who has the seven million dollars from the robbery, and if we do, all we'll do is make the FBI look smart when we turn him over, and we both know they're not all that smart."

"Don't you think it would be satisfying to find the guy who has all the cash?"

"Not particularly. He couldn't be charged with stealing it, because the guy we know stole it died a few weeks ago, and because the statute has run out on the crime. The very worst that could be done with him is a charge of receiving stolen property, and I'm not so sure that, after so long, it's even stolen property. And that particular crime isn't what we're tasked to investigate. Honest to God, boss, I don't know why you're so enchanted with this case. I mean, it's not even a case." Griggs could have gone on, but he sensed he was getting very close to the edge of insubordination, so he stopped.

"Al, if you were in possession of this money, what would you do with it?"

"I'd get it into a foreign bank, pronto," Griggs said. "Before I could spend another dime of it."

"Where?"

"The Bahamas, maybe, or the Caymans. Then I'd begin drawing on my balance in nice, new notes and start spending it like a drunken sailor. I think it's extremely unlikely that a foreign bank would even notice that the bills are old, and even if they did, why would they care? Pretty soon the money will be making its way around the world, from account to account and pocket to pocket. It probably already is."

The AIC heaved a deep sigh. "All right, Al, you've convinced me. You're off the case. Go find me some counterfeit money, or something."

"Thank you, boss." Griggs got out of there as fast as he could.

Stone got to the restaurant five minutes early, and Hank Cromwell turned up on time, in a smashing little black dress and pearls and a rather large handbag. They exchanged cheek kisses, and he liked her perfume.

"What would you like to drink?" he asked.

"An Absolut martini, straight up, with a fistful of olives. And then another, please."

"I'll try to avoid gaps between drinks."

Their drinks came, and they touched glasses and sipped.

"Are you armed tonight?" she asked.

Stone snapped his fingers. "Damn it, I forgot!"

"If somebody had fired at my front door, I'd be walking around with a shotgun," Hank said.

"I can't imagine where you'd hide it — certainly not in that dress."

"I'll bet if I carried it openly, nobody would bother me."

"Nobody but one or more police officers."

"Well, there is that. I did go armed for a while, during one period of my life."

"What period of your life was that?"

"The period when I was endeavoring to obtain a complete and final exit from the company of an Italian gentleman who had a lot of friends with broken noses and bulges under their silk suits."

"And how long did that period last?"

"About seven months, before he finally got discouraged. He was very persistent."

"How on earth did you become involved with him?"

"Well," she said, "I met him at the bar at P.J. Clarke's. How about that for a coincidence?"

Stone laughed. "You must spend a lot of time at Clarke's."

"Been there exactly twice — met him the first time and you the second. I'm hoping for better from you."

"I'll try not to disappoint you."

She patted his cheek with a cool hand. "You're sweet."

"How did you find out the Italian guy was connected?"

"Connected?"

"A Mafioso."

"It took me a little while, actually. He told me he was in the auto parts business, but I didn't realize the parts were all second-hand and that he was running something called a chop shop in Red Hook, Brooklyn. Still is, for all I know."

"Would it make you happy if I had him arrested?"

"I thought you were no longer a cop."

"I'm not, but my best friend in the world is. Would you like me to mention his name to Dino?"

She looked thoughtful. "I must admit, the notion of his being behind bars has a lot to recommend it, but the possible consequences don't. I'd have to testify against him, wouldn't I?"

"Did you ever visit his place of business?"

"No, I finally just put two and two together. He used only cash, no credit cards or checks, and he peeled it off a roll the size of your fist, which was secured with a rubber band. And, as an afterthought, there was the .45 in the shoulder holster."

"Then you wouldn't make much of a witness," Stone said, "since you don't know anything. He could be just an honest businessman with an unreasoning fear of the IRS and other people with guns. Still, the cops could nose around Red Hook and see what they find."

"I'm sure they'd find a garage full of

Porsche and Mercedes hulks. That was what he drove, and it was never the same car twice."

"Who was this guy?"

"One Onofrio Buono," she said. "Known as Bats, and not because he was crazy."

"Buono is a familiar name," Stone said.

"He's the only one of those I ever met."

"A gentleman of the same surname, one Eduardo Buono, led a heist at Kennedy Airport a long time ago, during which fifteen million dollars in cash abruptly changed ownership. Half of it was never recovered, and the elder Mr. Buono died in prison quite recently. Any of that ring a bell?"

"Not really. I mean, I suppose Bats had a father named Buono, but he hardly ever came up in conversation."

"Can you remember a time when he did?"

"Bats mentioned, once, that his father used to beat the shit out of his mother, a trait that I came to believe was genetically handed down from generation to generation."

"Was he abusive to you?"

"Just once. He slapped me around early one evening, and I got him slapped in jail for the remainder of it. I immediately took a two-week vacation to nowhere, and my car drove itself to an island in Maine. It was in February, and it wasn't much fun.

"When I got back there were a lot of dead flowers on my doorstep and a lot of unopened mail spattered with teardrops. That was when the persistence began, followed shortly by the obtaining of a temporary restraining order that was meant to keep him at least a hundred yards from me but, of course, didn't work, resulting in two further visits to Rikers Island by Mr. Buono."

"How did you finally get rid of him?"

"I had him visited in jail by a very large actor friend of mine, who specialized in portraying murderous hulks, and who explained to him what would happen to his various limbs and his brains if he did not immediately fall out of love with me."

"And that worked?"

"From what I heard later, it was my friend's finest work as an actor, a performance so convincing that it would surely have won him, in a different venue than Rikers, an Oscar nomination."

Their dinner arrived and was happily consumed. "Are you armed?" Stone asked at one point.

"Not tonight."

"Then what's in the giant handbag?"

"A fresh thong and a change of clothes for work tomorrow. I thought I might share your bed tonight, if there's room."

"I'll make room," Stone said.

27

Stone was awakened, as the first rays of dawn came through the slatted blinds, by a cool hand on his warm crotch, to which he immediately responded.

At the end of this encounter, Stone asked, "Do you always get up so early?"

"Seven is early?"

"It is around here."

"I'm usually at work by eight, eight-thirty at the latest."

"What would you like for breakfast?"

"What's available?"

"Almost anything you can imagine, in the breakfast line."

"Two eggs, over easy, sausages, toast, orange juice, and strong black coffee sweetened with a carcinogen."

Stone called down to the kitchen and ordered for both of them, then retrieved the *Times* and the *Daily News* from the dumbwaiter. He raised the head and foot of the bed sufficiently to cradle them while they read and ate. "Tell me," he said, when they were comfortable, "do you have any remaining friends in common with Mr. Buono?"

"If you knew his friends, you wouldn't have to ask."

"I was wondering if there's anyone you know who might be aware of any possible connection between Onofrio and Eduardo Buono."

"Nope. I should think your best bet for that sort of genealogy would be their respective police files. And I believe you have entrée, do you not?"

"I do, and a very good suggestion that is."

At eight o'clock, Hank rolled out of bed and into a shower, and fifteen minutes later, she presented herself, dressed and packed. "That was my kind of evening," she said, kissing him on the forehead. "Do you think we might repeat it in the not-too-distant future? I'm assuming you are not the sort of man who easily becomes violent and subsequently forms obsessive attachments to unwilling women."

"You assume correctly, and I'd love to."

"You have my number — in more ways than one," she said. She kissed him on the lips and fled the premises.

■ ■ ■ ■

After Stone had finished the crossword, he called Dino.

"Good afternoon," Dino said.

"It's nine in the morning."

"That's afternoon to someone who has to get up as early as I do."

"Dino, in your present position, nobody is going to keep a time card on you. Go in later, like a gentleman."

"I like to be in the office before things happen, not after. It's good for my in-house reputation."

"I need a favor."

"Consider it granted, if I feel like doing it."

"I'd like you to run a couple of names for me: Eduardo Buono and Onofrio Buono, who has the charming sobriquet of 'Bats.' "

"What is it you want to know about them?"

"Are they related? If so, how? Were they close? Ever pull any jobs together? Like that."

"I wouldn't dirty my hands with that," Dino said. "I'll have somebody get back to you."

"Many thanks."

They hung up.

Stone was at his desk, mid-morning, when his phone buzzed.

"A detective Donatello for you on line one."

"This is Stone Barrington, Detective."

"Good morning. The chief asked me to get back to you with some info on the Buonos."

"Thank you for calling. What did you learn?"

"Mostly what I already knew. Eddie is the uncle of Bats. The kid was a teenager when Eddie went away for the JFK heist, and he idolized his uncle. About a year before Eddie died in Sing Sing, Bats started visiting him every week, and a confidential informant told us the kid was bugging his uncle about what he did with the money from the heist. This attention apparently annoyed Eddie, and about a month before he died, when he was a patient in the infirmary, he cut the kid off, had him removed from his list of approved visitors. The kid made a scene on his next visit and got booted into the street for his trouble. Anything else you need?"

"Thanks, no, but I have a tidbit for you, if you don't already have it."

"I'm listening."

"Bats now has a high-end chop shop — Porsches and Mercedeses — in Red Hook. And he makes a practice of driving his merchandise before he chops it."

"That's very interesting," Donatello said. "I and the department thank you. I'll be sure the chief hears about it, too."

Stone hung up happy, having both learned something to his benefit and done his duty as a citizen.

Jack Coulter, née John Fratelli, was lunching at a table at the Breakers beach club with Hillary Foote when he saw a familiar face. He did not like familiar faces, especially since this one seemed to be looking for someone.

He riffled through his recent memories — this face seemed a recent memory — in search of a locale in which to place the face, and finally it came to him. Burger King. On the day that he had received an envelope, fat with new hundreds, from Manny Millman's messenger, he had seen that face a couple of tables away, and it seemed to be interested in him, and its owner seemed, somehow, familiar.

He cast further back in his memory and attempted to place the face in his pre-prison existence. Ex-something, he decided: ex-cop, ex-FBI, ex-something, he wasn't sure what. Fratelli's appearance had changed a great deal since that day at the Burger King: he was slimmer, tanner, and had a mustache and a good deal more hair, gray at the temples. He did not think of himself as recognizable in this setting by someone from his past. Still, he waited until the man's back was turned, excused himself, and went to the men's room, stopping to chat with an assistant manager long enough to tell him that he did not believe that man over there was a member of this club. When he came out of the men's room, he caught sight of the fellow being escorted rapidly toward an exit.

"What are you looking so thoughtful about, Jack?" Hillary asked.

He was trying to put a name to that face, but he had not yet succeeded when the question brought him back to the present. "I was thinking about how wonderful you were last night," he said. He meant it, too. It had been his first night in bed with a woman in more than twenty years, and the experience had more than lived up to his memories.

"You're a sweet man in bed," Hillary said, squeezing his hand.

"Thank you, my dear," Fratelli said, and he forgot about the familiar face. "I'm going to do some shopping for a car this afternoon. May I borrow your good eye for beautiful things?"

"Of course you may," she said.

28

Harry Moss's ears were burning. He had just been rudely escorted out of the Breakers beach club because he was not a member, and it was embarrassing. After all, he was nicely dressed in a shirt he had actually bought in Palm Beach, white trousers, and what he felt was a very attractive porkpie hat in straw, with a colorful band. In short, he was sure he was indistinguishable from any other sixtyish gentleman at the Breakers.

Harry had organized his search for Johnny Fratelli around his newfound fantasies about where he would go and what he would buy if he had suddenly come into seven million dollars. He had driven past the Breakers many times and admired it from afar as an unattainable venue for any part of his own life, and the Breakers had just confirmed that judgment by suggesting that he vacate the premises. He climbed into his Toyota Camry and thought about what to do next.

Harry had already combed the men's stores — Ralph Lauren, Maus & Hoffman, et cetera, plus the men's departments of Neiman Marcus and Saks Fifth Avenue, and without success. Perhaps this had been a waste of his time, since when he had seen Johnny Fratelli at the Burger King, the man had been wearing a loud Hawaiian shirt and baggy Bermuda shorts. And sandals, for Christ's sake — sandals with socks!

Clearly, Harry had better taste than Fratelli, so perhaps the Breakers would be a bit of a stretch for an ex-con with seven million dollars and no sense of style. Where else might one look for such a person? What would he buy, besides clothes? He drove out Okefenokee Drive, where all the car dealerships were. What would a guy who had just been sprung after twenty-two years think was a top-notch ride? He turned into the Cadillac dealership and had a stroll around the place, fending off salespeople as he went. Nah. Cadillacs weren't big enough anymore.

He tried the Mercedes dealership, with similar results. Then he had it: Rolls-Royce! A guy with seven million bucks stashed away could afford a Rolls! He continued out Okefenokee until he spotted the dealership. Here, he had no problem fending off salespeople because they either ignored him or looked right through him. His stroll was short, and he was soon back in his Toyota. As he waited at the exit for the traffic to subside enough to let him in, a black Lincoln Town Car turned into the dealership and drove past him, its windows black. Harry made his turn and headed back toward Delray Beach.

Fratelli and Hillary sat in air-conditioned comfort in the rear seat of a Breakers town car and watched the dealership hove into view. As they turned in, they narrowly missed a gray Toyota leaving the lot. The driver stopped outside the showroom and leaped out of the car to open Hillary's door.

"We'll be a few minutes," Fratelli said to the man, and a salesman was there to open the door to the showroom for them.

"Yes, sir, ma'am, how may I help you?"

"A Bentley, perhaps," Fratelli said.

"Normally, our sales are by order," the man said, "but as it happens, we have two new Bentleys on the showroom floor." He indicated two cars. "A Mulsanne, which is our larger model, and a Flying Spur, which, though still a large car, is more compact."

Fratelli had been on the Internet reading, so he was quite familiar with both cars. He and Hillary sat, first in the Mulsanne, then in the Flying Spur, then they got out and walked around both cars, very slowly. The salesman waited at a discreet distance, alert to any sign of a question from either.

"Well, Hillary, what does your unerring eye tell you?" Fratelli asked.

"Ummm," she said, looking critically at both cars. "I think that the white Mulsanne is gorgeous, but I'm not sure that white is the correct color for that car. It's just a teeny bit much." She turned her attention to the Flying Spur. "However, I love the soft green of the Flying Spur, and especially the saffron and green leather interior. The equipment list is extensive, too, and it's a hundred and fifty thousand dollars cheaper. Really, why would one need more car than that?"

"I concur," Fratelli said. "Will you excuse me while I have a chat with this fellow?" He turned to the salesman. "Why don't you and I sit down for a moment?"

"I'll rest in the Flying Spur," Hillary said.

Fratelli had a last look at the car's window sticker, then sat down at the salesman's desk, picked up a notepad and a pen, and wrote down a number.

The salesman looked at it and frowned. "I

really don't think that's possible, sir. I think . . ." He wrote down a larger number.

Fratelli made a point of gazing for a long time at the pad before writing down another number. "That's my final offer," he said. "Cash. Now."

"No trade-in, sir?"

"No."

"Just let me speak to my manager." He got up and went into a glass-enclosed office, where he exchanged some words with the manager, then he returned. "I'm very sorry, Mr. . . ."

"Coulter."

"Mr. Coulter, but my manager says it can't be done."

"Then I thank you for your time," Fratelli said, rising and shaking the man's hand. He went back to the car and helped Hillary out of it. "Shall we go, my dear?"

They left the showroom and walked toward the town car, where the driver waited, door open. Then there was a voice from behind them.

"Mr. Coulter?"

Fratelli turned to find the manager standing in the doorway. "Yes?"

"I believe we may be able to do business," the man said.

"You understand that my offer is to include all charges. No dealer prep, or anything of the sort. I don't need a thousand-dollar car wash."

"There is sales tax, of course," the man said.

"Of course." Fratelli walked back to the town car and gave the driver a fifty. "We won't be needing you for the trip back," he said.

An hour later, having initiated a wire transfer and signed a number of documents, and having been given a tour of the instrument panel by the salesman, Fratelli drove his new Flying Spur out of the dealership. "Shall we go for a spin?" he asked Hillary.

"Why not, darling," she replied, sinking back into the soft leather upholstery.

Harry Moss had another idea. He found the offices of the *Palm Beach Post* and bought a small display ad.

29

Now Stone was faced with a problem: he had an itch to go to London for a few days, but on the other hand, he had a very similar itch to stay closer to Hank Cromwell.

He hadn't prayed about it, but the phone rang and he got what he considered to be an answer.

"Good morning," Hank said.

"It certainly is," Stone replied.

"I haven't seen your kitchen. Describe it to me, especially the appliances."

"Okay, there's an eight-burner Viking gas stove with two ovens and a grill, a French-door refrigerator of commercial size, large and small microwaves, a large wine cabinet, a pantry, an ice machine, and a dishwasher. There's also a butler's pantry with a scullery, another ice maker, another dishwasher, and storage for dishes and silverware, mostly used for dinner parties."

"That beats my electric, two-burner stove

and half refrigerator," Hank said. "Why don't I cook us dinner at your house? Whenever you say."

"Tonight?"

"Fine. I'll leave work and do some shopping."

"I've got an account at Grace's Market," he said. "Charge the food to me. You're already providing the skill and labor. I already have the wine."

"Is Grace's a good store?"

"The best. It's a cab ride for you, but they'll deliver to the house, so you won't have to hump anything."

"I'll be there around five, if we're going to sit down at eight. You'll have to vanish while I'm cooking, I don't need a distraction."

"Very good."

"Would you like to invite Dino and Viv?"

"Why not? If you haven't heard from me in ten minutes, they're in."

"Bye." She hung up, and Stone called Dino.

"You and Viv up for dinner here, cooked by Hank?"

"Can she cook?"

"She's making all the right noises."

"What time?"

"Seven, in the study. We're banished from the kitchen until dinnertime."

"You're on."

They both hung up.

Joan buzzed. "There's a Mr. Onofrio Buono on line one, says he'd like to make an appointment for some business advice. You know him?"

"Of him," Stone said. "Tell him this afternoon. Hang on, make that early afternoon." He didn't want Buono and Hank to have sight of each other.

"Whatever you say."

Joan buzzed precisely at two o'clock. "Mr. Buono is here."

"Just a second." Stone took a small digital recorder from a drawer, set it on his desk, switched it on, and covered it with a file. "Send him in."

Stone rose to greet his guest, who was a solid six-footer in a black suit, white-on-white shirt, and a silver necktie. "Mr. Buono?" he asked, offering his hand.

"That's right." Buono shook his hand and took the chair opposite Stone's desk.

"What can I do for you?" Stone asked.

"I'm considering starting a new business," Buono said.

"Who recommended me to you?" Stone asked.

"I read about you somewhere — the *Post*,

I think."

"I don't think I've ever been written about for the *Post* in a business context."

"It was more like a mention, it was complimentary."

"I'm sorry, I interrupted you. What sort of business?"

"You might call it, ah, 'proceeds recovery.' "

Stone thought for a moment. "Proceeds of what?"

"Well, let's say you had a business, and you suffered a loss."

"What sort of loss?"

"Any kind of loss that cost you."

"All right."

"Well, I would offer to recover that cost for you, for a reasonable share of what I recovered."

"I'm sorry, Mr. Buono, I'm trying to put what you've said in some sort of context, but I'm failing."

"All right, let's say you own a store, and a couple guys come in with guns and empty your cash register and your safe. I would recover that for you."

"And how, as a storekeeper, would I know you were in that business and able to perform that service? Would you advertise?"

"Not exactly. Let's just say I'd send

around sales representatives, and that would make for word of mouth. I would also offer a service preventing that kind of loss, and insurance to get it back."

"And if I didn't hire you or purchase your insurance?"

"Then when things happen, you're stuck with your loss."

"In certain circles, Mr. Buono, that would be called 'the protection racket.' "

"Are you calling me a criminal?"

"I'm not calling you anything. I'm just pointing out that your description of your proposed business closely resembles a practice that is highly discouraged by the criminal justice system."

"I think that the scale is what's putting you off," Buono said. "Let me rephrase."

"Please."

"Let's say you offer a service that transports large amounts of cash from banks in one country to banks in other countries. We're talking millions, here."

"Go ahead."

"Okay, one day some guys with big guns and a forklift roll into your office, tie everybody up, and load a couple crates containing, say, fifteen million dollars, onto a truck and drive away."

"That sounds an awful lot like the robbery of my store," Stone pointed out. "Without the insurance provision."

"Well, it's the insurance provision that makes it illegal, right?"

"In a manner of speaking. And how do you get the fifteen million back?"

"Well, first of all, half of that money is recovered by the cops from several of the participants in the robbery. It's the other half we're talking about, and I don't recover that. You do. And I pay a reasonable fee."

"Well, Mr. Buono, it begins to seem as though we're no longer talking hypothetically, that you're referring to an actual event."

"That's a possibility," Buono said.

"Well, if I were in a position to recover half of fifteen million dollars, why would I need you?"

Buono spread his hands and smiled. "To stay alive," he said.

"Ah," Stone said, "I perceive that you might be the person who recently fired a shotgun at my front door. Or, if not the person, then persons in your employ."

Buono gave an affirmative shrug.

"I'm sorry, could you restate that?"

"Possibly."

"Possibly the person or the persons?"

"Either. Both."

"May I ask why you think I might be in a position to recover this money for you?"

"Because the guy who has it is your client, and he came to you for advice. Guy name of Fratelli."

"Well, Mr. Buono, as a matter of attorney-client confidentiality, I can neither confirm nor deny the name of a client."

"Sure you can," Buono said. "You just need to be motivated."

"And you feel that marring the paint on my front door is a motivation?"

"Oh, it gets worse. Next time, the shotgun could be aimed at your face."

"Okay, Mr. Buono, you've put your case. It's time I put mine."

"Please," Buono said.

"I've already covered the part about attorney-client confidentiality, so I won't bore you further with that."

"Gee, thanks."

"Now let me tell you the part about this." Stone took his badge wallet, put it on the desk and opened it. "This will tell you that I'm a retired police detective. Had you heard that from the *Post*?"

"Sounds familiar. Why should I give a shit?"

"That fact should tell you that I have friendly acquaintances in the NYPD, one of whom is the chief of detectives. Did that occur to you?"

"Again, why should I give a shit?"

"Suppose I tell you that, if I felt inclined, I could have your chop shop in Red Hook raided and all your personnel arrested before you can get back there? And, of course, you arrested in the stolen car you're driving."

Buono's previously mock-friendly face was suddenly devoid of expression. "How the fuck . . . ?"

"Mr. Buono, you have already invested me with amazing powers of perception regarding criminal activities. Why would I not know about yours?" Stone sighed. "Now it's time for you to go." He reached under the file folder and switched off the recorder. "And let me add this: if I ever again see or hear from you or any of your . . . employees, I will create such a shitstorm as to blow you and your business off the face of the earth. And if I get a chance, I'll blow your head off while I'm doing it. Do we understand each other?"

Buono continued to stare at him, but now his jaw had dropped.

"The door is over there," Stone said, pointing.

Buono got up and left without another word.

30

Dino and Viv showed up for drinks at the appointed time, as was their wont, let themselves into the house with Dino's key, and entered the study, where Stone was reading a book. He looked up as they entered, then got up and built them drinks.

Dino glanced at his watch. "Turn on the TV," he said. "Channel Two news. We've got about a minute."

Stone picked up the remote and tuned it. "What are we looking for?"

"It will be self-explanatory," Dino said.

Everybody settled down to watch, and a moment later an anchorman appeared, after a story about a dog who had saved a cat from drowning.

"A little more than an hour ago," he said, "the NYPD raided premises in Brooklyn that turned out to be a very large chop shop, which is where stolen vehicles are taken to be dismantled and have their parts sold."

The screen changed to a helicopter shot of a huge steel shed surrounded by vehicles with flashing lights and men and women in armored vests. "The shop housed more than thirty vehicles, all German cars, like Porsches and Mercedeses, and is said by locals to have been in operation for at least two years, disguised as an auto repair establishment." The camera switched to an indoor shot, showing a pile of multicolored fenders stacked like saucers. "Just pick one the color of your Mercedes and buy at a very significant discount from the dealer's price. The alleged owner of the shop was not present for the raid, but is being sought for an interview by police."

"Okay, you can cut it off now," Dino said.

Stone switched from the TV to some light jazz. "Well," he said, "I'm afraid I'm going to get the credit for your raid, and from all the wrong people."

"You mean us? You sure get the credit there. Donatello went out there and bought a Porsche alternator for a hundred bucks. You got any idea what that would cost new?"

"I don't know, five hundred?"

"More like a thousand. We put that raid together in less than four hours. What were you talking about, 'credit from the wrong people'?"

Stone took his recorder from his pocket, set it on the coffee table, and switched it on, replaying his conversation with Bats Buono. When it was finished, he switched it off. "I didn't record the part where I said if he messed with me I'd blow his head off."

"So he's going to think that you set up the raid! That's hilarious!"

"Well, I guess I'm responsible for it, but I sure as hell didn't set it up. You've certainly done wonders for my credibility with a certain segment of the community, Dino, but not a hell of a lot for my peace of mind."

"I'll put a car on you for a week," Dino said. "How's that? Or would you rather just get out of town?"

"I've been thinking about spending some time in London," Stone said. "Looks like it might be the right moment."

"Good move."

"You'll call me when you've bagged Buono?"

"Sure."

They chatted for a while longer, then, at the appointed hour, went down to the kitchen, where Hank Cromwell was just finishing setting the table. "Array yourselves," she said, "and we'll dine."

Everyone sat down, and a moment later, plates with sautéed fresh foie gras and sliced figs were set before them. There was much smacking of lips and many ooohs and aaahs around the table. Stone went to the wine cabinet and came back with a bottle of Le Montrachet, 1978, and opened it. Everyone sipped.

"The perfect companion to my dish," Hank said. "Wherever did you come by that?"

"It was the gift of my Parisian friend, Marcel duBois," Stone said, "along with some other grand bottles, one of which we'll have with our main course."

They polished off the foie gras in short order, and finished the wine while Hank put the finishing touches on the main course, which turned out to be a poularde, a fat, older hen, in a champagne sauce. Stone selected a bottle of Château Palmer, 1961, decanted it, and poured Dino a sip.

"Never had anything that good before," Dino said, "unless it was the white wine."

"Another perfect accompaniment," Hank said, serving the chicken. "From your French friend?"

"Yes, indeed, and there's a dessert wine to come."

It took them the better part of an hour, what with conversation and seconds, to get through the main course, then Hank served a crème brûlée, after sealing the sugar top with a chef's blowtorch. The crust was so thick, Stone had to hammer on it with a large spoon to break through. He served them a half bottle of Château Coutet, 1959, with the dessert.

Finally, over coffee and a vintage cognac, Stone played the recording of his conversation with Buono for Hank.

"My goodness," Hank said, breathless, when she had heard it. "I don't think anyone has ever spoken to him that way."

"There was a little more from my end," Stone said, "but I didn't record it, in case it ever is played in court."

"Was my name mentioned?" she asked.

"No, it was not. He has no idea we know each other."

"I wouldn't be too sure of that," Hank said. "After all, I may be the only civilian he's told about the chop shop."

"Then we shouldn't be seen together for a while," Stone said. "I have to go to London tomorrow on business, so that takes care of me. Now we have to take care of you."

"I'll put a police car on you until we've bagged Buono," Dino said.

"That would be a great relief. And I won't have to testify?"

"I think Stone's tape will cover it for the DA."

"Hank," Viv said, changing the subject, "I'd ask you for the recipes for everything we had tonight, but I'd never find the time to prepare it all. Where did you learn to cook like that?"

"From my mother and Julia Child, and an Englishwoman named Elizabeth David, who wrote wonderful cookbooks."

"You certainly learned well. You could easily be a pro."

"I wouldn't find that fun," she said, "doing it every day for strangers. I prefer doing it occasionally for people I like."

"We're always available for that," Viv said.

"Hank, pardon my asking, but are you staying the night with Stone?" Dino asked.

"Yes," Stone answered for her.

"What time do you go to work?"

"At eight."

"Then there'll be an unmarked police car outside at that hour, and he will transport you to and from work and wherever else you need to go, until Mr. Buono is safely locked up."

"Thank you, Dino."

Later, in bed, Stone and Hank showed their

gratitude to each other for good food and police protection.

31

The following morning at seven-thirty, Stone walked out his front door and had a look up and down the block. An unmarked car waited at the curb, idling, two men in the front seat. He saw no threat, so he went and got Hank, kissed her, and put her into the backseat. "I'll be back in a few days, maybe a week, and I'll call you then," he said. The car drove away.

Joan backed Stone's Bentley out of the garage, and he put his luggage in the trunk. She drove him to JFK while he leafed through the *Times*. There was a report on the Red Hook raid of Buono's chop shop, and Stone savored every detail. He made the morning flight to London and managed to get in a nap to replace some of the sleep he had lost by rising so early. His flight picked up a brisk tailwind across the Atlantic, and he was at Heathrow by eight-thirty PM, London time.

As he left customs with his luggage cart, he saw a chauffeur holding a card with his name on it. Shortly, he was in the backseat of a large Mercedes, on his way into the city.

He arrived at Emma Tweed's house in Holland Park, an elegant neighborhood with large houses, and the chauffeur carried in his luggage, while Emma kissed him, took his coat, and walked him into the kitchen, where she served him a light supper of cold meats and a salad. He stayed up as late as he could, so that he would get a good night's sleep and temper the jet lag, then they went to bed.

"You're too tired to take me on tonight," Emma said. "Sleep, and I'll see you tomorrow. Take this," she said, handing him a small pill.

He took it and was asleep in minutes.

He awoke in a bedroom darkened by drawn curtains, with no idea what time it was. He got out of bed and drew the curtains and was nearly knocked down by the brilliant sunshine streaming in. When his eyesight recovered, he found a clock that told him it was after ten AM.

He showered and shaved and then felt not so fuzzy around the edges. He was getting dressed when his cell phone rang.

"Hello?"

"Good morning, Stone, it's Evelyn Throckmorton."

"Good morning, Evelyn."

"I hope you had a good flight and a good night's sleep."

"I had both, thanks." It was unlike the crusty ex-cop to be so solicitous.

"May I take you to lunch today, if you've no plans?"

"Of course."

"Do you know the Grenadier, in Wilton Row, Belgravia?"

"I do. It's my favorite pub."

"May we meet there at one PM?"

"Perfect."

"See you then." Throckmorton hung up.

Stone made himself some toast and coffee and read the London papers, which Emma had left on the kitchen table. She rang him later in the morning.

"I hope I didn't wake you."

"No, I've been up for an hour or so."

"Can you entertain yourself for the rest of the day?"

"Sure. In fact, Throckmorton has invited me to lunch."

"Good. I should be home around six. Did you bring a dinner jacket, as requested?"

"I did."

"Then we'll be having dinner at the home of friends at eight. Try and get a nap in this afternoon, so you can stay on your feet."

"I'll do that."

They both hung up.

Throckmorton was already seated at a table in the small dining room of the Grenadier when Stone arrived. They shook hands, and Stone ordered half a pint of bitter ale.

"You drink our stuff, do you?" the ex-cop asked.

"Helps me acclimate," Stone replied.

"I want to thank you for recommending me to Mrs. Tweed."

"You're very welcome, and thank you for solving her problem so swiftly."

"It was our Russian friends, in Paris, stealing her designs," Throckmorton said. "I understand you've had some dealings with them in the States."

"I'm afraid that's correct," Stone said. "And I hope I've heard the last of them."

"One can hope. From what I hear, you have new friends to play with, in New York."

"What do you hear?"

"Some fellow named Buono?"

"You have excellent hearing."

"I had occasion to speak to your friend

Dino. Good job, his getting the big promotion to chief of detectives."

"Yes. I believe he's enjoying it. Did he call you?"

"T'other way 'round. I called him to get your number. When I called your office, your secretary wouldn't give it to me."

"I'm sorry about that, Evelyn. Joan is a tough gatekeeper."

They ordered lunch from a short menu.

"How long will you be in London?"

"A few days."

"Dino wanted you out of town, it seems."

"Yes."

"I'm not sure you're much better off over here," Throckmorton said.

"And why would that be?" Stone asked.

"During my investigation of Mrs. Tweed's problem, I had occasion to spend a day in Paris, and I visited a well-placed acquaintance in the Prefect of Police. Your name came up."

"I'm surprised to hear that," Stone said.

"You were there last year and had some dealings with them, I believe."

"That's true."

"My acquaintance there is leading an investigation of Russian Mob elements operating in Paris, and as a result, did some wiretapping. Your name was being bandied about as being connected to the death of a man named Majorov, one of their own."

"I'm extremely sorry to hear that," Stone said. "My name being bandied about, I mean. Do you have any further information?"

"Just that these fellows seem to blame you, somehow. There were no further details."

"Majorov was in Los Angeles, trying to force me to let him into the hotel business that I'm involved with out there. I read of his death in the *New York Times.* A heart attack aboard his private jet, I believe, Moscow. How could they possibly think I was involved?"

"Apparently, they believe his heart attack was instigated."

"And they believe I instigated it?"

"Apparently. Or that you instigated the instigator."

"Good God!" Never mind that it was true; the Russians weren't supposed to expect it.

"Well, yes. I think you should be on your guard while you're on this side of the Pond."

"I'm unarmed on this side of the Pond," Stone said.

"And you will have to remain so. See those two gentlemen in the bar? Blue suits, white socks?"

Stone looked over his shoulder. "Yes."

"They are not unarmed, and one or more of their number will be around while you're here. They are the first staffers of my new investigative service, which I have started with the proceeds of my work for Mrs. Tweed. They are here with my compliments."

"Thank you, Evelyn. I hope they won't turn out to be necessary."

"In my experience, the Russians have long memories, extending over generations. Once crossed, they remain crossed."

"What an uplifting thought," Stone said, glancing at his watch. "I've got to run."

"My men, Derek and Charles, will drive you. Good day, Stone."

32

The car belonging to Derek and Charles was an old London taxicab with the taxi sign removed. "Is this a legal vehicle?" Stone asked.

"Perfectly legal," Derek replied. "Why do you ask? Are you uncomfortable?"

"No. In fact, I'm more comfortable than I would be in most cars. You seem to have rebuilt the seats."

"We've re-engined it, too," Charles said. "It's now wearing a lightweight, twin-turbocharged V8, from an old Porsche 928 wreck, that puts out about 425 British horsepower." He floored the cab for emphasis, and Stone was snapped back into his seat. He fumbled for the seat belt and fastened it.

"Zero to sixty in about five-point-six seconds," Derek said. "In time we'll trim another second off that, then we'll be in Ferrari territory."

"I hope you've redone the suspension as well," Stone said. "These things have a high center of gravity, don't they?"

"Fully independent, roll bars, the works," Charles said. "And the COG is much lower than you'd think." They took a corner faster than Stone would have believed possible without tipping over the big black thing, and shortly, they arrived back at the Holland Park house.

"One of us will keep an eye outside, the other will come in with you, if that's all right."

"Perfectly all right with me," Stone said. He used the key Emma had given him to let himself in.

"Hello, down there?" Emma called from upstairs.

"You'll be all right down here," Stone said to Derek, then he went upstairs, to find Emma at her dressing table, her hair pinned back, applying her makeup. She was dressed only in a bra and panties.

"How was your lunch with Throckmorton?" she asked, as he kissed her on the back of the neck.

"Charming," Stone said. "The DCI has concerns about the Russians who were stealing your designs."

"He thinks they have designs on me?"

"No, designs on me, and not fashionable ones. He's supplied us with a pair of his former police colleagues to watch over us, and they've brought along a very comfortable refurbished taxi."

"Well, at least we'll blend in with the traffic."

"You're taking this better than I thought you would," Stone said.

"Oh, Throckmorton explained the facts of life to me — about the Russians — when I hired him. I've no problem with armed guards, have you?"

"My only problem is with the necessity of having them," Stone replied. "If you'll excuse me, I'll change." He got into his dinner clothes, tied his black bow tie, filled his pockets with the usual detritus, and started downstairs. "I'll wait for you in the study," he said.

"Righto. Down in half an hour."

He went into the study, found the ice machine, and poured himself a Knob Creek, which Emma had thoughtfully provided. He had just eased into a soft chair when his cell phone rang.

"Hello?"

"It's Dino."

"Hey, pal, how are you?"

"I'm okay. How's Hank?"

"She's in New York, remember? I'm in London."

"Then where is she? My people showed up at eight yesterday morning to drive her to work, but she wasn't there."

"That's because I put her into the car at seven-thirty. Then I was on the way to the airport with Joan."

"That would explain why there was nobody home when my guys arrived at eight."

"You keep saying eight, but they were there early, and I put Hank into their car."

"What kind of car?"

"The usual, a dark Crown Vic."

"Stone, the department got rid of the last Crown Vic a couple of years ago. Everything is new since then."

Stone froze. "Then who . . . ?"

"Exactly. Who? Have you heard from Hank?"

"Not a word, but I didn't expect to."

"Call her," Dino said. "Right now."

Stone broke the connection and dialed Hank.

"Miss Henrietta's line." A man's voice.

"Let me speak to her."

"I'm afraid she's indisposed at the moment, Mr. Barrington. What took you so long to call?"

"I'm in London. Let me speak to her."

"London in Canada?"

"London in England. Let me speak to her."

"Hang on. Hank? Say a few words to your friend Stone."

Her voice seemed to come from across the room. "Go fuck yourself, Onofrio!" This was followed by a smack and a groan.

"Listen to me," Stone said.

"No, Mr. Barrington, you listen to me," Onofrio replied. "You and I are going to do a little swap."

"What?"

"You're going to give me my uncle's money, and I'm going to give you Hank. All that's in question here is how much of her you get back, and in what condition. Call me when you've got the money ready to move. Since you're in London, I'll give you forty-eight hours." He hung up.

Stone called Dino back.

"Yeah?"

"Dino, we've got a big, big problem," he said.

33

Emma was on her cell phone all the way to the dinner party, at a house in Eaton Square, so Stone didn't have to talk, which was just as well, as he was dumbstruck.

The dinner party was not small and intimate; there were a good two dozen people there, including a couple Members of Parliament, a government minister, half a dozen tall, impossibly thin young women in very expensive dresses, and some sort of rock star in a spangled dinner jacket. Stone fixed a smile on his face and managed to keep up a line of automated chat as Emma propelled him around the room, introducing him. Fifteen minutes passed before he snagged a waiter and got them drinks.

He was insanely hungry — probably something to do with his rattled internal clock — and the waiters always seemed to run out of canapés before they got to him. The ex-cop Derek stood by the drawing room door with a glass of ginger ale in his hand, casting a beady eye over whoever entered his line of sight, as if daring them to make a move on Stone or Emma. Supported by an underlayer of recorded pop music, the noise level was off the charts. Stone wanted nothing more than to find a quiet corner, if such existed, and think. A picture of Hank, bound and gagged in a small room somewhere, kept crowding everything else out of his mind.

"Are you all right?" Emma shouted into his ear.

"What?"

"You seem preoccupied."

"What?"

She gave up and entered into a conversation with another woman, conducted mostly in some sort of sign language. Stone spied an ajar door that seemed to lead to a study and made for it. He closed the door behind him and leaned against it, breathing deeply. The door was thick enough to bring the noise on the other side down to a tamed roar.

"You couldn't stand it either, eh?" a man's voice said. Deep, with an upper-class drawl.

Stone jumped, then saw a man in a chair before the fireplace, lit only by a flicker of flame. All the lights in the room were out.

"Would you like a brandy?" the man asked. "There's a decanter over there, between the bookcases."

"I don't mind if I do," Stone said. He set down his empty glass, found the decanter, and poured himself a snifter.

"Join me?" the man asked, indicating the chair opposite where he sat.

"Thank you," Stone said, sinking into the leather.

"Noisy in there, eh?"

"My ears are still ringing," Stone said.

"I'm Alistair Brooke," the man said. "With an 'e.' "

"Stone Barrington."

"A Yank, eh?"

"New York."

"What brings you over the water?"

"Visiting a friend."

"Emma?"

"Yes."

"I saw you come in together. I've a wife somewhere in the drawing room. Are you in business?"

"The law."

"I, as well — barrister."

"Ah."

"Well said. Have you visited our courts over here?"

"No. What knowledge I have of them

comes from films like *Witness for the Prosecution* and a number of BBC dramas. They seem to be more elegant than most of our courtrooms in New York."

"Perhaps. We've been using the same ones for a long time. Do you try cases?"

"I've spent most of my career avoiding the courtroom, whenever possible," Stone said. "Are you hiding from the noise, too?"

"The noise and a rather noisy Russian gentleman. Did you notice him?"

"I'm not sure," Stone said, but he found the thought of a Russian in the next room disturbing. "Which one was he?"

"Six foot, closely clipped hair, thick of body and mind."

"I'll try and avoid him," Stone said.

"His solicitor has been pestering me to represent him in a criminal case, and I've no wish to be involved with him, considering what I've heard."

"What have you heard?"

Brooke shrugged. "Thuggery, brutish behavior, foul business practices, the odd murder — that sort of thing."

"What's he charged with?"

"Conspiracy, financial misdeeds, et cetera."

"What's his name?"

"Yevgeny Majorov. Said to be the son of a

Soviet-era KGB general."

Stone sat up. "How old is he?"

"Perhaps late forties."

"Does he have a brother?"

"Did have. It was all over the papers a short while ago. The man landed on a private jet in Moscow, having died en route from somewhere-or-other."

"Yes, that news made its way to New York, too."

"Did you know the brother?"

"Not really. He attempted to do some business with me in the States. I resisted the notion."

"Oh? How did he take it?"

"Not well."

"I hope the threats weren't carried out."

"Fortunately not." Stone's cell phone vibrated on his belt; he ignored it, and it stopped.

The door opened and Stone looked over his shoulder to see Emma, bearing two plates, enter the room, followed by another woman, also bearing two plates. "I saw you come in here, Stone, and I can't blame you. Rita and I have brought you two dinner. Hello, Alistair."

"Hello, Emma." Air kisses were exchanged.

The two women bore the plates to a table

across the room and pulled up chairs to it, and the men joined them. Brooke introduced his wife to Stone.

"Wine is on its way," Rita said, then the door opened and a waiter entered with a bottle of champagne and four glasses. He set them on the table and left.

Stone opened the champagne and poured them all a glass.

"So you two have become acquainted?" Emma asked.

"We toil in the same vineyard," Alistair replied. "More or less."

Then civilized conversation ensued, the combination of brandy, champagne, and food worked its wonders, and Stone was able to forget about New York and Hank and Yevgeny Majorov for a little while.

An hour later, the four of them made their way out of the large flat, preceded by two men in suits. Alistair nodded at their backs. "Majorov," he mouthed. They all stopped at the elevator.

"I'll walk down," Stone said, wishing to avoid the Russian. He started down the stairs. Unfortunately, he reached the ground floor at the same time as the elevator, and as its doors opened he found himself fixed in the gaze of Yevgeny Majorov. Neither man averted his gaze.

"May we drop you?" Emma said to the Brookes.

"We're in Ennismore Gardens," Alistair said. "If it's not out of your way."

Majorov and his companion got into a new-looking Rolls and tooled away. Stone held the cab door open for the Brookes and Emma, then took a jump seat.

"This is quite a taxi," Alistair said.

"Belongs to a friend," Stone said.

"Must be an interesting friend."

Stone couldn't argue with that.

34

Emma woke Stone the following morning by the simple device of biting him on a nipple. Nature took its course, a couple of times.

Stone lay, gazing sleepily at the ceiling, while Emma showered. For no particular reason, he checked his iPhone on the bedside table. He had had a phone call, and there was a voice mail.

"Stone," Hank's voice said. "If you can do something, please do it." The connection was broken. She had sounded desperate. Stone looked at the bedside clock; it would be the wee hours in New York, so there was no point in calling Dino again. He called his American Express travel agent and asked to change his return ticket to the next flight out of Heathrow. There was one at noon that reached New York at three. He booked it, then called his office number and left a message for Joan to meet him at JFK at three-thirty.

Stone hung up, got to his feet, and started for the bathroom. Last night's drinks were hanging on, if not over. Emma came out of the shower as he entered.

"I've got to go back to New York," he said. "Client emergency."

Emma reached for a towel. "When?"

"Noon plane from Heathrow."

"But I've got theater tickets for tonight," she said. "The big new hit play."

"I'm so sorry, Emma," he said, kissing her, "but this one is life or death. It can't be avoided."

"Oh, well," she said, obviously exasperated. "Shall I send you to the airport in my car?"

"Throckmorton's taxi is outside, remember?"

"Oh, yes."

Stone showered and shaved and packed, while Emma dressed for work. "Can you come to New York soon?" he asked.

"I can't predict just now," she said. "I'll call you, though."

"I'm sorry I was here for such a short time," he said, hugging her. "Believe me, I'd rather stay than have to deal with this situation."

"I believe you," she said, kissing him.

"Have a good flight." And she was gone.

Stone made himself some breakfast and read the papers, then at nine-thirty, he grabbed his luggage and went outside to where Derek, having gone home to sleep, then returned, sat at the wheel of the cab. "Heathrow," he said.

"Righto," Derek replied, and made a quick U-turn past a black BMW parked down the street a few yards. He checked his rearview mirror. "I think we've picked up company," he said.

"Swell. I hope this tank is sufficiently armored to repel small-arms fire."

"The doors have Kevlar inserts, but the glass we ordered hasn't arrived yet. Anything happens, hit the deck."

They made it to Heathrow without an exchange of gunfire, and as they stopped, the BMW drove slowly past them. The driver was the man who had accompanied Yevgeny Majorov to the party the night before.

Stone thanked Derek, grabbed his luggage, waved off a porter, and ran for check-in. Half an hour later he was through security with his pass and in the VIP lounge. He checked his iPhone address book for John Fratelli's throwaway cell phone number and called it. The call went straight to voice mail. "Mr. Fratelli," he said, "a friend of mine has been kidnapped by an acquaintance of yours, a Mr. Onofrio Buono. He wants your money in exchange for her. Call me, and let's see if you have any ideas."

That done, he called Joan at home; she would be up by now.

"Hello?"

"It's Stone. I left a message at the office for you to pick me up at JFK at three-thirty."

"Can do."

"There's something else: call my broker and tell him I may have to free up five million dollars in cash."

"Are you being held hostage by al-Qaeda?"

"Tell him not to do anything yet, just to figure out how to raise the cash with as little tax damage as possible. If I need it, it'll be on short notice."

"Okay," Joan said. "I'll look forward to hearing all about this when I meet you."

"Believe me, you don't want to know," Stone said. "See you at three-thirty." He hung up and called Dino at home.

"Bacchetti."

"It's Stone. Any news of Hank?"

"Not a word, not a peep — our efforts to track down Buono have not succeeded. He probably had a hidey-hole prepared, just in case."

"I may have to give him some money," Stone said.

"Whose money?"

"Mine. All right, Arrington's." She had willed him a considerable fortune.

"I think it's time for me to call the FBI," Dino said.

"Not yet," Stone said. "I'm at Heathrow now. When I get in, I'll call you. I don't want to turn this into a whole big thing with a lot of feds screwing it up."

"I sympathize with your view, but are you really going to try to handle this by yourself?"

"With your help, yes. I don't see how the feds can improve the odds."

"Frankly, neither do I," Dino admitted.

"Talk to you later."

They hung up.

Stone's flight was boarding when his cell phone vibrated. He stepped out of line and took the call.

"It's John Fratelli," the voice said. "I got your message. How did this happen?"

"Buono came to see me," Stone said. "I pretty much told him to go fuck himself, but then I think he — or one of his — saw a woman he knew at my house. They've taken her, and he's demanding your money — as if I had access to it."

"If I were handling this," Fratelli said, "I'd just kill him."

"I have every sympathy with that plan," Stone replied, "but I don't know where to find the man. The cops raided a chop shop that he owns, and they're looking for him everywhere as we speak, but so far, no joy."

"Let me see what I can do," Fratelli said. "I'll get back to you."

"I'm in London, boarding a plane for New York right now. I should be within cell phone range by four o'clock, Eastern time."

"Right." Fratelli hung up, and Stone got on the airplane with a sense of deep foreboding.

35

John Fratelli sat on the edge of his bed, feeling sick. Everything had been going so well; now this. His first impulse was to fly to New York, find Bats Buono, and beat him to death. Instead, he ordered breakfast from room service, then showered, shaved, and dressed for golf. Breakfast arrived as he cleared the bathroom.

He ate slowly, thinking hard. Who could he call about this? Who did he know anymore? Everybody was dead, almost. Almost. He knew exactly the right person to call, but not if he was alive. He called information and asked for Gino Buono, Eddie's brother, Onofrio's father. There was a number in Queens, and he called it.

"Hello?" He sounded old and sleepy.

"Gino?"

"Yeah, who's this?"

"This is . . ." He stopped himself, about to say Jack Coulter. "It's Johnny Fratelli."

There was a brief silence as Gino computed the name. "Jesus, Johnny. I heard you were out."

"For a while now."

"How was Eddie when he went?"

"Not too bad. You and I should do so well."

"I'm glad to hear it. I went to the funeral, of course."

"Of course. I was sorry not to be there, but I was, ah, indisposed at the time."

Gino chuckled.

"How's Onofrio doing?"

"He was doing great until a couple days ago. The cops raided his chop shop out in Red Hook."

"I didn't know he had a chop shop. Last I knew he was doing protection."

"Times change. He was doing Porsches and Mercedeses only — a great business."

"I heard he was looking for me, but I don't have a number."

Gino was suddenly wary. "Looking for you? Why?"

"He thinks I have Eddie's money from the heist."

"Do you?"

"About three hundred grand, from a safe-deposit box in a bank. That's all."

"Where's the rest?"

"Eddie didn't tell me about that. I figured he must have gotten a message to you or some other family."

"I didn't hear a fucking word from him."

"Well, he wouldn't haven't written a letter, given his circumstances. When did you last see him?"

"Easter weekend, a year ago. It was only the third time I saw him while he was up there. We weren't that close, you know. Eddie was always too elegant for the likes of me."

"Onofrio came to see him now and then, he might have told him something."

"Then why would the boy want to talk to you?"

"You tell me. You got a number, Gino?"

"He's out of state. Tell you what: give me your number and I'll give it to him when I speak to him."

"When is that gonna be?"

"Soon. He'll call."

"Okay." He gave Gino the number. "That's what you call a throwaway cell number. It's good for today only, not after that."

"I'll pass it along."

"Thanks, Gino. How you holding up?"

"I'm old, that's how."

"Tell me about it. Bye-bye."

Fratelli hung up and looked at his watch. Time to meet Hillary at the golf club. It would be their first round together.

Hillary hit first, about 220 yards, straight down the fairway. Fratelli was next; longer, but it sliced into the long rough.

"Nice distance," Hillary said.

Fratelli laughed. "You're very kind. My instructor and I are working on the slice, but I'm not there yet."

Hillary, with 180 yards to the pin, hit a three wood to about six feet.

"I'd just like to point out that we're not playing for money," Fratelli said. She laughed. He found his ball, and it was resting on a bare patch in the long rough, 160 yards out. He took a club from his bag and hit the ball straight and true to just inside Hillary's. Then he rejoined her, the club still in his hand.

"What's that?" she asked, nodding at the club.

"An eleven wood," Fratelli replied. "It's my secret weapon."

"How does your instructor say you're doing?" she asked, as they got into the cart.

"He's says I'm the best middle-aged beginner he's ever coached."

"You don't have a handicap, yet?"

"He says I'm playing to about an eighteen."

"Not bad for a short-timer," she said. Then she sank her putt and he took two putts to hole his.

They took a break at the ninth hole, and Fratelli was having a diet soda when his phone vibrated. "Excuse me," he said, then stepped away from the table. "Hello?"

"Hey, Johnny, it's Onofrio."

"Hiya, kiddo, what's happening?"

"The old man said you wanted to talk."

"I got a message *you* wanted to talk."

"Yeah, I guess so. I went to see your shyster lawyer."

"Yeah? Your uncle Eddie recommended him. He gave me some basic advice, I paid his bill, and that was that."

"Nah, it was more than that, Johnny. He's in on it, isn't he?"

"Eddie's money? That what you're all atremble about?"

"That's it."

"Well, Eddie left me a little something in a bank deposit box. I had just got it out when you or yours took a shot at me, remember?"

"Yeah, I'm sorry about that, Johnny, you know how it goes."

"Your old man seems to think I got the whole bundle."

"Sure, you did. Who else?"

"I thought he would have left the big part to his family, but you know what? Nobody came to see him when he was in the infirmary for his last four months."

"Last time I tried, they threw me out. He took me off his visitors list."

"Gee, I wonder why he did that."

"I guess he liked you better."

"He liked me three hundred grand's worth — that's what was in the box."

"So, according to you, there's seven mil plus out there somewhere."

"Must be."

"Where are you, Johnny?"

"I'm on my way to the Coast — Greyhound bus. You oughta try it sometime, kid — see America."

"Bullshit."

"America?"

"Nah, you headed for the Coast."

"I hear it's nice out there, and I've got my little stake."

"Yeah, let's talk about that. Your shyster tell you I've got his girlfriend?"

"He mentioned it."

Fratelli heard a sound like a splash and what seemed like a woman laughing.

"Did the shyster tell you what's gonna happen to her if you don't cough up?"

"What do I care? She's nothing to me. I wouldn't give you a plugged nickel for her ass. That's why I called, kid, to tell you that. And don't try me on this number again, it won't work." He hung up. "I hope that does it," he said aloud to himself, then he rejoined Hillary for the second nine holes.

When he got back to the Breakers, he tossed the cell phone and got another out of his underwear drawer.

36

Stone was back at his house before John Fratelli called.

"Welcome home."

"Thanks."

"I talked to Onofrio Buono."

"Have you got a number for him?"

"No, I spoke to his father, Gino, who lives in Queens. He called his boy and gave him my number. By the way, I tossed that phone. Write this one down." He recited the new number.

Stone wrote it down. "What was the result of that call?"

"I told him I got only three hundred grand from the safe-deposit box, and that I didn't know where the rest was."

"Was that true?"

Fratelli ignored the question. "He told me that if I don't give him all the money, he'll kill the girl. I told him pretty much what you told him."

"To go fuck himself?"

"Pretty much. Listen, I heard something in the background of our call — at least I think I did."

"What was that?"

"I thought I heard a splash and a woman laugh."

"Does that mean anything to you?"

"Maybe. Eddie used to talk about a cabin he had on a lake, in Connecticut. He owned it until he died, and some of his family used it now and then."

"Where in Connecticut?"

"A few miles north of Danbury, near a wide place in the road called New Fairfield. The lake was privately owned and it was really more of a pond — eight or ten cabins on it. I don't remember the name, or even if it had a name."

"I'll look into it," Stone said.

"I wonder about something."

"What?"

"The woman laughing. Why would a woman who was being held hostage laugh?"

Stone thought about that. "Maybe he has a female accomplice."

"Could be. I was you, I'd like to know more about that before I gave Bats any money."

"So would I."

"Do you have a lot of money, Mr. Barrington?"

"Yes."

"Does the girl know you have a lot of money?"

Pause. "Probably."

"Let me give you the best advice I can."

"Please do."

"Call the guy's bluff."

"You think he's bluffing?"

"It's fifty-fifty. I saw in a movie once, where the FBI told a father whose kid had been kidnapped: you can pay the money and get your kid back, or you can pay the money and not get your kid back. Or, you can not pay the money and not get your kid back, or you can not pay the money and get your kid back."

"That's probably good advice. You think Buono is bluffing?" Stone asked again.

"It would be just like him," Fratelli replied. "On the other hand . . ."

"Thanks for the advice, I think."

Fratelli laughed. "Let me know how it comes out." He hung up.

Stone called Dino and told him about the conversation.

"I'm looking in my road atlas at a map of Connecticut," Dino said. "I see a very small lake near New Fairfield."

"Maybe it's worth a trip up there," Stone said.

"I know the head of the Connecticut State Police. I'll give him a call. Have you heard any more from Bats Buono?"

"No, but I just got back to the house."

"If he calls, stall him."

"Stall him how?"

"Tell him you just got back in town, and it's going to take a couple of days to get ahold of the money. I know you've already made the arrangements, but don't tell him that."

"You know me too well."

"It's what I would do, if I had a few million available. On the other hand, like Fratelli says, you can just call his bluff."

"I thought about it. I don't think I can do that."

"What about the laughing woman?"

"It could very well be another woman, not Hank."

"Could be. Look, Hank knows you're loaded, she might be looking to cash in."

"I don't read her that way."

"I don't either, but you never know."

"Sometimes you do."

"Think back to when you met her at P.J. Clarke's."

"Okay."

"Who got there first? You or Hank?"

Stone thought about it. "I did."

"Maybe Bats Buono is smarter than you think he is."

"I doubt it."

"How did Hank come to tell you about Buono?"

"It came up in a conversation we had at dinner. She said she had met him at Clarke's, and he became obsessed, and she had to take out a protection order to get rid of him."

"And when did Buono come to see you?"

"The next day."

"I've got to make a couple of calls. I'll get back to you when I know more. If Buono calls, stall him like we talked about."

"Okay." Stone hung up. Joan was standing in the doorway. "Your broker is on the phone. He wants to know how you want the cash."

"Tell him I'll call him back."

Stone went through his mail, trying to keep his mind off Hank and Bats Buono. Less than an hour later, Dino called.

"I talked to Colonel Dan Sparks, head of the Connecticut State Police."

"And?"

"And he's going to send a SWAT team to

New Fairfield. There's a little grocery store — you and I can meet him there, it's a couple of hours from your house."

"Dino, we don't know which cabin to hit. Fratelli said there are eight or ten."

"Dan knows the guy who owns the property that the lake is on. He's the one who built the cabins and sold them. By the time we get there, he should know which cabin."

"You going to pick me up?"

"In half an hour. I'll use the siren, if I have to."

As Stone was hanging up, his cell phone vibrated. He let it ring three times before answering.

"Yes?"

"Have you got the money?" Buono asked.

"There's a problem about that. You talked to Fratelli, so you know he hasn't got it."

"I don't care if he's got it," Buono said. "Your money will do just fine."

"Let me speak to Hank."

"She's in the ladies'."

"Have her call me when she gets out." Stone hung up.

Five minutes later, she called. "Stone? Are you going to help me?"

"Yes," he said. "Is there another woman there?"

But Buono had taken the phone from her.

"Are we clear now?"

"It's going to take a couple of days to put together that kind of money. Unless you'll take a check."

Buono laughed heartily. "I'll give you until noon the day after tomorrow. I'll call you with instructions, and you'd better follow them to the letter."

"I won't give you a dime, unless Hank is at the meet, and healthy. And in my car. If she's so much as bruised, I'll take it out on you."

"I'll call you at noon, day after tomorrow."

"Don't call, unless Hank will be there."

But Buono had hung up.

37

Dino was out front in his unmarked police SUV on time. Stone got into the car.

"Are you armed?" Dino asked.

"Damn straight, I'm armed," Stone replied. The driver got moving.

Dino was silent until they got on the West Side Highway and headed north. "I did a search of the court records for the past five years," he said.

"The court records? Why?"

"I was looking for a protection order filed by Henrietta Cromwell against Onofrio Buono."

"And?"

"There wasn't one."

"Shit."

"My reaction exactly. Then there's the matter of another woman up there, or rather, the lack of one. I don't think you ought to give this guy any money, Stone."

"That's hard," Stone said.

"I know, but if she's in cahoots with him, there's a chance you could make things worse for her."

"Worse? How?"

"Suppose Buono wants *all* the money?"

Stone sighed. His cell phone went off.

"Yes?"

"It's Joan. I've got your broker on the line, and he insists on talking to you."

"All right, put him on."

"Stone?"

"Yes, Jim?"

"Do you want this cash?"

"Yes, I do."

"You've got enough stocks that are losing or static that we can sell without paying a capital gains tax."

"Sell them."

"How do you want the money?"

"In tens and twenties — nothing bigger."

"That's going to be very bulky."

"I know. Send your secretary out to get some leaf bags."

"What are leaf bags?"

"Great big, heavy-duty garbage bags. Put the cash in one of those, and I want the bills loose, not banded. Mix 'em up."

"All right. When do you want to pick up the bag?"

"Send it over to my office tomorrow

morning. Joan will sign for it."

"I'll have to bill you for the armored car."

"Come on, Jim, take a cab."

"I'm not getting into a cab with five million dollars in a leaf bag."

"Tell you what: I'll get someone from Strategic Services to pick up the money at your office."

"No, at the bank downstairs. Ask for the manager, Mr. Crockwell."

"Tell him to give it to someone with Strategic Services ID. Call Mike Freeman over there and tell him when it's ready."

"All right, Stone. Whenever this — whatever it is — is over, let's have a drink and you can tell me what the hell was going on."

"Deal, but you're buying." Stone hung up and called Mike Freeman.

"Welcome home, Stone. You are home, aren't you?"

"I've been home, now I'm on the way to Connecticut."

"Okay."

"Mike, I need the services of Strategic Services."

"What can I do?"

"Tomorrow morning, you'll get a call from my broker, telling you that the money is ready. Please send some people over to my bank. Ask for Mr. Crockwell. Your men will show Strategic Services ID, and Crockwell will give them five million dollars in tens and twenties, in a leaf bag."

"All right, Stone, I'm baffled. What's going on?"

"I may have to pay a ransom to someone."

"In tens and twenties?"

"It may be to my advantage, if he has to count it."

"Do you want me to pay it to somebody?"

"Just hang on to it until I call you back and give you instructions on where to deliver it."

"You want me to send an armored car?"

"Do it any way you like."

"Stone, do you need some backup?"

"I don't think so, but I may reconsider. I'll let you know when I call back."

"Is Dino in on this?"

"I'm in his car right now."

"Good, that makes me feel better."

"There'll also be a SWAT team from the Connecticut State Police."

"I feel even better."

"Bye."

"Bye."

"Am I beginning to sense the outlines of a plan?" Dino asked.

"If you are, then you're a gifted seer, because I don't have one."

38

New Fairfield was an actual wide place in the road, not a metaphor. A large, unmarked black truck and an unmarked black sedan were parked next to each other outside a small market. Men in black uniforms were leaning on the truck and sitting on the car, as if waiting for something terrible to happen. Dino's driver parked next to the unmarked car, and a man in a dark suit came over. Dino got out, and Stone followed.

"Hello, Dan," Dino said, offering his hand. "Thanks for turning out. This is my friend and former partner, Stone Barrington. Stone, Dan Sparks."

Stone shook his hand, too; his paw was large, his grip iron. "Hi, Dan."

"We've got a little problem," Sparks said.

"I would be surprised if you didn't," Dino replied.

"I can't find the owner of the land and

the lake, and there are ten cabins."

"Uh-oh."

"I don't think we can go knocking on doors."

"No, you can't."

Stone spoke up. "He can." He was pointing at a Federal Express delivery truck. The driver was taking a package into the market. "Dan?"

"Right." Sparks walked over to the truck in time to intercept the driver on his way out of the market. A badge was flashed, a conversation conducted. The driver produced an envelope and filled out a waybill according to Sparks's instructions.

"Stone?" Sparks called.

"Yes, Dan?"

"Any message?"

"Tell him I'm not going to give him any money."

"Right." Sparks wrote that on a sheet of paper, stuffed it into the envelope, sealed it, and handed it to the driver. More conversation, then he returned to the group. "All right, everybody, saddle up. We're going to follow the truck to where the entry road joins a loop around the lake. We'll wait there until the driver returns, then I'll have further orders. Dino, Stone, you're with me."

The men got into their body armor and helmets, then into the truck. Dino and Stone piled into the backseat of Sparks's car, while Dino's driver followed in his car.

"Just follow the truck," Sparks said to his driver.

The little caravan followed the truck half a mile down the highway, then turned off onto a gravel road. They entered the woods, and another half a mile down the road they stopped, while the delivery truck turned right. They could see water fifty yards ahead, through the trees.

"Now we wait," Sparks said. "He'll go house to house, asking for Buono. If this works, he'll deliver the envelope, then come back here. If it doesn't work, he'll still come back here."

They sat quietly for a minute. "How's the new job going, Dino?" Sparks asked.

"Better than I expected," Dino replied. "I'm actually enjoying it."

"Next, you'll be the commissioner."

"God forbid."

They went quiet again. Half an hour passed. The truck reappeared and pulled up next to Sparks's car.

"Turn left, first house on your right," the driver said.

"Did Buono sign for it?"

"I didn't see a man. A woman signed." He handed over a receipt.

"H. Cromwell," Sparks read aloud.

"There was no car there, either," the truck driver said.

Sparks got out of the car and rapped on the rear door of the police truck; it opened. "Okay, we're going on foot from here," he said to the men, and they began to file out, shouldering weapons.

Stone got out of the car and walked over to Sparks. Dino followed. "Dan, let me drive down there in Dino's car."

"What's your point?" Sparks asked.

"She knows me."

"What about Buono? Does he know you?"

"Yes, we've met."

"Are you armed?"

"Yes, but Buono won't shoot me — he wants the money."

"You okay with this, Dino?"

"Why not? It's Stone's ass."

"I'll give you five minutes, Stone, then we're going in."

"Five minutes it is."

Dino's driver got out of the SUV, and Stone got in. He started the car and glanced at his watch. He turned left and drove slowly down the road until he came to a mailbox emblazoned with a large B. He turned into the drive and continued downhill another thirty yards, until it opened into a clearing, with the lake behind. It was dusk, and there was a porch light on. No car in sight.

Stone got out of the car and walked slowly to the house, looking carefully around. He climbed a few steps onto the porch and walked to the door. Closed. He opened the screen, took a deep breath, and knocked. Not hammered, like the cops, just a polite knock. Nothing happened. He knocked again.

The door opened, and Hank stood there, wearing a bathrobe. Her eyes widened, then she rushed into his arms. "Oh, Jesus," she said. "I knew you'd come, but not this fast."

"Are you alone?"

"Yes, Onofrio went to the grocery store."

"In New Fairfield?"

"I don't know, he said it was nearby."

"Get some clothes on. We're getting out of here, and there's a SWAT team three minutes behind me, so hurry!"

She ran into another room, and Stone had a look around. There was a bedroom to his right with twin beds, bare of linens.

He walked farther into the small living room; a woodstove was on his right. On his left he could see into another bedroom, where Hank was getting dressed. She was too far along for him to know whether she had been naked under the robe. There was a double bed in the room, neatly made up.

Hank came back. "Let's go," she said.

Stone put her into the SUV, turned around, and started up the road. A cop stepped into the road and put a hand up. Sparks and Dino came out of the woods.

"I've got her," Stone said. "Buono is at the grocery store we just left."

"Shit," Sparks said. "Everybody back in the vehicles!"

Dino got into the rear seat of the SUV. "You know this guy by sight, don't you, Stone?"

"Yes, but I didn't see him." He turned to Hank. "What's he driving?"

"A silver Mercedes, the big sedan," she said.

"Do you know the plate number?"

"No."

Stone shouted to Sparks: "Silver Mercedes S Class!" He followed the police car and truck back to New Fairfield, and everybody spilled out of the vehicles again. He looked around the parking lot. No Mercedes. He couldn't remember if there had been one before. "Dino, do you remember seeing a Mercedes when we got here?"

"No," Dino replied, "but I didn't not see one, either."

"All right, Hank," Stone said. "Start from the beginning."

39

Stone watched Hank take a deep breath.

"You put me into that car, and they drove away. Before I could say anything I was on the floor with somebody's foot on my neck. We drove for, I don't know, twenty minutes, half an hour. I was disoriented, I don't know where we went.

"Then we were in a garage, and Onofrio was there. I was blindfolded, my hands tied behind my back, and stuffed into the trunk of a car. We drove for a long time, first stop and start, then obviously on the open road, probably an interstate. I made myself as comfortable as I could and dozed for a while.

"The trunk opened, and I was hustled into the house, untied, and the blindfold came off. There were groceries brought from the car, and I was told to cook."

"What were the sleeping arrangements?" Stone asked.

"I know you saw the double bed — that's where we slept. I know the guy well, I knew what he wanted, and I decided to give it to him. It made life more bearable, if it wasn't hostile all the time. If I hadn't give in to him, I would have been tied up and blindfolded again, and I didn't want that."

"Did anyone else visit the house?"

"No, there were just the two of us. He got some phone calls, and I talked to you twice."

"What did you do with your time?"

"There was a TV, with a satellite dish, and some magazines. We fucked a lot."

Stone winced. "Were you ever left alone there?"

"Not until today. I thought about running, but I had no idea where we were. I don't know *now,* come to that. I never saw a soul, not even on the lake. It was starting to get late in the day, and I didn't want to try the woods or the road in the dark. I thought he'd be back any minute."

"You're in the lower left-hand corner of Connecticut," Dino said.

At the store in New Fairfield, Stone and Dino got out of the car and went to Sparks. "Buono is gone," he said. "He probably saw your vehicles before we got here, then took off."

"What do you want me to do?"

"You could issue an APB on the silver Mercedes," Dino said. "But Buono is either halfway to New York by now, or to some-place else."

"Okay," Sparks said. "You got the girl?"

"We'll take her back with us," Stone said.

"I wouldn't let her go home without a police detail on her."

"We'll go to my place," Stone said.

Everyone was quiet on the drive back to the city. Dino sat up front, and Stone and Hank were in the backseat. She put her head on his shoulder and seemed to sleep, so he didn't question her further.

As they approached Stone's house, Dino asked, "Do you want some cops here?"

"I don't think so," Stone replied. "He'll probably think we have them anyway, and he can't get into the house."

Hank stirred. "Where are we?"

"Almost to my house," Stone said. "You're staying with me."

"I need some clothes," Hank said. "All I've got is what I'm wearing. He had bath-robes in the house, so I was able to wash things."

"You're about Joan's size," Stone said. "Taller, but she'll have something you can wear."

"All right."

"Dino, you want to come in? Helene can fix us some dinner."

"Nah, I'd better get home to Viv."

Dino's driver had a look around before Stone and Hank got out of the car. Stone opened the door to a darkened house and closed the door behind them. Then he tripped over something soft and fell. Hank found a light switch, and Stone was sitting on the floor in the foyer, next to two fat leaf bags.

"What's that?" Hank asked.

"Five million dollars," Stone replied.

"Onofrio seemed to be expecting seven or eight."

"Five million was all I was willing to pay for you."

Then they began to laugh.

40

John Fratelli was dressing for dinner when his cell phone rang.

"Yeah?"

"It's Stone Barrington."

"How'd it go?"

"We got the girl back. Buono got lucky — he went to the grocery store and saw the police there and took off."

"Did he hurt her?"

"No, not so's you'd notice."

"I'm glad of that."

"I appreciate the tip-off about the cabin. It made all the difference."

"You're welcome."

"You sound different since you got to wherever you are," Stone said.

"I *am* different: new name, new house, new girl."

"What more could any man ask for?"

"You're right about that. Call me if Bats acts up again. I'll help if I can."

"Thanks." They hung up.

Fratelli met Hillary downstairs, and the Bentley was waiting for them. They drove to Café L'Europe for dinner, and the valet drove the car away. Fratelli thought to himself: *You'd better not scratch it.*

They were seated immediately, and Fratelli ordered them martinis. After looking at the menus and chatting quietly, they ordered, and Fratelli cleared his throat.

Hillary looked at him askance.

"There are some things I have to tell you about me."

"I had a feeling something like that was coming," she said. "Shoot."

"I told you some lies about my background — in fact, everything I told you was a lie."

"You didn't tell me much, and I had the feeling I shouldn't ask."

"I grew up in Brooklyn. My father worked as a shoemaker for a place that made custom shoes. He paid the rent, put food on the table, gave me an allowance. My last year in high school I . . . fell among thieves."

"Did they steal from you?"

"No, together we stole from others — financial institutions. We made some money, I bought some clothes and a car. We did about two jobs a year. Nobody ever got hurt. I was the driver, I never went inside, never carried a weapon. Then, when I was in my mid-twenties, something went wrong inside. I heard shooting. I wanted to drive away, but I was a standup guy, and I didn't. I sat there and waited until my three partners stumbled out of the bank. Two of them had been shot by a guard.

"I drove them to a doctor we knew, then left the car on the street and went home. That night, the police came. The partner who didn't get shot told the police everything. The two wounded partners died in the doctor's office. I went to prison. My tattletale partner walked, as we say.

"I served twenty-five years. Inside, I met a man named Eduardo Buono, who was from Brooklyn, too, but he was smarter than I, better educated, better read. We made a bargain: I protected him from . . . assaults by other prisoners, he gave me what amounted to a university education. We both got jobs in the library, and I spent most of my time reading."

"What did you read?"

"Everything. I started with the Harvard Classics — that's supposed to give you a liberal education. I read the Durants' *Civilization.* I read other histories, especially American history, and biographies. Pretty soon I was educating myself.

"I never applied for parole because of Eddie, who needed me to survive in there. Then he died, and I completed my sentence and went free."

"So you have no . . . what is it they say — debt to society?"

"None."

"So where did the money come from?"

"From Eddie. He was inside because he had masterminded the robbery of a cash transfer business at JFK airport. They stole fifteen million dollars. Half went to Eddie, half to his crew. All the crew spent money and got noticed. When they started getting arrested, Eddie knew he was next. He hid his money and went to prison. He thought he could buy a pardon, but that didn't work. Before he died he told me where the money was, and the statute of limitations on the robbery had expired. When I got out, I collected it and left New York. Came here, changed my name, invested the money offshore, bought an apartment, and met you." Fratelli shrugged. "I think that brings us up to date."

"Well," she said, "that was a much more interesting story than I had anticipated."

"I'm sorry I deceived you."

"I'm glad you did," she said. "I would

have been put off. But now I've gotten to know you, and I'm glad you told me."

"I would understand if you didn't want to see me again."

She took his big hand in hers. "That, my dear, is not the case."

"I would be grateful if you would keep this in confidence. I wouldn't want Winston and Elizabeth to know."

"Of course. You're a good man, Jack, and I'm terribly, terribly fond of you. You're an honest man, too. Do you know how I know?"

"How?"

"You don't cheat at golf. Almost everyone else I know does, but not you."

Fratelli laughed.

"May I know your real name?"

"Jack Coulter is my real name. I have a birth certificate, a passport, and a driver's license to prove it. I was born John Fratelli."

"That's a pretty name, it's a pity you can't use it." Then she frowned. "Why can't you use it?"

"Because there are a few people who know that I'm out, and they believe I have Eddie's money."

"And you don't want to meet them again?"

"That is correct."

"You don't see any old friends?"

"The only friends I have are Winston, Elizabeth, and you."

"And we will always be your friends," she said, squeezing his hand.

Dinner arrived, and Jack tasted the wine and approved.

Hillary raised her glass. "To a bright future," she said.

He raised his glass. "I'll drink to that."

The following morning, as Jack was having breakfast in bed and reading the papers, he was finishing the *Palm Beach Post* and he was suddenly riveted by a small display ad.

JOHN FRATELLI
I know who and where you are. You would be wise to contact me before I find it necessary to collapse your world.

There was a name, Harry Moss, and a phone number.

41

Stone was at his desk when Dino called.

"Thanks for the road trip," he said. "How's our victim?"

"Better than I would have thought," Stone said. "She insisted on going to work this morning — after going home to change clothes."

"Well, it's unlikely that we're going to hear from Buono again."

"You think so?"

"Pretty soon he'll find out he's a federal fugitive, and that should scare the shit out of him."

"How'd he get to be a federal fugitive?"

"Kidnapping is a federal crime, and I turned the case over to the FBI, since Hank is no longer at risk."

"And how will Buono know he's a federal fugitive?"

"He'll see it on TV tonight, along with an interview with an FBI agent, or somebody he knows will see it."

"You do good work," Stone said. "Was Viv mad at you for keeping her up last night?"

"Yes, and now she wants to come along when I see you, so she'll know where I am."

"Okay by me."

"I'll tell her."

"See you later."

They hung up.

Joan came to his door. "What's in the two huge bags upstairs?" she asked. "They were delivered late yesterday afternoon, but I didn't open them."

"Five million dollars," Stone replied.

"Ooh! May I have it, please?"

"No."

"I said 'please.' "

"Politeness will not get you everywhere. That reminds me, I have to get rid of that money." He phoned Mike Freeman.

"Good morning."

"Good morning, Mike."

"I'm still waiting for the phone call from your broker."

"He won't be making the call, I have the money here. Can you have it picked up and delivered to my bank in a secure fashion?"

"Security is what we're all about."

"Have your men see Joan when they arrive. She knows where it is. There are two bags, instead of one, and please have your men get a receipt from my banker. They may have to wait a bit while he counts it."

"Those bankers! They don't trust anybody, do they?"

"They certainly don't."

"Are you ready to tell me what this is all about? I'll buy dinner."

"Sure. Where?"

"I'm feeling flush, how about at Daniel?"

"Great."

"Eight?"

"Fine, see you then."

Jack Coulter found a Palm Beach area telephone book in a desk drawer in his suite and looked up the name. He was listed: Harry M. Moss. Coulter had remembered the name that went with that face. The address was on Ocean Drive in Delray Beach, a little south of Palm Beach. Pretty tony neighborhood for a retired FBI agent. Moss must have come into money: certainly, he wanted to come into more.

Jack called Manny Millman, the bookie, and while the number rang, he became John Fratelli again, in accent and attitude.

"Yeah?"

"Manny? It's John Fratelli."

"Hey, there. Everything okay?"

"Almost. I'd like somebody investigated without him knowing. Anybody you know can handle that?"

"Sure. I've got an ex–Miami cop who bets with me. What do you need?"

"Got a pencil?"

"Always."

"Name is Harry Moss." He gave Manny the address and phone number, and his own number. "Retired FBI. I want to know everything there is to know about him. Everything. I'll pay ten grand for a very thorough investigation. He's got three, maybe four days. Have him call me at this number when he's ready to report. If you'll pay him, you can deduct twelve grand from my next payment, okay?"

"Okay."

"What's your man's name?"

"Willard Crowder, black guy, first-rate human being."

"Then go!"

"You got it, pal. I'll call him right now."

"Thanks, Manny."

"You okay, Johnny?"

"Never better — Vegas is sensational!" He hung up.

42

Manny called the number, and Willard Crowder answered on the second ring.

"Yeah, Manny, I know, I'm overdue. I'm good for it."

"Don't sound so grumpy, Will, this is a good-news call."

"Good news I could use."

"How'd you like me to scrub your tab of, let's see . . ."

"Six and a half large."

"Right, and I'll throw in another two grand in cash."

"Who do I have to assassinate?"

"Not a soul. All you have to do is pretend to be a private eye."

"Manny, I *am* a private eye, remember? I've got a plastic badge and everything. What do you need?"

"There's a guy up in Delray Beach named Harry Moss. Write this down." Manny gave him everything he had. "He's a retired FBI guy. A friend of mine wants to know everything there is to know about him."

"Everything? Like what?"

"Everything you can find out by the end of the week. Think of it as an employment investigation. My friend especially wants to know the dirt."

"I'm gonna need expenses."

"I think my friend will spring for another grand."

"Okay, I'm on it."

"Call me when you're done. I'll give you my friend's number."

"Who's your friend?"

"Don't ask." Manny hung up.

Crowder hoisted himself out of bed and looked around. Good thing the woman was coming in this afternoon. He picked up the beer bottles and treated himself to his first shave and shower in three days, ignoring the thirst that lived at the back of his throat.

That done, he stuck a couple of days' clothes into a duffel and ripped the plastic wrap off a dry-cleaned suit. He left the woman's money under the pepper mill on the kitchen counter, and filled his pockets with the usual crap. He hesitated when he came to the 9mm and decided to go with his old snub-nosed Smith & Wesson Airweight revolver that he had worn on his ankle for years as a backup piece. He Velcroed it in place, put on a necktie, grabbed a straw fedora and his duffel, then went down to his car, a 1968 Mercedes convertible that made him look classy to the women. On his way up U.S. 1, he ran it through a car wash, which felt almost as good as his shower.

After that, since he had hocked his laptop, he stopped in a computer café and rented himself an hour of running down his target on Google and Facebook. He was amused that Harry Moss had what had to be a fifteen-year-old photograph posted, along with a plea to hear from eligible ladies. That done, he drove to Delray and found the elderly beachfront apartment building that was home to Mr. Moss.

Question: how did the guy buy this place and handle the property taxes on an FBI pension? A trip to the courthouse solved that riddle. Then he looked for the nearest coffee shop that a sixty-one-year-old guy would have breakfast at every day. He found just the right place, went in, sat at the counter, and ordered a big breakfast. An attractive black woman in a neat uniform took his order, then succumbed to his charms and started talking.

"You a cop?" she asked.

"You're smart — ex-FBI, retired a couple years ago. I'm Will, Madge." Her name was on a plastic tag pinned to her yellow uniform.

"Hey. I got another regular customer used to be FBI. Maybe you know him?"

"Name?"

"Harry Moss."

"Sure I knew him a little: not too tall, balding, early sixties?"

"He's not balding anymore, he's bald."

And in forty-five minutes, between eggs and bacon and the occasional other customers' needs, he got a lot. He left a big tip.

"You come back, now, hear?"

"I hear ya. You want to have dinner one of these nights?"

She handed him a card. "Call me and find out."

Crowder hung around the apartment building long enough to see Moss leave the building. He followed from way back and watched the man park at a shopping center and go into a Publix market. He left with half a basket of what Crowder thought was probably frozen dinners.

Crowder didn't wait for him to go out in the evening; he could make that up later.

He drove home, found his apartment clean and neat, then sat down and wrote out his report. He hung his suit in the closet and fell into his reclining chair in his shirt and shorts with a large bourbon. Tiger Woods was playing in California, and he was looking good.

Harry Moss walked into the diner at five o'clock for his usual slice of key lime pie and coffee. "Hey, Madge," he said, climbing onto a stool.

"Hey, Harry," Madge said. She put the pie and coffee on the counter without being asked. "Friend of yours came in here this morning."

"Friend?" Who would that be?

"Well, he said he knew you a little from the FBI days. Name of Will. Black dude."

Moss paused with the first bite of pie nearly to his mouth, then he put down the fork. "I only ever knew two or three black agents, and none of 'em was Will."

Madge shrugged. "I guess he got the wrong guy, then. He described you like he knew you, though."

Moss made a second attempt to eat the first bite of his pie, but his mouth tasted funny, and he put it down again. "Madge, you been talking about me to somebody?"

"Nah, he brought you up," she lied.

"What'd he ask you?"

"He wanted to know if you lived around here, said he wanted to look you up." She was getting into the swing of her lie, now, to see if she could get a rise out of Harry. She did.

Moss's face was turning red. "What did you tell him?"

"Just that I knew you. I told him I don't know where you live."

"You sure you didn't tell him that?"

"Now that I think of it, I don't know where you live."

"What was he driving?"

"An old Mercedes convertible, real old. He parked it across the street."

"What color?"

"Kind of off-white."

"Describe him."

"Big black dude, six-two, on the heavy side. Sharp dresser."

Moss tried again with the pie and got down a bite. Who the hell was this guy?

43

Stone got downstairs to his office at the usual time, and there was a pink memo slip on his desk: call Dan Sparks. Stone called. Out of the office, leave a message. He did. A week had passed since he had been up to Connecticut, and he hadn't seen Hank, which was okay with him. He was oddly disturbed that she had been sleeping with her captor. What was that? Stockholm syndrome?

He called Dino. "Morning."

"Yeah, it is."

"You heard anything from Dan Sparks?"

"I had a message on my desk when I got in. He was out when I called back."

"Me, too. You think his people picked up Buono?"

"I'd be real surprised if Bats was still in Connecticut. You see him on the news?"

"I saw a report."

"I ran him against the database, and he

had no arrest record," Dino said.

"I would have thought he did," Stone said. "I mean, the guy's a career criminal, and he's, what, forty? How'd he avoid arrest for so long?"

"He must be real careful. You know, it's funny, his uncle Eduardo never got busted, either, until his pals gave him up after his big heist."

"Maybe caution runs in the family. He's got a father named Gino, lives in Queens. Run him, will you?"

"Hang on." There was the sound of computer keys clicking.

"Nada," Dino said. "He's clean."

"That's puzzling. You think it means anything?"

"Means what? I can't think of anything. Either they were all three extremely smart and careful, or they all got very lucky."

"That's too lucky," Dino said. "Hang on, Dan Sparks is returning my call. I'll tie you in, if I can remember how to work this phone."

There was a click. "Dan?"

"Yeah, Dino."

"I've got Stone on the line, too. Save you a call."

"Thanks, I need to talk to the two of you."

"Shoot."

"My crime-scene team went through the house on the lake, and they found traces of blood in the kitchen drain."

"I don't think Hank was hurt," Stone said.

"Well, it's not a mystery. We found a body about fifteen yards into the trees."

"What kind of a body?" Dino asked.

"White male, five-eight, maybe, a hundred and forty, maybe, sporty clothes."

"Did you take prints?" Stone asked.

"Yeah, we can scan and run 'em pretty much instantly these days. No hit on our computers or the national."

"What about dental?"

"That'll be tough," Sparks said. "The guy has no head."

It got real quiet for a few seconds.

"Cause of death?" Dino asked.

"Multiple knife wounds in his back. A knife in the kitchen matches the wounds — that's one possibility. An ax was leaning against a woodshed at the side of the house — that's another."

"Any sign of the car?" Stone asked.

"Sign, yeah. There were tracks running into the lake."

"Could you see anything in the water?"

"Nah, lake's about thirty feet deep there. We've got divers on the way. They can probably float it."

"How do they do that?" Stone asked.

"They'll take big bladders down there, put 'em in the car and inflate 'em from compressed-air bottles. That should pop it right up, and we can tow it to shore. You fellas thinking what I'm thinking?"

"Probably," Dino said.

"Maybe," Stone chipped in.

"My guess, the lady didn't take kindly to being kidnapped, so she took the first opportunity."

"She didn't want to drive away in the car," Dino said. "She knew he drove stolen cars from his chop shop."

"Nice point," Sparks said.

"If I were a lawyer," Stone said, "oh, that's right, I am — I could make a case for self-defense in court."

"I would buy that," Sparks said, "if the guy still had a head."

"Kidnapping rage?" Stone suggested.

Both Sparks and Dino laughed heartily.

"You got an APB out on her?" Dino asked, when he had recovered himself.

"Yeah, but we're playing that tune softly: we're seeking her for information about a possible crime."

"That's polite," Dino said.

"We thought so. I'd like to hear her story, before we paint her as an ax-wielding, backstabbing homicidal maniac."

"Very restrained," Dino said. "Stone? You still there?"

"I'm thinking," Stone said.

"Good idea," Dino replied.

"Was there a cell phone in the house?"

"No," Dan said, "but there was one in the corpse's pocket."

"Who did it belong to?"

Short silence. "Good question. I'll have to check."

"I'd really like to know."

"Hang on." He put them on hold.

"This doesn't sound good," Dino said.

"Tell me about it."

"Maybe my guys should talk to Hank before Dan's do."

"It couldn't hurt."

Dan came back on the line. "I was wrong," he said. "There were two cell phones — one his, one hers."

"So she wasn't able to call for help," Stone said. He wanted to make that point.

"Well," Dan said, "I can see how a lot of things could happen in a situation like hers. A lot of people would panic in the circumstances, and rage can be a product of panic. My money's on you in court, Stone."

"Gee, thanks."

"She's going to need a lot better lawyer

than Stone," Dino said.

"From what I'm hearing, she could do a lot worse," Dan replied.

"Thank you for that vote of confidence," Stone said.

"I'm just saying a jury might be very sympathetic to her plight."

"But not to her skill with tools," Dino said. "And there's the cleanup to consider, and the fact that she didn't confide in Stone." He paused. "Did she, Stone?"

"She did not."

"You want a couple of hours to feel her out?" Dino asked.

"That won't be much fun."

"Not as much fun as feeling her up, I'll grant you."

"Don't be a smart-ass, Dino."

"I don't have to send out the detectives just yet."

"I'll get back to you," Stone said, and he hung up.

44

Stone thought about it for a few minutes before he made the call. He tried the office number and asked for Hank.

Another woman came on the line. "Who's calling?"

"Stone Barrington. I'm a friend of Hank's."

"She called in sick some time back. I haven't heard from her, and her cell phone went straight to voice mail."

"I see. Thanks for your help." He hung up and called Hank's home number. It rang four times, then went to voice mail. "It's Stone. We need to talk right away, before you talk to anybody else." He left his office number, though he knew she had it.

Half an hour later, Hank called back. "Hi, I'm sorry I haven't been in touch."

"Are you ill?"

"Not exactly."

"What does that mean?"

"I'm just a little shaken up, and I'm not thinking very clearly."

"Are you at home?"

"Yes. I was in the shower when you called earlier. I just saw the flashing light on the phone. Can we get together? I need to talk with you."

"Then you'd better talk to me now, because soon you'll be talking to the police, and it won't be fun."

"I don't mind talking to them, I'm the victim, remember? Not a perp, to put it in yours and Dino's graceful and expressive language."

"You'd better be prepared to convince the police of that, or not talk to them at all."

"Are you giving me legal advice?"

"I will, if you like, on the basis of a client-attorney relationship."

"Should I hire you?"

"You should hire somebody. Do you know any very good attorneys?"

"I don't know any attorneys at all, except for you."

"I think it would be a good idea for you to be represented by someone else, in the circumstances."

"What circumstances?"

"An attorney who might be more sympathetic to your plight."

"What plight? What are you talking about, Stone?"

"All right, let me ask you one question — as an attorney."

"Okay."

"Where's the head?"

"The head of what?"

"The head of Bats Buono."

"As far as I know, he's self-employed."

He thought she seemed perfectly calm, maybe a little exasperated with him.

"I'm talking about the head that used to rest on his shoulders."

"You're saying that Onofrio has lost his head? Metaphorically?"

"Not metaphorically — actually."

"Stone, you're not making any sense."

If this is a performance, he thought, *it's a good one.*

"Are you sitting down?"

"No, should I be?"

"Yes. The Connecticut State Police sent a crime-scene team to the lake cottage. They found traces of blood in the kitchen sink."

"And what conclusion did they draw from that?"

"That somebody did some bleeding."

"I didn't, I'm wound-free."

"Did Bats cut himself shaving?"

"Not that I noticed. What aren't you telling me, Stone?"

"They searched the property and found a corpse in the woods."

She gave a little gasp. "Onofrio's?"

"It was carrying his wallet and two cell phones, yours and his."

"He took it away from me. He's actually dead?"

"Yes, and his head is missing."

"Oh, shit!"

"Well, yes. His car was missing, too, and there were tire tracks leading into the lake. A dive team is on the way there now to raise it."

"And you're saying the police think I had something to do with his death?"

"They're considering it. Is there anything you want to tell me?"

"Look, he was alive when he drove away from the house. That was the last I saw of him, and he hasn't called."

"Well, he wouldn't, would he?"

"Now that you mention it, I guess not. Am I really a suspect?"

"I think they would probably describe you as 'a person of interest' in the case, but that's only one bad answer from 'defendant,' so when they come calling, tell them the truth."

"I am telling the truth. I always tell the truth."

"They're going to ask you about the protection order you took out against Buono."

"Now, look, Stone . . ."

"Stop right there. Consider your answer."

She was quiet for a moment. "All right," she said finally, "I almost took out the order, but I didn't actually do it."

"Then why did you lie about it? Don't you know there are court records of protection orders?"

"I was on the point of doing it, but he suddenly stopped calling, so I waited for a couple of days, and when he didn't call again, I didn't take out the order."

"All right, I'll accept that answer."

"That's very good of you," she said, and there was acid in her voice. "You checked up on me, did you? Or Dino?"

"Yes. Do you blame me?"

"I apologize for lying to you."

"Thank you. The good news is, the cops, generally speaking, don't know about your lie. The bad news is, Dino does."

"And he would rat me out about that?"

"I don't know. At least you haven't lied directly to a cop, only to me. Keep it that way."

"All right. Any other advice?"

"Do you want me to find a lawyer for you?"

"I thought you would represent me."

"That is not in your best interests, given our personal history, however short. I say again, I think you need to be represented by another attorney."

"Do I really need a lawyer right now?"

"That's my best advice."

"But then he'll tell me not to answer any police questions, won't he?"

"Very possibly."

"And if I don't, that will make me look guilty, won't it?"

"It's a conundrum. The advantage lies in not having any lies on the record. If you want to answer their questions, he'll be in the room, to keep you out of trouble."

"All right, recommend somebody."

"His name is Herbert Fisher. He's with my firm, Woodman & Weld. He's young, smart, and shrewd."

"All right, Herbert Fisher."

"He's called Herb." He gave her the number.

"I'll call him."

"Do that."

They both hung up. Stone was still confused, but there was enough in her answers to keep him believing that she had not killed Buono.

45

Jack Coulter was in the Breakers' gym, working out, as he had done every day in prison, except he did not now use weights to achieve bulk. He glanced at the mirrored wall and was pleased to see himself as a well-built, fit forty-year-old. He had had his suits altered twice to adapt to his decreasing weight.

His cell phone rang on the stool beside him, and he picked it up. "Yes?"

"Who is this?" A male voice, deep, raspy.

Jack hung up and waited. The phone rang again. "Yes?"

"I'm sorry, this is Will Crowder. Are you expecting my call?"

"Yes."

"Manny Millman said —"

"Stop. Report."

"Yes, sir. The subject, Harry M. Moss, is a sixty-one-year-old white male, five-nine, one-sixty, in apparently good health. He retired from the FBI at fifty-nine and lives on his pension, plus benefits from an inheritance."

"What benefits?"

"His mother married twice. Her first husband, Martin Moss, was a carpet salesman for a big furniture store in New York. He died of a heart attack at fifty-four. Her second husband, William Hood, was the owner of the big furniture store. Not long after their marriage, he retired at the age of sixty-nine and sold the business. They moved to Delray Beach, Florida, to a beachfront condominium in a building constructed in the 1920s. He proceeded to gamble away much of his capital, and he shot himself at the age of seventy-two, on the beach in front of their building late at night. Mrs. Hood continued to live in the apartment until her death, three years ago, in much-reduced circumstances. She left her son, Harry, the apartment and enough in a trust to pay the maintenance, taxes, and fees on the apartment, but not much else.

"There was some considerable feeling in local law enforcement that Mrs. Hood murdered her husband, her motive being to conserve what was left in his estate before he threw it all away. The theory of the case is that the two of them went for a walk on the beach after midnight, and that she took along a .32 caliber revolver belonging to her husband that he kept in a bedside drawer, that she shot him in the right temple, knowing that he was right-handed, wiped the gun, put his fingerprints on it, and left it in the sand next to his body. She returned to her apartment via a service elevator, which was very little used at night, then went to bed and waited for someone to come to the door and inform her of her husband's suicide. She was awakened by the police around eight AM the following morning, roused from a sound sleep, she maintained, after the discovery of Mr. Hood's body by a maintenance worker who had come to rake the beach.

"Repeated interrogations failed to shake her story — that she had gone to bed at her usual hour of eleven, and that her husband must have taken a late walk after that time, then, depressed by his financial woes, taken his own life. The case was closed after a coroner's inquest ruled Hood's death a suicide.

"Moss lives entirely on his pension, as he had saved little, and he is not yet old enough to collect Social Security. He has listed the apartment with a local firm, naming a price of three million nine hundred and fifty thousand. He probably hopes to realize three and a half million. It has been on the market for fifteen months with two offers of less than two mil. He blames local market conditions following the recession. He drives a two-year-old Toyota Camry Hybrid and frequents the five-dollar window at Hialeah racetrack, wins some, loses some.

"Contact with a close acquaintance says that he does little with his time other than hang out at a local coffee shop and the public library in the daytime and a local bar in the evenings, watching sports on TV and trying to pick up women, almost always unsuccessfully. His attitude toward life is one of being thwarted — especially by his stepfather's gambling habit. He feels that, if not for that, he would be a wealthy man today, driving an expensive car, dressing well, and having sex with beautiful women.

"His defining characteristic is that he is always looking for a windfall that will restore him to that position, but he seems unlikely ever to achieve that.

"That concludes my report. Do you have any questions?"

"No." Jack hung up.

Will Crowder stared at the phone in his

hand as if to rebuke it. He had no idea whom he had been talking to and no idea why. He called Manny Millman.

"Yes?"

"It's Will Crowder. I've made my report. Your friend seemed satisfied."

"Good. Your debt is canceled. I'll have your three grand for you this afternoon at the track. Come see me." He hung up.

46

Herbie Fisher sat in his office, cradled by his Eames lounge chair, reading a letter for his signature. His secretary buzzed. "Yes?"

"Stone Barrington for you."

He pressed the SPEAKER button. "Stone?"

"How are you, Herb?"

He had trained Stone not to call him Herbie anymore. "I'm just great, thanks. You?"

"So-so."

"That doesn't sound good."

"I just got off with a friend who may be in trouble."

"Anybody I know?"

"Her name is Henrietta Cromwell, calls herself Hank."

"Does she look like a Hank?"

"Not a bit."

"Anything I can do to help?"

"I'd appreciate it if you'd see her, talk to her. If you can help, please do."

"What's her number?" Herbie saw the

light on his second line flashing. “She may be calling now. Hang on.” He buzzed his secretary. “If someone called Hank Cromwell calls, get her in here.” He went back to line one. “Okay, give me some background.”

Stone started with his meeting Hank at Clarke’s, then took him, step by step, through everything that had happened.

“All right,” Herbie said, “I think I get the picture. Do you have an opinion about this?”

“I’d rather let you form your own after you see her.”

“There is the possibility, as I see it, that after you left the lake cottage with Hank, Buono could have returned to the lake and been murdered by somebody else — either someone who came with him or someone who knew where he was and came after him.”

“I think that’s her way out of this.”

“Is she a truthful person?”

“I’ve caught her in only one lie, about the protective order. Everything else could be true, or she could be lying about all of it.”

“Well, you’ve certainly made my day more interesting. Maybe we’ll talk again after I’ve seen her.”

“I think you’ll make better decisions if I don’t contribute to them.”

"As you wish. See you."

They both hung up.

His secretary was standing in the door. He signed the letter and handed it to her.

"*Ms.* Hank Cromwell will be here in a few minutes," she said.

"When she arrives, show her straight in."

Once again, Herbie admired Stone's taste in women. He took Hank to the other side of the room, sat her on his sofa, and took a chair opposite.

"Stone thinks I may be in trouble," she said.

"I heard. Do *you* think you're in trouble?"

"If there's a God in heaven, I'm not."

"That could go either way."

"Do you want to ask me if I'm a murderer?"

"No, I don't. If I do that, and you answer in the affirmative, then I can't put you on the stand at trial without becoming your accomplice after the fact. It's my hope that your version of the facts is sufficient to convince me that you're entirely innocent."

"Entirely innocent," she said flatly, as if she were considering her condition. "Is anyone ever entirely innocent?"

"Certainly. But some people who are innocent of a crime still feel guilt about their behavior, and whether they've somehow contributed to the event."

"In my case, which event?"

"Let's start with the kidnapping."

She repeated what she had told Stone.

"If that's a true story, or alternatively, if it's a story that cannot be proven to be untrue, then I don't think you are complicit in your own kidnapping."

"Thank you."

"Now tell me about your rescue."

"Onofrio left the cabin to go grocery shopping."

"Hold it right there. Let's examine that. Why would a kidnapper leave his victim alone to go to the grocery store?"

"You've heard of the Stockholm syndrome, when a kidnapped person begins to feel sympathy for her kidnapper?"

"Of course."

"This is sort of the opposite of that. I, ah, treated in him such a way that he began to trust me."

"By having sex with him?"

"That was part of it. I just didn't behave like a victim. I behaved the way I did when I was seeing him."

"How long did you see him?"

"About seven months."

"And the relationship was like what?"

"Pleasant, amusing — he did have a sense of humor — and attractively sexual."

"And you tried to make it all those things again?"

"Yes, I did, and it worked. Also, besides trusting me, he knew that I had no idea where I was, not even what state I was in, having arrived there in the trunk of a car. He knew that I'm a city person, unaccustomed to the woods, and he knew that I'm a little afraid of the dark."

"A little?"

"All right, more than a little. Enough that I was well anchored in the cottage. He knew I wouldn't try to walk out of there at night."

"So, what is your theory of what happened after you left the cottage with Stone?"

"Well, obviously Onofrio returned to the cabin and someone else killed him. I certainly didn't, and somehow I don't think he committed suicide."

Herbie laughed. "Probably not. Do you have a theory of who killed him?"

"He had associates, he ran a chop shop, which is a criminal enterprise, is it not?"

"It is."

"Then his associates were criminals. I should think he knew a number of people who would kill him for several million dollars. I think that Onofrio would have killed me for several million dollars, but I don't think he intended to, or that he thought he had to to get the money. Stone had already said that he would bring the money, but that he would have to see me alive before he'd hand it over."

"Did you ever meet any of Onofrio's associates?"

"One man, once. Onofrio picked me up at my apartment for dinner, and we drove to an Italian restaurant in Red Hook, a little mom-and-pop place. I can't remember what it was called, except that it was the possessive of a male Italian's first name — Gino's, for instance, but not actually. But it was a very common Italian name."

"And did he meet someone there?"

"We had just sat down and ordered wine when a man in a sharp suit came into the place, walked over to our table, and handed Onofrio a plain envelope, rather thick, as if it contained money. He introduced the man as Marty, no last name. The two talked for a minute in a kind of code, not mentioning names or places. The effect was that someone who owed him money had paid him. Onofrio put the envelope into his inside suit pocket, and the man left. He didn't refer to him again."

"Did you have any other impressions of

the man?"

"He was rather handsome, seemed to be Italian, and Onofrio seemed to respect and trust him, as if he were a valued associate."

"Yes," Herbie said, "if you've got a few million bucks in cash lying around, you've gotta watch out for those valued associates."

"What should I do?"

"Nothing," Herbie said. "Let's let the police make the next move. Do you know how to make a conference call?"

"You enter some sort of code, don't you?"

Herbie explained the process. "If you get a call from the police, either Connecticut or New York, ask them to hold and call me. If they come to your home or your place of work, or if they take you or ask you to come to a police station, call me and I'll meet you there. Tell them you don't want to answer questions until your attorney arrives, and don't let them charm or threaten or trick you into talking to them before I arrive or am on the phone."

"All right."

"If they don't contact you, then you're probably in the clear. Go live your life. But I think you'll hear from them, if only because they'll want more information."

"Should I tell them about Marty?"

"After I'm on the phone or present. Only

then. I'll introduce the subject."

"All right."

Herbie walked her to the elevator, shook her hand, then returned to his office and called Stone.

"What did you think?" Stone asked.

"I was impressed with her. She told me something she hasn't told you."

"What was that?"

"I tell you this as a collaborator in representing her, so as to avoid client-attorney confidentiality."

"Of course."

"She was out to dinner one evening when an associate of Buono's, who he introduced as 'Marty,' brought him an envelope that seemed to hold a lot of money. She said that she thought that Buono respected and liked him and regarded him as a trusted associate. I think that Marty sounds good for the killing, if he knew that Buono was coming into millions in cash. They may even have been collaborating, and Marty wanted it all. I think that Hank would have been killed, too, if you hadn't just taken her out of the cottage."

"Okay, I'll see what I can learn about that. What do you think Hank's future looks like?"

"I think she'll get through this without

getting arrested and charged — unless there's something she hasn't told me."

"Well, there is that, isn't there?"

"All too often," Herbie replied.

47

Stone called John Fratelli on his throwaway cell phone.

"Yes?"

"It's Stone Barrington."

"What can I do for you?"

"Bats Buono is dead."

"Hey, that's good news! Who offed him?"

"Somebody arrived at the lake cottage sometime after I left with the girl. He was stabbed repeatedly, and his head was cut off with an ax. His car was rolled into the lake."

"That doesn't make any sense. If I was his murderer, I'd put the body in the car before I rolled it into the lake."

"That's a very good point."

"Was Bats driving one of his stolen cars?"

"Very possibly."

"Then here's how it might have gone down: Bats is partners with some guy in the kidnapping for ransom. He calls the guy and tells him you're bringing the money, to get up to the cabin. The guy arrives and finds Bats, but no money and no girl. He takes this badly, then one of two things happens: either he goes into a rage and stabs Bats and cuts off his head to make ID harder, or more likely, he believes that Bats has gotten paid and released the girl, so he puts a gun to Bats's head and tells him to cough up. Bats swears he didn't get paid, and the guy puts one in his head, then he cuts the head off so the cops can't do a ballistics match on the bullet. Maybe it's his favorite piece."

"Okay, I'll buy that. There's a suspect. Bats had a close associate named Marty. Ring a bell?"

"I don't know any of his associates, but tell you what: I'll call Bats's old man, Gino, and ask about Marty, see what I can get from him. Call you back?"

"Sure." They both hung up.

Fratelli called Gino Buono.

"Yeah?"

"Gino, it's Johnny Fratelli."

"Did you kill him, Johnny?"

"So you heard."

"Some cop from Connecticut called me. Did you, Johnny?"

"No, Gino, I'm in Vegas. I had nothing to do with it."

"I didn't think you did, but I had to ask."

"It's okay. I've heard something, though, might be useful."

"Tell me."

"Did Onofrio have an associate called Marty?"

"Yeah, Marty Parese. Marty was his right-hand man. They've been tight since they were kids."

"I heard that Marty and Onofrio might have been in this together and were going to split the money."

"Onofrio didn't tell me nothing, but that makes a lot of sense."

"You think Marty would off Onofrio for a few million in cash?"

Gino was quiet for a moment. "Maybe. Come to think of it, who *wouldn't* off him for that much money? I can't think of anybody *I'd* trust around that kind of money."

"Just a thought. My condolences, Gino, for your loss."

"Thanks, Johnny."

Fratelli called Stone back. "I spoke to Bats's old man, Gino."

"And?"

"Gino says the guy is Marty Parese, and he and Bats were tight since they were kids. Gino also thinks Marty is good for the killing, since there were millions involved."

"I'll see that it gets looked into," Stone said. "Thank you, John."

"Anytime. Oh, and I'll give you two to one that when they find Bats's head, there'll be a bullet in it." They hung up.

Stone called Dino.

"Hey."

"Are your people working the Buono murder with Dan Sparks?"

"Yeah."

"I've got a suspect for you."

"I accept free gifts."

"I didn't say it was free, it's going to cost you a couple of dinners."

"Okay, one dinner — don't get greedy."

"There's a guy named Marty Parese, who was Buono's best friend since childhood."

"So, your theory is that the best friend did it? Why not the butler?"

"It's not my theory, it's Gino Buono's theory — Bats's father."

"Yeah? Are you and Gino best buddies these days?"

"I didn't say he told *me.*"

"So this is what you lawyers call hearsay?"

"In case you didn't know, Dino, hearsay works when you're investigating a murder, just not in a courtroom."

"You're just trying to get Hank out of this, aren't you?"

"I don't represent Hank, Herb Fisher does."

"I wonder how that happened."

"I recommended him, he's good."

"Yeah, he is, I guess."

"Somebody I know thinks that Bats and Marty were in the kidnapping together, and that when I agreed to give Bats the money, Marty came running, but when he got to the cottage both Hank and the money were gone. After that, there was a disagreement."

"I can imagine," Dino said.

"There's a theory about Bats's head, too."

"I can't wait to hear it."

"Marty put one into Bats's head, then remembered he'd used his favorite gun, so he took off the head because he didn't want anybody to find the bullet."

"Great. That explains all the knife wounds in Bats's back."

"Marty didn't want it to look like a shooting."

"Anything else?"

"That's about it."

"Okay, it's good for a dinner, but it's not *that* good, so you'd better order something cheap."

"When have you known me to order

something cheap?"

"That's what I'm afraid of."

They both hung up.

Dino called the lead detective on the Buono case.

"Yeah, Chief?"

"You ever heard of a Marty Parese?"

"Yeah, he and Buono were partners in the chop shop. Allegedly."

"There's a theory — this is about fourth-hand by now — that Parese and Buono were partners in the kidnapping, too, and when Parese got to the lake cottage and found Buono there but without the money or the girl, he put one in his head and cut off the head so we couldn't make a ballistics match. What do you think?"

"It does make a weird kind of sense," the detective said. "I mean, the medical examiner says the knife wounds in Buono's back were postmortem. We'll pick up Parese and have a chat with him."

"Hey, that's a good idea," Dino said. "And Dan Sparks might like to have somebody there when you question him."

"Sure, Chief."

"Have a good time." Dino hung up.

48

Joan buzzed. "Mike Freeman on one."

"Did his people pick up the money?"

"Half an hour ago."

Stone pressed the button. "Hey, Mike."

"We have a problem with your money, Stone."

Stone's stomach lurched. "What is it, Mike?"

"Your bank won't take it."

"That doesn't sound like my bank, turning down a five-million-dollar deposit."

"The manager said he'd call you. Meanwhile, the truck is on its way back to your house, so be prepared to receive it. I'll be happy to send the truck back to you when you've sorted out the problem."

"Thanks for the call, Mike." Stone hung up and buzzed Joan. "The two bags of money are on their way back to us, so be ready to get them inside fast."

"What's going on?"

"My bank manager is going to call."

"He's on the other line."

Stone pressed line two. "This is Stone Barrington."

"Mr. Barrington, this is Charles Crockwell, your bank manager."

"Good morning, Mr. Crockwell. What's the problem?"

"Good morning. The problem is, we can't accept that kind of unsorted cash deposit."

"I don't understand, you cashed my check, why won't you take it back?"

"The problem is, you asked for the sum in tens and twenties, which we were happy to arrange, but then you asked us to unband everything and mix it up."

"That's right, I did."

"Well, we'd have to close down the branch and put everybody to work sorting it in order to be able to accept the deposit. I don't think you realize how difficult that would be."

"I thought you folks had machines that did that work."

"We have such a machine, but it's gone back to the manufacturer for repairs. The only place I know that might do that is the Federal Reserve Bank of New York, and their only customers are banks."

"Mr. Crockwell, I'm a pretty good customer of your bank, am I not?"

"Mr. Barrington, you are an extremely good customer, and we value your trust in us, but I'm telling you that what you're asking is beyond our ability to accomplish at this time, and our counter and sorter won't be back for another ten days, I'm told."

"What do you suggest I do?"

"Well, if you know a couple of dozen people that you would trust with five million dollars in small bills, invite them over and ask them to help you sort it. You could make a sort of party of it."

"That's an amusing suggestion, Mr. Crockwell."

"I don't mean to make light of the situation. I suppose you could call the chairman of the board. He could convene a board meeting, and they could count it, but I should mention that there are a couple of people on that board that I wouldn't trust with a large sum of loose cash."

"Thank you, Mr. Crockwell," Stone said, and hung up. "Joan!" he screamed.

Joan came running and entered the office with her trusty .45 in her hand. "What?"

"You don't need to be armed."

"All right, then, what is it?"

The doorbell rang.

"That's gotta be your cash," she said, then

left the room. She came back a moment later with two men and a steel cart that barely squeezed through the door. "Right over there," she said, pointing at the sofa. The two men hefted the leaf bags and a cardboard box onto the sofa, Joan inspected the seals, approved and signed a receipt, and the two men left. "Now what?" she asked.

"What's in the cardboard box?" Stone asked.

Joan read the label. "Cash-binding bands."

"I don't know what to do," Stone said.

"What's the problem?"

"The bank won't take the money unless it's sorted into tens and twenties and banded."

"Won't the bank do it?"

"They don't have the people, and their equipment is broken."

"Who's going to do it, then?" she asked.

"That's the problem."

She looked at the bags. "Let me know when you figure it out," she said, then went back to her office.

Stone sat, staring at the bags. Joan buzzed. "Hank is on line one."

Stone picked up the phone. "Hi."

"You sound a bit disconsolate," she said. "Something wrong?"

"The bank won't take the money back."

"The five million?"

"Yes. It has to be sorted and banded or they won't take it back. Right now, the two bags are sitting on my office sofa."

Hank began to laugh. "You're the only person I know who could possibly have this problem."

"I'm the only person you know with five million dollars in small bills in the house?"

"I can't think of another soul. You want to have dinner tonight?"

"Okay."

"Don't sound so enthusiastic about it."

"I'm sorry."

"Where should I meet you?"

"Come here for a drink, say seven?"

"How do I dress?"

"Let's keep it in the neighborhood — how about the Four Seasons?"

"You talked me into it. I'll see you at seven." She hung up.

Joan came into the office holding an office supply catalog. "Here's a machine that could solve your problem," she said, handing him the catalog.

Stone read the description; the thing would count currency and separate it into piles. "Order one," he said, handing the catalog back to her.

She left the room. Five minutes later she was back. "They don't have it in stock," she said. "I called the manufacturer, but they closed for business at five o'clock, which was three minutes ago. I got a recording."

"Call them tomorrow morning."

"Today's Friday, and Monday is a national holiday."

"Oh, shit," Stone said. "What am I going to do with it?"

Joan stared at the two bags. "We could put it in the wine cellar," she said. "It has a lock."

"I don't know where the key is, I never lock it."

"Well, I guess you could just leave it there on the sofa. Nobody knows it's here but Mike Freeman. I guess it's as safe a place as any, except a vault, and we don't have one of those, and it won't fit in any of our safes."

"Would you sleep in here, with your .45?"

"No, I would not."

"Well, I guess I'll have to sleep in here."

"Do you and Hank have a date tonight?"

"Yes."

"Then I'd bet against your sleeping down here. I'm off. You and your five million have a nice weekend." She left.

Stone continued to stare at the bags for a while, then he went upstairs.

49

Harry Moss sat on his usual stool at his usual sports bar and had his usual Cutty Sark and water. He was trying to watch a golf tournament on TV, but his vision kept blurring.

When it got a little quieter in the bar, Jerry, the bartender, drifted over. "Hey, Harry," he said. "Some guy was in here asking questions about you a few days ago."

Moss sat up straight. "Was it a black guy?"

"Yeah, he felt like a cop of one kind or another."

"What do you mean by that?"

"I mean, cops all have something about them that I don't like."

"I was a cop," Moss said.

"You were a fed — they have a different thing."

"What do feds have?"

"Pressed suits, white shirts, boring ties, clean shaves."

"Like me."

"Yeah, like you, except I've never seen you in a suit."

"And this guy wasn't federal, you think?"

"Nah, city cop, state cop, probably."

"What did he ask you about?"

"He mentioned knowing you, and then he just poked around a little: you know, how's Harry doing? What's he up to? Where's he hang? Like that."

"What did you tell him?"

"Practically nothing."

"Come on, Jerry, what'd you tell him?"

"Nothing, really. He seemed to know a lot already. What's it about, do you think? You schtupping somebody's wife?"

"I wish," Moss said. His cell phone went off, and he dug it out of his pocket. "Harry Moss."

"No kidding, *the* Harry Moss?"

The guy had a New York accent. "I'm the only one I know. Who's this?"

"The Harry Moss who puts strange ads in the Palm Beach paper?"

"You saw that, did you? You calling from Palm Beach?"

"I'm calling from Vegas. Even way out here we get the Palm Beach papers."

"You got some information for me?"

"What's it worth to you?"

"Depends on what you're selling."

"How about this: I know somebody who was sitting out on the beach at Delray a few years back, late at night, and these two people came along, and they were having an argument of some sort."

"What are you talking about?"

"Patience, Harry, I'm getting there."

"All right, go on. What were they arguing about?"

"Seems the woman was real upset with her husband about his gambling habit. Seems the guy was a degenerate gambler. You know anybody like that?"

"What's your point?"

"I'm getting there, Harry. Then this woman did something that really surprised the witness."

"What?"

"She reached into her handbag, pulled out a gun, and shot her husband in the head."

Moss didn't know what to say.

"You're going all silent on me, Harry."

"This was not the subject of my ad. How'd you know I placed the ad, anyway?"

"In a minute, Harry. Next, the woman took a handkerchief out of her husband's pocket, wiped the gun down, put his fingerprints on it, and dropped it next to his body. Then she walked away very quietly and returned to the building where she and her husband lived."

"Why are you telling me this?"

"I thought you ought to have the true facts. There are other people who might like to have the facts, too."

"So what? She's dead. Nobody can touch her now."

"Maybe not, but they could touch you. I hear the husband has relatives who thought they might have some of his estate coming."

"Good luck to them with that."

"But, Harry, if the police knew what really happened, there'd be an investigation. And if they talked to the witness and found that the woman murdered her husband, then, under Florida law, she couldn't have legally inherited her husband's money or property, since she caused her husband's death. And — think about this, Harry — you wouldn't have been able to inherit from her. Everything would go to his relatives."

"What do you want?"

"That's a pretty nice apartment you inherited, isn't it, Harry? Worth what? A couple of million? More when the real estate market recovers."

"You want my apartment?"

"No, Harry, but remember, it's the husband's apartment, and his relatives would sure be interested, I'll bet."

"Why would you do something like that?"

"Why would you run an ad in the Palm Beach paper?"

"You're Fratelli, aren't you?"

"Is that what you think, Harry? Tell me, are you sitting in the sports bar, having a Cutty Sark and water? That's where you could be found any evening, isn't it? Or in your apartment later, fast asleep. And the service elevator isn't manned at night, is it? And all those elderly retirees are asleep, just like you."

"Are you threatening me?"

"You bet your sweet ass. I'm in a position to shut your life down, Harry. This time next year, you wouldn't be sitting in the sports bar drinking scotch, you'd be sitting on a curb somewhere, drinking muscatel from a bottle."

"Listen to me, Fratelli."

"You listen to me, Harry. First of all, that name never passes your lips again, for *any* reason, you got me?"

"All right."

"And another thing — even if you sell the apartment and get your money out of it, I can always find you, and believe me, I could snap your neck like a twig. You getting the message?"

Moss was sweating now. "I understand."

"From now on, then, it's live and let live?"

"Live and let live," Moss said, mopping his face. "I'm sorry I disturbed you."

"Thank you, Harry. *Never* disturb me again. You won't like the consequences."

The man hung up. Moss went to his recent calls and found it. Private number.

"Jerry," he said, "give me another Cutty Sark and water."

"Sure thing, Harry. You feeling okay? You're looking kind of pale."

"Just give me the drink," Moss said.

50

Stone's bell rang a couple of minutes after seven, as he was walking down the stairs. He turned off the alarm and opened the front door.

"Hi," Hank said. "I'm thirsty. Can a girl get a drink here?"

"Very possibly," Stone replied. "Come right in." He closed the door behind her and set the alarm again.

"You always do that?" she asked.

"Just a habit," he said. "Only one button to push, ARM."

"Better safe than sorry," she said.

"You read that somewhere." He led her into the study. "What would you like?"

"A very dry vodka martini, please."

He shoveled some ice into a glass and filled it with water, and while it chilled, speared a couple of anchovy-stuffed olives with a long toothpick. He emptied the ice and water from the glass, dropped the olives into it, and poured the martini from a premixed bottle in the freezer. He handed it to her, then he filled an old-fashioned glass with ice, filled it again with Knob Creek, and raised his glass. "To the resumption of your normal existence," he said.

"God, I'll drink to that!" She took a big sip from her martini. "That is breathtaking!"

"Are you settling down yet after your ordeal?"

"I am. I'm going back to work on Monday."

"Tuesday. Monday's a holiday."

"Right, so I get another day off. What will I do with myself?"

"Hang around here, why don't you? We can . . ."

"Fuck our brains out all weekend?"

"Good idea!" He opened the desk drawer, took out a key, and handed it to her. "You can come and go as you please."

"I don't suppose I'll need a change of clothes."

Stone smiled. "As far as I'm concerned, you won't need clothes at all."

"A naked weekend," she said, smiling. "I like it."

"We can cook for each other."

"You cook?"

"Not as well as you, but I dabble."

"I suppose I'll have to put clothes on to go up to Grace's Market."

"Yes, unless you want a ride home in a police car."

"On my way, I'll pick up something more casual. I haven't been shopping for way too long."

"As you wish."

They settled into the sofa and sipped their drinks.

"How have your spent your time off?" Stone asked.

"Mostly just vegging and watching old movies on TV."

"What did you watch?"

"Singin' in the Rain, Gone with the Wind, The Best Years of Our Lives."

"All favorites of mine, too. My son is a moviemaker. Did I tell you?"

"No. What's he done?"

"A little independent called *Autumn Kill* that cost nothing to make and earned sixty-something million, worldwide."

"Wow, he must be very good."

"He certainly is. He has a deal at Centurion Studios, and he's out there now, completing his second film."

They nattered on for an hour and had a second drink.

■ ■ ■ ■

Dino was working late when he got a phone call from the lead detective on the Bats Buono murder. "What's happening, kid? Any luck on nabbing Marty Parese?"

" 'Fraid not, Chief. Apparently, he took a powder when we raided the chop shop. Nobody will admit laying eyes on him. We're running down some leads, though."

"Anything new on the girl? Hank?"

"Not a thing. Her only involvement is as a victim, far as I can tell."

"Okay, keep me posted." Dino hung up and called Stone.

"Excuse me," Stone said to Hank, picking up the phone. "Hello?"

"Hiya, pal."

"Hey, Dino."

"Just wanted to give you an update. We haven't been able to find Marty Parese. He blew after the raid on the chop shop."

"Oh, well," Stone said.

"Better news — Hank is no longer considered a suspect."

"That is good news. She's here now, we're having a drink and going to the Four Seasons. You and Viv want to join us?"

"Can't do it — we're both working late. Tomorrow night? We'll drink some of your booze."

"Sure."

"We'll let ourselves in."

"See you then."

They both hung up.

"How's Dino?" Hank asked.

"He's good, and he had a couple of pieces of news: they've been looking for a guy named Marty Parese, who was Buono's partner, but no luck. Apparently, he made himself scarce after the raid on the chop shop."

"Oh, yeah, I met him once. Onofrio introduced us in a restaurant."

"The good news: you're no longer a suspect."

"That's a relief, I guess. I'd better let Herb Fisher know."

"You ready for some dinner?"

"I'm starving. I've never been to the Four Seasons."

"It will be my pleasure to introduce you."

Stone let them out the front door. "You saw how to arm the system going out. This is how you disarm it when you come in." He showed her the six-digit code, then rearmed the system and locked the door behind them. They cabbed it the few blocks to the restaurant and were soon seated at a poolside table in the main dining room.

An hour and a half later, Hank dabbed at her lips with a napkin. "That was just wonderful," she said.

"I'm glad you enjoyed it."

"I have to go to the little girls' room."

"It's on the way out. I'll show you." Stone signed the check, then led her downstairs. "I'll get a cab and wait for you outside."

Hank disappeared into the ladies' room, and Stone asked the doorman for a cab. Nearly ten minutes passed before he found one, and Hank was just coming out the door.

Minutes later, Stone let them into the house, and after he had rearmed the system, they took the elevator upstairs.

They made love for half an hour or so, then collapsed in each other's arms. Sometime in the night, Stone rolled over and was surprised to find her side of the bed empty, but she returned from the direction of her bathroom and crawled back in with him.

Still later, Stone was half wakened by what sounded like an electronic beep, but then he drifted off to sleep again.

■ ■ ■ ■

In the morning, Helene sent up a big breakfast on the dumbwaiter, along with the morning papers, and they dawdled in bed. Halfway through the morning, the phone rang.

"Hello?"

"Stone, it's Bill Eggers. I'm doing some work on the Arrington account, and I can't find the year-to-date statement. Have you got a copy?"

"Sure, Bill. I'll go downstairs and fax it to you."

"Thanks. See you later."

Stone got out of bed and put on some pants, a shirt, and a pair of slippers.

"Going somewhere?"

"I just have to run down to my office and fax a document to my law partner, Bill Eggers. He's doing some weekend work."

"Don't be long," she said.

As Stone approached his office door, he heard the sound of machinery running and wondered if Joan was doing some weekend work, too. He opened the door and saw some sort of business machine on his desk and realized it was counting and sorting money. Joan must have found a machine after all.

Then something solid struck him on the back of the neck. He didn't remember falling to the floor.

51

Stone smelled leather, and he couldn't understand why. There was a murmur of voices from somewhere and the fluttery sound of a machine running. He opened his eyes and found himself facedown on his office sofa; his hands were chained behind him and his feet clamped together. He had a headache centered at the base of his skull, and he was having trouble thinking clearly.

He decided not to move for a while, just to listen and get oriented.

The machine stopped, and there was the sound of something tapping from the direction of his desk. He turned his head sideways so that he could see. There was a strange man seated at his desk; he was removing stacks of bills from the machine, tapping them on the desktop to square them, then banding them and arranging them in a suitcase that lay open beside the desk, while reading numbers from the machine and noting them on a yellow legal pad. Then he heard a voice he hadn't expected to hear.

"How long do you think this will take?" Hank asked.

Stone moved his chin down enough to allow himself a view of the other side of the desk. Hank was removing a double-handful of money from one of the leaf bags, squaring batches of the bills, then stacking them into the machine. That done, she switched it on, and it began separating and sorting the tens and twenties.

"Shit," the man said, "even with the machine, it's going to take us all day, at least."

"I guess there's no faster way to do this," she said.

"Not unless we had a couple more counter-sorters and more people to help, and we sure as hell don't want more people in on this."

"No," she said, "we don't."

Stone saw her begin to look his way and closed his eyes.

"He's still out," Hank said. "How hard did you hit him?" Her tone was one of idle curiosity, not of concern.

"Jeez, I don't know. Hard enough to put him down and out, but not hard enough to kill him, I hope. We may need him at some point."

"I can't imagine why," Hank replied.

Okay, Stone said to himself, *I think I'm getting this.* He rewound his memory to earlier in the evening and watched the replay on the inside of his eyelids. They had drinks; he gave Hank a key; he showed her how the security system worked; she spent ten minutes in the Four Seasons' ladies' room while he got a cab; she must have made a phone call. Who else could the guy be but Marty Parese? They stopped talking and worked, and that gave him more time to think. He had come down to fax Eggers the year-to-date statement. If Bill didn't receive it, would he send somebody over here? Stone's question was almost immediately answered.

The phone rang three times, and the voice mail system picked up. "Stone? It's Bill. Never mind faxing the document, we found our copy. Sorry to trouble you." Eggers hung up.

Shit. No cavalry arriving from that direction. He did some more thinking. *God knows where Joan is; long weekend.* No conceivable cavalry from any other direction, either. Assuming they didn't kill him — and that, he thought, might be an unwarranted assumption — nobody would find him until Tuesday morning. Where would Hank and her friend be by then? Acapulco? Rio? Answer: anywhere they damn well pleased. They would have a lot of luggage, of course, given the bulk of his five million dollars, even neatly stacked in suitcases. Unlikely that they would take a commercial flight; they wouldn't want to be separated from their bags. So, they'd drive. Somewhere they could exchange the money for hundreds. Where the hell could they do that? They couldn't just wheel it into a bank and make reverse change. Any banker in his right mind would call the FBI.

Wait a minute; why would Marty Parese have a cash counter-sorter handy on short notice? You couldn't rent one at a tool rental place. Chop shop had to be a cash business; if you sold somebody a few thousand bucks' worth of Mercedes bits and pieces, you wouldn't take a check, and you wouldn't put the cash in the bank. You'd launder it, somehow. Run it through a legit business account, maybe? One that dealt in a lot of cash? Casino? Check cashing service? Dirty bank? There must be dirty banks.

"Marty, tell me you got the groceries," Hank said.

"A week's worth."

"I gave you a list."

"Yeah, I got most of that. I couldn't find truffle oil."

She gave him a shopping list. When? On the phone from the ladies' room, or maybe before that. She had a plan; she called him for dinner, not the other way around. Where would they need groceries, especially Hank's kind of groceries? Someplace with a kitchen.

A wave of nausea struck Stone. Could a blow to the back of the head do that? He answered his own question by vomiting over the edge of the sofa.

"Jesus," Marty said.

"Oh, Stone, poor baby," Hank said. She went into his office bathroom and came out with a couple of towels and a trash can. She wiped his face with a damp facecloth, cleaned up the mess, and put the towels in the trash can. "Let's sit you up," she said. She rolled him onto his side, put his feet on the floor, and sat him up. "Is that better?"

Stone nodded and looked as dazed as he could, which, given the circumstances, wasn't hard. He moved his hands: cuffs. He looked down at his feet: duct tape. He was secured.

"You want some water, Stone?"

He nodded. She went to the bathroom and came back with a glass. He took a sip, swished it around in his mouth, and spat into the trash can. "More." He drank half the glass.

"Put some of that duct tape on his mouth," Parese said.

"I can't do that," Hank replied. "If he vomits again, he could choke on it."

"So what? I don't care if he chokes, I'd just as soon put a bullet in his head."

"Marty, I've told you before: if we kill him they'll never stop looking for us, wherever we go. It's not like killing Bats — nobody cares about him. Stone has friends in the police, and they'd really come after us. Stone can take the five-million-dollar hit without blinking. He might even be too embarrassed to tell anybody."

"Whatever you say, babe. Now keep feeding the machine money."

"How much are we up to?"

"Two hundred and twenty thou."

"God. We'll be here until Tuesday."

"Not that long — we're getting the hang of it now."

They went back to work.

Stone felt better for throwing up; his head was clear now; he could think. Trouble was, he couldn't think of any way out of this. There were things in the office he could use, but he couldn't move. They could do with him as they willed.

That thought made him nauseous again, but he fought it down. He took some deep breaths.

"You okay, Stone?" Hank asked.

"Just confused," he said.

"Yes, I guess this is pretty confusing for you."

"So, was it you and Bats or you and Marty?"

"It was always Marty," she said. "Bats was just a schmuck."

"Ah," he said, "all is revealed." He was a schmuck, too. Now all he could do was sit here and wait to find out who won the argument over whether or not to kill him.

52

Jack and Hillary finished their round and went back to the clubhouse for lunch.

"You beat me on handicap," Hillary said, after they had ordered.

"Come on, I don't even have a handicap yet."

"You're playing consistently, though, which nobody with your experience ever does. I think your instructor is wrong about your playing at the eighteen-handicap level. I think you're closer to a fifteen."

"From your lips to God's ear," Jack said.

"You seem very much at peace today, Jack. I had noticed a little tension the past few days. Did something good happen?"

"Yes, something good happened. I just cleared up a little of the underbrush of my past life."

"Underbrush? That's a funny word."

"Now everything is just smooth, freshly mown fairway. I don't think I've ever felt quite so free."

She squeezed his hand. "I'm happy for you, Jack. I'm happy for both of us." She looked out at the golf course for a moment, as if she had something on her mind. "There's something I have to say to you."

Oh, God, he thought. And it had been going so well. His greatest fear had been something like this. He had been thinking of marriage, but now he was about to be cut down to size. "What is it?" he asked, as steadily as he could.

"Will you marry me, Jack?"

He nearly spilled his iced tea. "I was going to . . ."

"I know, you were going to back out. I was afraid that you were afraid of me."

"Oh, no," he said.

"You haven't answered me. Do you want to know about my circumstances? I love you, Jack, and I'll tell you anything you want to know."

"There's nothing I need to know about you, Hillary. I love you, and I'll marry you just as fast as we can do whatever it takes to get it done."

"Oh, that's such a relief," she said. "I was afraid you were afraid of my wealth."

"Not your wealth, hon, just our different stations in life."

"There's no difference, Jack. We live in the same community, in the same building, even. We play at the same golf course, we have the same best friends."

"You're a very generous person, Hillary."

"You're right, I am, but I'm not exercising generosity. I feel that we are absolute equals. I'm sorry about the difference in our fortunes, but it wasn't my fault — I inherited it."

"I promise I won't hold it against you."

"There are some things you need to know about my life and the way I live it."

"I don't need to know anything."

"If we're to be married, you need to know *everything.* I was married twice before I met you: divorced once, then widowed. Bob was a very wealthy man, and neither of us had children. After the estate was wound up and the taxes paid, I had a stock account with about seventy million in it, and four houses. I sold the one in Scottsdale. Now I live here in the winter and in Northeast Harbor, Maine, in the summer, and the spring and autumn on Fifth Avenue in New York, across from Central Park. Do you think you could live like that? I mean, I can sell any place you don't want to live."

"Excuse me, I'm a little breathless," Jack said. "I'm sure that any place you love will be fine with me."

"There's a lovely sailboat in Maine. Have you ever sailed?"

"Only on the Staten Island Ferry."

"I think you'll like it. I'm also the largest stockholder in Bob's company and on the board, and I have the use of the corporate jet, so we don't have to bother with the airlines. Have you done any traveling?"

"Almost none."

"Let's take a look at Paris, London, and Rome — for a start."

"You talked me into it."

"I've checked — we need to go to the courthouse and get a license, then there's a three-day waiting period, and then anybody who's a notary public can marry us. I thought my lawyer could do it."

"That's fine with me. Let's ask Winston and Elizabeth to stand up for us."

"Yes, of course. My apartment is so much bigger than yours — will you move in with me?"

"Of course."

"The sooner the better, as far as I'm concerned."

"Great."

"I haven't felt so good in years," she said.

"I've *never* felt so good," he replied.

"You know when I knew?" she asked.

"When?"

"When you bought the Bentley. I liked it that you included me in your decision, and especially that you had no problem taking my advice. A lot of men wouldn't want a woman's opinion."

"I will always want your opinion, and I'd be a fool not to follow your advice."

"That's it, then."

"Yes," he said, "that's it."

"Would you like to play another round after lunch?"

"I'd love it."

Two women in golf clothes got up from a table on the other side of the restaurant, and Hillary waved them over. "Hi, girls," she said. "Let me introduce you to my fiancé, Jack Coulter. Jack, this is Nikki Seybold and Gail Barley, both of whom I've known since college."

Everyone shook hands.

"Would you like to join us and make a foursome?" one of the women asked.

"Thanks," Hillary said, "but I want Jack all to myself."

They laughed and went on their way.

"They're jealous," Hillary said.

53

Stone had managed to doze off. He awoke slowly and kept his eyes closed, so as not to inhibit their conversation.

"Looks like we're making good progress now," Hank said.

"Yeah, we've cracked four million. We'll be there in another hour. Let's take a break."

"What for?"

"I'm starved," he said. "It's five-thirty, and I haven't eaten since five o'clock this morning."

"All right," she said. "Let's get these four bags into the van, then we'll get something to eat and come back and finish."

"Deal," Parese said.

They zipped up the four suitcases, stood them on their wheels, and began rolling the first two out of the office. A minute later, they came back for two more.

"Is one more bag going to be enough?" she asked.

"Yeah, we've got less than seven hundred grand to go, then we'll be done."

"Okay, let's go. Stone!"

Stone appeared to jerk awake. "Huh?"

"We're going to get some dinner. We'll be right back."

"Just a minute," Parese said. He picked up a roll of duct tape and walked over to Stone. He passed three lengths around the sofa and across Stone's chest, pinning him there, then he ripped off a short strip and slapped it over Stone's mouth. "There, that'll hold him."

The two left the office by the street door.

Stone waited a full minute to let them clear the block, then he started his struggle. He leaned as hard as possible against the tape across his chest, trying to stretch enough to give him some wiggling room. It seemed to work, but he remained taped to the sofa. Then he started thrusting his feet and pelvis forward, to get more stretching and to make it possible for him to slide under the tape and onto the floor. This took a good ten minutes, but he remained stuck to the big piece of furniture. He had his old handcuff key from his cop days somewhere in his desk, but he couldn't get up and walk over there to get it. He was huffing through his nose and sweating. Half an hour after they left, they came back with cartons of Chinese food.

"Hey, there," Hank said. "You doing okay?" She came over and ripped the tape off his face.

Stone took some deep breaths. "Yeah."

"You want some Chinese?"

"Not hungry."

"Suit yourself." She went back to the desk, and they made room for the food, then served themselves and opened a couple of beers.

Stone watched them and tried to relax.

They finished and Hank resealed the cartons. "In case you want some later," she said to Stone.

"Okay," Parese said, "it's six-fifteen. I want to be done and out of here by seven. We'll be out of the state by eight-thirty."

"Then let's do it." They resumed their stacking, counting, and sorting, and the last suitcase began to fill up. Stone watched them helplessly. Promptly at seven, Parese closed the last suitcase. "You wheel this to the van, and I'll get the machine. Who knows, somebody might want a recount when we do the swap."

"Okay." She wheeled the suitcase out of the office, and Parese picked up the machine, which looked heavy.

"Need a hand with that?" Stone asked.

Parese set down the machine and laughed. "You're something, Stone. Hank told me you was a card."

"A laugh a minute," Stone replied.

Parese picked up the machine again. "I'll be back in a minute to say goodbye." He staggered out of the office with his load. Three minutes later, they were back.

Parese got into his coat.

"We'll get out of your way," Hank said, putting on her coat.

But then Parese had a Glock in his hand. "Time to say bye-bye," he said to Stone.

Hank put her hand on the gun and pushed the barrel down. "No. I said no, Marty, and I meant it. We're leaving no corpses behind. Nobody will see him until Tuesday morning, and if he could get out of that tape he would have while we were gone."

"Sorry, babe, but there will be no witnesses." He racked the slide on the Glock.

Stone looked around desperately for help, but there was none. Then the phone rang. Parese turned and looked at it, and on the third ring the voice mail kicked in.

"Hi, Stone, it's Kate Lee. Will and I are going to be in New York over the weekend. Can you have dinner with us at the Carlyle on Sunday night? Call me on the private cell number, don't go through the White House switchboard. Hope to see you Sunday!" She hung up.

Parese was still staring at the phone. "Was that who I think it was?"

"Now are you getting the picture?" Hank asked. "The feds will be after us, too!"

"This is a mistake," Parese said, but he shoved the gun back into its holster on his waist. "All right, let's go."

"You first," Hank said.

He started for the door.

Hank ran across the room, took Stone by the chin, and kissed him on the lips. "Bye-bye, darlin'," she said. "It's been more fun than I can tell you."

"A word of advice, Hank," Stone said.

"What's that, darlin'?"

"You'd better kill Parese before he can kill you."

"That crossed my mind," she said. "Don't you worry about me, and thanks for all that money!" She turned and ran out of the office. A moment later, Stone heard the racing of a motor, then the vehicle drove away.

He started with the tape again, thrashing around with all his strength, and finally he was able to slide under the tape to the floor: a triumph! Except that he was still handcuffed and his feet taped together. He returned to a sitting position, then stood up and hopped toward his desk, flopping down in his chair. There were two things he wanted: the handcuff key in one of his desk drawers and Joan's .45, which lived in the middle drawer of her desk, always loaded. In case they came back. He decided to find the key first. That would make everything else easier.

He swiveled to his left in the chair and reached as far sideways as the handcuffs would allow, then got his desk drawer open. He rummaged among the drawer's contents with his nose and chin, checking every cranny, but he found no key.

He started with the left-hand top drawer and repeated the process. It had to be here somewhere. Half an hour later, he still had two drawers to go, and he was exhausted. Then he heard the door open: they were coming back. He laid his head on the cool desktop and waited for Parese and his Glock.

54

"What the fuck?" a man's voice said. He walked across the room, took hold of Stone's shoulder, and sat him up in his chair.

Stone looked up at the man with bleary eyes. "Dino?"

"You're some kind of host, you know that? We let ourselves in, as usual, and went to the study — no lights on. We went upstairs hollering for you, and then we come down here and find that you're playing some sort of sex game. Where's Hank? Gone out for lubricant?"

"Dino, please uncuff me."

"Won't that spoil things for Hank?"

"Dino, please."

Dino rummaged in his pocket for his keys, came up with a ring, selected the smallest key, and unlocked the cuffs. "There you go. You want me to leave your feet taped?"

Stone shook his head wearily, rested his

elbows on the desk, and put his face in his hands. Dino took a box cutter from a coffee mug on Stone's desk, emblazoned with the legend NEW YORK CITY MORGUE, and cut through the duct tape binding Stone's feet.

Viv came through the door. "What's going on?"

"You wouldn't believe me if I told you," Dino said. "Stone and Hank have been playing games. He was wearing the cuffs." He held them up.

"Oh, stop it, Dino. Stone, what's happened?"

"I hardly know where to begin," Stone said. He reached across the desk, grabbed a Chinese takeout carton and a pair of chopsticks, and shoveled some fried rice into his mouth. "Starved," he mumbled. "Nothing since breakfast."

Dino went to Stone's office bar, filled three glasses with ice, poured them all a drink, and brought them back to the desk. He took away the fried-rice carton and handed Stone a Knob Creek. "Wash it down with this, and tell us what the fuck happened." He and Viv took chairs and sipped their drinks, waiting for Stone to swallow.

"Okay," Stone said finally, after taking a big breath and a big swallow of bourbon. "Hank and her boyfriend, Marty Parese, just stole five million dollars from me."

"What five million dollars is that?" Dino inquired.

"The five million I was going to use to ransom Hank from Bats Buono — or to pretend to ransom, until I got a shot at him."

"You said Marty Parese — we're looking for him already. He blew when the chop shop got raided."

"Hank and I had dinner last night, came home, went to bed, as usual. This morning Eggers called and asked me to fax him a document. I got dressed and came down here and somebody — make that Parese — hit me with something and knocked me out cold. When I woke up, Parese and Hank were using a counting and sorting machine to put the five million in order. My bank had scrambled it, and they wouldn't take it back until it was sorted."

"When did they leave?"

"Just after seven. You were due here at seven, weren't you? Where the hell were you? You might have grabbed them."

"The vagaries of being a public servant," Dino said. "I worked a little late."

"They sorted and banded the money — it was in two large leaf bags — and packed it into five or six suitcases on wheels. They took the machine with them, too. Parese wanted to kill me, but Hank stopped him."

"I guess she's just a sentimental softy," Dino said. "Except for the part about stealing your money. Any idea where they went with it?"

"I figure they can't take a plane, the bags might get X-rayed. They were in a van."

"Make, model, and color?"

"I never saw it. They said it was a van."

"Any idea where they're driving to?"

"Parese said he had a week's groceries in the van, so someplace with a kitchen."

"Can you narrow that down for me?"

"Parese said they'd be out of the state by eight-thirty."

"So, they weren't going to New Jersey. That pretty much leaves Connecticut, if we're talking bordering states. You thinking what I'm thinking?"

"The lake cabin? That's the only thought I've had."

"A good choice, probably. They reckon that the Connecticut State Police, having gone over the place thoroughly, won't be going back there. Oh, I forgot to tell you, they found Bats Buono's head in the Mercedes when they floated it."

"Did the head have a nine-millimeter slug in it?"

"Good guess, Stone."

"When you catch up with them, run Parese's Glock through ballistics."

"I'll see that that happens. You want some more Chinese now?"

"I want a steak," Stone said. "Let's go to the kitchen."

Stone found steaks in the fridge and, after seasoning the meat, threw them onto the Viking grill, while Viv boiled some potatoes and made a salad. Dino was on the phone with Dan Sparks, in Hartford.

"Oh, Dino," Stone said, "I forgot to mention that one of them is probably going to kill the other, as soon as they're at a safe place."

Dino covered the phone. "You got a bet on who does the killing?"

"My money's on Hank," Stone said. "But you never know."

"Right," Dino said, "you never know." Then he went back to his conversation with Sparks.

"Dino," Stone said, and Dino covered the phone again. "Now what?"

"I got the impression they were planning some sort of money laundering, swapping the small bills for larger ones. Ask Dan if there's anybody anywhere near the cabin that would deal in large sums of cash."

Dino asked Dan Sparks and got an answer, then he hung up. "Dan says there are a couple of Indian-owned casinos within an hour or two's drive of the cabin. The Indians don't necessarily run them, they hire experienced managers, people with casino experience."

55

Hank and Parese were driving north on the Sawmill River Parkway in the van.

"Slow down, Marty," she said. "There's a fifty-five-mile-an-hour speed limit up here, and we don't want to get pulled over tonight of all nights."

Parese slowed a little. "Awright."

"See that switch on the steering wheel? That's the speed control. Set it at fifty-five and leave it there."

"Awright, awright." He looked at the steering wheel and nearly missed a curve.

"Watch the road, I'll do the speed control." She leaned over and turned it on, then slowed the van to fifty-five and pressed the SET button. "There, take your foot off the accelerator."

"You're right," he said. "You're always right, babe."

"I'm not smarter than you," she said,

softening her voice, "I'm just better at details."

"I'm not going to argue that point," he said.

"So, Marty, tell me how we're going to do this."

"Why don't you just leave it to me, baby?"

"Details, Marty, I need to know the details."

"All right: did Bats ever mention a guy named Tommy Dion to you?"

"Sounds vaguely familiar."

"Tommy is an old-school Vegas guy. He grew up working the casinos out there, ended up managing a couple of them. When the Indians started opening casinos upstate, he signed on as a consultant to a couple of them, and they were so impressed they made him a manager. Tommy and my old man were tight all their lives, and I've done a deal with him."

"What's the deal?"

"He brings us four and a half million dollars in hundreds, and we give him five million in tens and twenties."

"We're giving him *half a million dollars*?"

"It's a good deal, trust me."

"The thing is, can we trust *him*?"

"He's making half a million bucks in one night, and it's all his, tax-free. He just borrows the cash from the casino for a few hours, and he returns it in small bills. It's a wash, literally, no bookkeeping problems."

"And you really trust him?"

"Trust is a relative word when you're talking this much money," Parese said. He looked at his watch. "I'm due to call him now." He took out his cell phone and pressed a button.

Hank kept her hand on the wheel and her eyes on the road.

"Hey, Tommy, it's me. We're on. You got the cash ready?" He listened for a moment. "Good work. We'll be there in an hour. Okay, got a pencil? I'll give you directions." Parese dictated precise driving instructions. "You got that? Repeat it to me." He listened some more. "Now listen to me, Tommy. You know I trust you, but you can only be two guys. We're two, you're two. Got that? Good. Now, if there's more than one guy besides you, and if anybody but you gets out of that car, he will die." He listened some more. "I'm glad you understand. Did you get the suitcases? The ones with wheels? How many? Two is good. We'll give you five. Now we've done a complete machine count of the money, and it's exactly five mil. I've got the printouts for you to see, but if you want a recount, the machine will be there, and you can run it yourself. All right, two hours. Don't be early or late. We're gonna be nervous, and we don't want any mistakes. See ya, pal." Marty hung up.

"Are you satisfied that he's going to do the right thing?" Hank asked.

"I'm satisfied, but there are two shotguns and an Uzi in the back of the van, where the spare tire lives. We'll be ready for anything."

"I suppose you've thought of killing him and keeping both his money and ours."

"I thought about it, but it wouldn't be good practice, you know? We do that and we'll have not only the cops looking for us, we'll have a lot of made guys all over the country watching for us, and probably a lot of Indians, too." He laughed.

"Tell me about tomorrow."

"Tomorrow is pretty straightforward. We drive to Oxford Airport, maybe half an hour's drive from the house. Nobody's looking for the van, so we just leave it there. The airplane is a Hawker 400, has enough range to get us all the way to South America, but we're going to stop in the Cayman Islands, just south of Jamaica, and open a bank account. Then we'll go on to South America. Rio okay?"

"I think Rio sounds lovely. What's the

airplane costing us?"

"A hundred and fifty grand."

"Jesus! Can't we fly commercial from the Caymans?"

"We don't want to leave a paper trail from there. Sure, we're overpaying for the airplane, but it's a long flight, and the pilots have to be taken care of up front."

"What's to keep them from abandoning us when we leave the airplane in the Caymans to go to the bank? They could just take off again and fly home, and we'd be out a lot of money."

Parese thought about that and sighed. "All right, we'll give them half up front and half when we land in Rio. Worst case, we'll give them the second half when we're ready to take off from the Caymans. Oh, we have to buy fuel, too. That could run another eight, ten grand."

"What time are we meeting the airplane at Oxford?"

"Nine AM."

"Where at the airport?"

"At the main terminal."

"Are we clearing out with customs?"

"No, the pilot files a form with the feds before the flight."

"Does it have our names and passport numbers on it?"

"Yes, no getting away from that. But it shows us going only to the Caymans. Once we land out of the country, we can fly anywhere with no record of it. The pilots will say they picked up somebody else in the Caymans for the Rio leg."

"Who owns the airplane?"

"A guy I know runs a charter company. He buys time on airplanes from various corporations, time when they'd otherwise be sitting on the ground waiting for some CEO to fly somewhere. We've got the airplane for three full days."

"That's good work, Marty, I'm proud of you."

He grinned. "Thanks, babe. Oh, and you were right about not offing Barrington. At first I thought you were getting sentimental over him, but after thinking about it, he can't hurt us."

"We don't want to kill anybody at the cabin, either," she said.

"I know, but we have to be ready to do it if it's called for. I mean, if there's more than one car, or three or four guys get out of the car, then we're at war. No way around that."

"Let's don't get into that position," she said. "Remember to be charming. Charm works."

"Up to a point."

"Oh, what are we going to do with the counter-sorter?"

"We'll dump it in the lake as soon as we make the cash swap."

"Good. We don't want to leave it in the van or the cottage, and we want to Windex the van all over to get rid of prints."

"I've never been arrested," Marty said, "so I've never been printed. You?"

"Nope. I'm squeaky clean."

"Squeaky clean, I like that. Oh, I got a number in Rio — we can get new passports."

"Fine. Maybe we'll go to Europe from there. You'd like Rome. You speak Italian?"

"I grew up speaking it half the time. Couple weeks, you'd think I was a native Roman. Listen, babe, this is gonna work, don't worry about a thing."

She leaned over and kissed him on the ear. "I'm not worried, Marty, I'm safe in your hands."

56

Stone, Dino, and Viv had a good dinner and waited for Dan Sparks to call back. "Listen," Stone said, "I want to get a shower and a change of clothes."

"Hurry up," Dino said. "And bring a weapon."

Stone went upstairs and let the hot shower run on his face, then he got into some comfortable clothes, holstered his lightweight Terry Tussey .45, and went downstairs. Dino was on the phone.

"Okay," Dino was saying, "at the convenience store in about an hour. This time, don't bring police vehicles. If we get there first, let's don't scare them off." He hung up. "Everybody ready?"

They went outside and got into Dino's car; his driver already had the engine running. "You get something to eat?" Dino asked the man.

"Yes, sir."

"Good. It's going to be a late night. Let's hit the West Side Highway."

"Drive by the convenience store," Hank said. "If there are police vehicles there, we'll have to call it off and meet Tommy somewhere else."

"Okay," Parese said. They drove past the store at forty miles an hour. "I don't see anything that looks like cops," he said.

"Neither do I, but when we get to the lake, let's drive around the shore road to the right and approach the house from the other direction."

"Sounds good."

They turned off on the road to the lake, and a couple of minutes later they came to the T junction and turned right.

"So far, so good," Parese said. "And we've still got an hour before Tommy is due."

"Look for clusters of vehicles," she said. "Any kind of vehicles parked in driveways or side roads."

Parese did as he was told. "I don't see anything," he said.

"Then let's drive on around the lake," Hank said. "And turn off your lights, there's enough of a moon to see."

Twenty minutes later, they were approaching the cottage.

"Pull into the drive and stop," she said. "I want to walk down there first."

He pulled into the drive; they could see the house, and it was dark.

"Never mind me walking," Hank said, "just turn off the engine and coast down to the front of the house, then turn around and back up near the porch. I'd like to be pointed the other way if we have to move."

They got out of the van and stood in the dim moonlight, listening. Nothing but an owl somewhere. Parese unlocked the front door and turned on a light. "Looks okay," he called back.

"Let's get the bags inside," Hank yelled. Parese came outside, and they wheeled in the five suitcases and their own bags. They set three of the bags containing the money in the middle of the living room, and put two of them on the dining table.

Parese went back to the van and came back with the counter-sorting machine, then he went back and brought in two grocery bags.

"That's not a week's groceries," she said.

"I just said that for Barrington's benefit," Parese replied. "There's enough for a snack tonight and breakfast tomorrow."

"You hungry?" she asked.

"I'm too excited to eat. This is gonna happen, I can feel it." He went back to the van and came back with the two shotguns and the Uzi. "They're all loaded," he said, putting them behind the front door.

They put their own bags in the bedroom, and when they came out, they could hear the crunch of tires on gravel.

"This is it," Parese said. He pulled out his Glock and stood by the door, his back to the wall. A car door slammed.

"Marty?" a man's gruff voice called.

"I'm here, Tommy. Come on in."

Hank stood where she could be seen. A man appeared on the porch, and Parese turned on the outside light. "Who's with you?" he called.

"Just the guy who drove me. He won't move."

"Come on in, then."

Tommy walked into the living room and stopped. "I'm unarmed," he said, opening his jacket and turning around. He also hoisted his trouser legs so Parese could see there was nothing strapped to his ankles.

"You brought the four and a half?" Parese asked.

"In the trunk of the car. Where's yours?"

"Right over here." Parese led him to the dining table and unzipped the two suitcases.

Tommy dug down into the bundles of bills

and made sure it was all money. "Good," he said, zipping up the bags and moving them to the floor. "Now let's see the others."

The two men hoisted the other three bags onto the table, and Tommy inspected them, then set them on the floor. "Funny how much money weighs," he said.

"It's just paper," Parese replied. "You satisfied, or you want to run it all through the machine again?" He handed Tommy some folded sheets of paper. "Here's the count as it went through the machine."

Tommy took the paper and put it in his pocket. "I'm okay," he said. "Let's go get my bags."

"The lady will go with you," Parese said. "I'll wait here." He nodded at Hank. "Don't worry, babe, you'll be okay with Tommy."

Hank followed the man out to his car and around to the trunk. He opened it with a key and hoisted a bag onto the ground. "Take it in," he said. "I'll bring the other one."

The two of them wheeled the bags into the house and to the dining room table. Parese put them on the table and opened them. They were filled with banded stacks of hundreds. He went through random stacks to be sure there was no newspaper in them.

"You want to put them through the machine?" Tommy asked.

"I'm good. You delivered, Tommy, and I appreciate it."

"I appreciate the action," Tommy replied.

The two men hugged, and Parese stood in the doorway and watched him walk back to the car. The driver started it, turned around, and drove up the drive. They could see his taillights through the woods as he drove away.

Parese turned and took Hank in his arms. "It's done, babe."

"Let's get those two bags into the van, in case we need to make a hasty departure," she said. They each took a bag and wheeled it outside, and Parese hoisted the bags into the van and closed the door. "Now," he said, "I want to fuck you in the worst way."

"And I want to fuck you, too, Marty," she said.

57

Stone sat in the backseat with Viv. He didn't know why he was so tired; after all, he'd spent the day on the sofa in his office. He wished he'd gotten more sleep.

"You're awful quiet, Stone," Dino said when they were on the Sawmill.

"I'm just thinking, what if we're wrong about the lake cottage?"

"Then we're wrong — it'll cost you five million dollars, but the world won't end. I bet your insurance company will cover you. I mean, it's a straight-up armed robbery."

"I don't know what the limits are on my policy."

"Dino," Viv said, "suppose Stone is right about being wrong. What's our backup plan?"

"Gee, I don't know, Viv. Stone, you got a backup plan?"

"I'm thinking," Stone said.

"Think faster, we're half an hour out."

"I'm thinking as fast as I can."
"Oh, well, that's all right, then."
"You could think of something, you know, Dino."
Dino got quiet.

They got to the convenience store at New Fairfield more or less on time. There were no police vehicles.
"I'll bet Dan is inside," Dino said.
They all got out and walked into the store. It was empty of customers. Dino walked over to the lone cashier. "Is Colonel Sparks of the State Police here?"
"Who wants to know?" the man asked.
Dino showed him his badge.
The man nodded toward the rear of the store. "Stockroom."
They walked the length of the place and pushed open a swinging door. Sparks and seven or eight men were sitting around on crates and folding chairs, looking bored.
"Hey, Dino," Sparks said. "You remember my team."
"Hi, guys," Dino said. "You remember Stone Barrington. This is my wife, Viv. She's a retired NYPD detective."
Viv's credentials established, everybody nodded.
"When do you want to go in, Dino?"

"Well, I don't want to get there first," Dino said. "Let's see, they left Stone's house around seven, and it's an hour-and-a-half drive up here, so that would be eight-thirty. It's eleven now. If they've made the swap, they'll probably spend the night, and they're still there. If they haven't made it, then they're staying up late. Let's go now."

Sparks stood up. "Okay, everybody, saddle up. Put your gear on in the cars, not in the parking lot. We don't want to attract attention. We'll do this like last time — we'll leave the cars after a right turn at the lake road, out of sight of any approaching vehicles, then we'll walk down the road and take to the woods before we get to the cabin."

Everybody got into the cars. They drove to the entry road and made the turn to the right, without headlights or incident. As quietly as possible, they left the vehicles around the first corner and began to walk up the road. Stone brought up the rear with Viv.

Stone and Viv waited in the road until the SWAT team had filtered into the woods, then Dan Sparks came back to get them. They followed him down the road. There was a light on in the living room.

"No van," Stone said.

"No vehicle of any kind," Sparks replied.

They followed him up onto the porch and into the living room. Nothing, nobody, except the counter-sorting machine on the floor next to the dining table, and two shotguns and an Uzi behind the front door. Stone went into the bedroom and turned on a light; there was a leather duffel on the bed. He unzipped it and pulled out a few things. "A man's clothes," he said to Sparks.

"I don't see another bag," Sparks said.

"And no five bags of tens and twenties," Stone pointed out.

"There's nothing in the place that says a woman was here," Dino said. "There are two bags of groceries on the kitchen counter, untouched."

"They've been here," Sparks said.

"They've been here and gone," Stone replied.

"At least, one of them did," Sparks said. He walked back into the living room. "Everybody got a flashlight?" he asked.

Everybody held up flashlights. "I want a search of the woods," he said. "Work your way out from the house. Remember what we found the last time we searched the woods."

Ten minutes later, Sparks came back into the house and beckoned to Stone, Dino, and Viv, who were sitting at the kitchen table, drinking coffee from the grocery bags. He led them outside and a short distance into the woods.

"Is that your Parese guy?" Sparks asked, playing his powerful little flashlight on a figure on the ground. "He's got an empty holster on his belt, and we found a single nine-millimeter shell casing on the ground in front of the house."

"That's Marty Parese," Stone said. "And that's a knife sticking out of his chest."

"You're very observant," Sparks said drily. "Now, where's Henrietta Cromwell?

"In the wind," Dino said.

58

The group sat around the living room of the lake cottage. It was after one AM, and the medical examiner's wagon had already left with Parese's body. They were all having a drink from the cabin's booze supply.

"So," Dino said, "where are we?"

"I like Stone's idea about the chartered airplane," Dan Sparks said. "My people are checking every airport in the western half of the state, as far as and including Hartford's airports. Danbury and Oxford are the closest ones. Danbury closes at dusk, and Oxford is quiet. I've got men on the runway at each, should anybody try to land, and the New York boys are covering White Plains, Newburgh, and Albany."

"Hank could be headed for Mexico," Stone said. "We don't know anything about the vehicle, except that it's a van — no make, year, or color."

"Yeah," Sparks said, "and I'm not issuing

a nationwide APB for a van. I don't need that kind of trouble. We are checking every nearby motel, hotel, and B&B for a woman in a van, though."

Dino spoke up. "And I've got people watching her apartment building in the city." He sighed. "I guess we ought to head back soon, late as it is."

"Listen, you guys shouldn't be driving back to the city this late," Sparks said. "Why don't you sleep here and get an early start? Our crime scene is outside, and we've already shut it down. Nobody's going to disturb you."

"Suits me," Viv said, and nobody argued with her.

"I want another drink," Stone said, getting up and heading for the kitchen. "Can I bring anybody anything?"

"The bottle," Dino said, "and some ice."

Stone brought back the makings and set them on the dining table, then poured for everybody.

"Not for me," Sparks said. "I'm headed home." He shook everybody's hand, then left.

"Where would you go with five million dollars in cash?" Viv asked. "I mean, the airplane makes the most sense. But Dan has a lid on that. Where else?"

"That's the five-million-buck question," Dino said, "and I'm too tired to think. I put in a twelve-hour day before we got here."

"Yeah," Stone said. "And you'd be surprised how exhausting it is to be bound hand and foot all day. I'm really beat."

"No more great ideas?" Dino asked.

"None. Zip. Nada."

They finished their drinks, then Dino and Viv took the double-bedded room, and Stone and Dino's driver took the twin-bedded one. Stone didn't bother looking for sheets; he found a blanket and slept in his clothes. Everybody was down and out in fifteen minutes.

Stone woke up to sunlight streaming through a window onto his bed. He struggled out of bed, went into the bathroom and splashed some water on his face, then he put on his shoes and walked outside.

It was a beautiful spot, he thought. The sun sparkled on the little lake, and a light breeze rustled the trees around the house. It didn't look like the sort of place where two men had died over the past few days. He went back into the house and, using the groceries from the two bags, started breakfast. The smell of bacon got everybody up, and soon they were having scrambled eggs.

They had just finished when Dino's phone rang.

"Bacchetti," he said. He listened for a minute, then turned toward Stone. "You know where Oxford Airport is?"

"Yes," Stone replied. "Don't you remember? You and I attended a shoot-out there a few years back. It's a twenty-minute or half-hour drive."

"Oh, yeah. Dan, we'll be there in half an hour." Dino hung up. "Let's get going."

"What's happening there?"

"He didn't say."

Dino's driver brought the car to the house and they piled in.

"I hope they caught her," Stone said.

"You hope they caught your five million bucks," Dino said.

"That, too."

The drive took less than half an hour. "Go to the main terminal," Stone said. They drove down the road for half a mile, and some buildings hove into view at the top of a hill.

"That's it," Stone said.

There were two police vehicles in the parking lot below the terminal building, and one van, a black one. They pulled into the lot and got out.

Sparks was standing next to the van, looking in through the driver's window. He turned as they approached. "Well," he said, "we've got your woman." He stepped back so they could look inside.

Hank Cromwell was lying across the bench front seat, her head resting on her crooked arm. She looked asleep, but the seat was soaked with drying blood that had dripped onto the passenger-side floor, as well. Nobody said anything.

The medical examiner's van pulled into the lot, and everybody stood back to let them pass.

"A jet landed at eight-thirty this morning," Sparks said. "The pilots refueled and waited another half an hour, made some phone calls, then took off again. We've got the tail number and are checking it out. After the jet had gone, somebody parked down here, saw the body, and called us."

The ME left the van and approached Sparks. "Single gunshot wound, right side," he said. "If she'd had reasonably prompt medical attention, she would have survived. Looks like she parked here, went to sleep, and bled out." He held up a Glock in a plastic bag. "This was underneath the body. We didn't find a shell casing, so I don't think she shot herself."

"We found the shell casing last night,"

Sparks said.

They stood back to let the stretcher be wheeled past and put into the state van. "It's your scene now," the ME said to Sparks.

Sparks put on some latex gloves and opened the van's side door. There were two suitcases on the rear seat. He opened them both and found only a woman's clothing, then he went to the rear door and opened that. Two black nylon suitcases with built-in wheels sat in the luggage compartment. Sparks tipped one on its side and unzipped it. The case was filled with stacks of hundred-dollar bills.

"Mystery of the money solved," Sparks said.

"Stone," Dino said, "it was nice of Hank and Parese to change all that cash into hundreds. Much more convenient to deal with."

"You're right, Dino. I wonder how much they paid whoever did the swap."

"You can count it all over again when it gets to your house."

"As far as I'm concerned," Sparks said, "you can take it with you. Just give me a receipt, I don't want it on my hands."

Dino took out his notebook and wrote out a receipt. "Received of Dan Sparks two black suitcases, contents: uncounted." He signed it and ripped off the page. "There you go, Dan," he said. He grabbed one of the bags and set it on its wheels. "You get the other one, Stone."

Stone followed Dino to his car with the other bag, and they stowed them both in the baggage compartment of the SUV.

"I want to go straight to my bank," Stone said to Dino as he got into the car.

"Your bank is closed," Dino said. "Holiday weekend, remember? You're going to have to take the money home with you."

Stone made a loud groaning noise. "Then you're going to have to help me count it."

"Fat chance," Dino said.

59

Stone and Dino got the two suitcases out of the SUV and rolled them into Stone's office.

"There you go," Dino said. "Have a good time." He left.

"Shirker!" Stone called after him, but the only reply was the slamming of the office door.

His office smelled faintly of vomit, and his desk was a mess of papers and currency bands. He swept everything off and emptied a suitcase on the top. As he did, Joan came into the room.

"I saw Dino outside the window, and I got curious."

"That's your misfortune," Stone said. "Now you have to help me count the money."

Joan picked up a stack of bills and examined them. "All hundreds? What did you do? Wave a magic wand?"

"Don't ask, just count." He found a legal pad and a calculator. "Each bundle is a hundred hundred-dollar bills, or ten thousand dollars. It'll be easy."

"You always say that when it's hard," she replied, taking the legal pad and calculator from him. "Did you sleep in those clothes?"

"As a matter of fact, I did."

"What happened with Hank?"

"Hank is dead."

"What? You killed her?"

"Of course not. She and her boyfriend had a little tiff, and she brought a knife to a gunfight."

"Boyfriend?"

"Buono's buddy Marty Parese, who, incidentally, killed Buono and cut off his head. Hank managed to knife Parese before he shot her. Neither survived."

He filled in the rest of the details for her.

"So you were in this office, trussed up like a turkey, when I was watching Tiger Woods play golf on TV? I should have been helping you."

"That crossed my mind, but don't worry about it. If you had happened upon us, you would have been trussed up, too."

"Well, at least you'd have had some company."

Stone finished counting the bundles,

stacking them back in the suitcase as he did so. He closed and zipped it, then he set it on the floor, picked up the second case, unzipped it, and started again.

"Neither of us would have been much company, since our mouths would have been taped."

"Why didn't Parese shoot you?"

"He was about to, but he was interrupted by Kate Lee leaving a message on the voice mail. That stopped him in his tracks and helped Hank talk him out of it."

"Poor Hank," Joan said.

Stone continued his count, and Joan continued to mark down the results and do the arithmetic. "I warned her before she left the house that he'd kill her if she didn't kill him first. She just didn't do it soon enough. If she had, she'd have been on a chartered jet bound for God-knows-where, with five million in cash."

"No," Joan said, adding her final column and noting the balance on her legal pad.

"What?"

"She'd have had four and a half million — that's the total."

"Oh, so Parese paid somebody five hundred thousand to bring him all hundreds. I guess ten percent wasn't a bad deal."

"It was for you," Joan said.

"Call my insurance agent tomorrow and explain things to him. I don't have the heart. If he wants to see the money, tell him to get over here pronto, because I'm sending it back to the bank before lunch."

"I think the deductible on your household policy is fifty thousand," she said. "So you won't get hurt too badly. Are you going to leave the money in the office again?"

"No, yesterday when I was rummaging with my chin in my desk drawers, I found the key to the wine cellar." He opened a drawer and held it up. "So at least it will be out of sight and under lock and key."

The phone rang, and Joan picked it up. "Woodman & Weld, Stone Barrington's office." She listened for a moment. "Please hold. It's somebody named Jack Coulter," she said. "He wants to come with his wife to see you tomorrow about legal representation. He says Eduardo sent them."

Stone laughed. "Eduardo again?"

Joan laughed, too. "No, this time it's Eduardo Bianci."

"Make the appointment for late morning."

Joan pressed the button. "Mr. Barrington can meet with you at eleven AM, if that's convenient. Fine, let me give you the address. Then we'll see you and Mrs. Coulter at eleven." She hung up.

"Who are Mr. and Mrs. Jack Coulter?" Stone asked.

"I don't know, but his voice sounded oddly familiar. I don't know of anyone by that name, though."

Stone rolled first one suitcase, then the other into the wine cellar and locked the door.

"It smells not so hot in here," Joan said.

"Yes. Please get Helene and Fred in here first thing in the morning to clean the carpet around the sofa. There was a little accident yesterday."

Joan pressed the VOICE MAIL button on the phone. "Stone, it's Kate Lee. I haven't heard from you, but we're changing our dinner to Monday evening at seven, if you're available. Call me on the cell number."

"Was that the first lady?"

"Yes. I didn't have the opportunity to call her back." He did so and got her voice mail. "Kate, I'm sorry I couldn't get back to you sooner, but I was . . . tied up. I'd love to see you this evening at seven." He hung up.

"You look tired," Joan said.

"Yes, that's why I'm going to go upstairs to bed. I didn't get a lot of sleep last night, and counting bags of money is tiring."

"See you tomorrow, then. Don't oversleep and forget your dinner."

Stone took the elevator; he was too tired to walk up the stairs.

60

Stone slept through the afternoon. He woke around six PM and reflected on the past few days and weeks. Three people were dead, one of them someone he had grown fond of, before she had betrayed him for money. Still, she had saved his life, after endangering it, so he couldn't feel too badly toward her.

He struggled out of bed and got into the shower and shaved, then got a cab to the Carlyle.

Special Agent Griggs of the Secret Service met him at the elevator when he reached the Lees' floor.

"Welcome back, Agent Griggs," Stone said.

"Thank you, Mr. Barrington," Griggs said. "I was reassigned last week, this time for the duration. By the way, while I was serving in Florida, we came across some more of those old hundred-dollar-bills my partner and I visited you about."

"Any resolution of the case?" Stone asked.

"I'm afraid not. I did some looking around, but I just told my boss that it was a waste of our time, and he agreed."

"I'm glad it's off your mind," Stone said.

"The president and Mrs. Lee are expecting you," Griggs said, then walked him down the hallway to the door, motioning for another agent to step aside. Griggs rang the bell. "Good to see you, Mr. Barrington."

"And you, Agent Griggs."

Kate opened the door and pulled him inside. She gave him a big hug. "Exciting news," she said. "We'd like to tell you together." She took his hand and pulled him into the living room, where Will Lee already had a glass in his hand. He stood up to greet Stone with a warm handshake.

"The usual?" Kate asked.

"Please."

She handed him the drink, and they all sat down. "The others will be here in a little while," Will said, "but we wanted to see you first."

"Oh?"

"First, there's this." He picked up a white envelope and handed it to Stone.

"What's this?"

"Read it, then forget about it. I have."

Stone opened the envelope and extracted a heavy sheet of paper. Across the top were emblazoned the words PRESIDENTIAL PARDON. And under that was printed the name THEODORE THOMAS FAY.

"The pardon is sealed, as you suggested," Will said. "It will not be released to the press. And I have seen that his name has been removed from every law enforcement and intelligence database."

"Thank you, Mr. President. I'm very grateful to you."

"And we are very grateful to you, Stone, for your friendship and good advice over the years. Now, I will trust you to see that the document is delivered into the right hands at an early date, and we'll say no more about it, ever."

"Now, our other news," Kate said. "I have decided to run now, not later, for the Democratic nomination for president, and we're making the announcement tomorrow. The others of the Group of Twenty-one will be joining us for dinner shortly."

"What changed your mind about the timing?" Stone asked.

"A reporter for the Washington Bureau of the *New York Times* got somebody — who cares who? — to talk. Confronted with the impending publishing of the story, Will and

I talked it over and decided to go now, even if we have missed some primaries."

"This is going to be very exciting," Stone said. "I congratulate you, and I promise you my vote and as many more as I can muster up for you."

"We'll be handing out other envelopes for everybody after dinner, outlining my positions on just about every issue in detail. If you have time to read them, they will give you much ammunition for mustering those votes and, especially, for fund-raising."

"I'll start phoning my unsuspecting friends tomorrow," Stone said.

The doorbell rang again, and people began to file into the penthouse apartment. The Lees and Stone joined them, and Stone folded the envelope and put it into an inside pocket.

61

Stone was at his desk at ten AM, and his first call was to Mike Freeman.

"Good morning, Mike."

"Good morning, Stone. Good weekend?"

"I haven't decided yet, but now I'd like to make one more attempt to make a bank deposit."

"I'll send my people immediately."

"I'd be grateful if you'd come with them, if you're free. I have something to pass privately to you."

"I can manage that. Half an hour?"

"Perfect." Stone hung up and buzzed Joan. "Now, please get me Eduardo Bianci."

Peter, Eduardo's butler, took the call, ascertained that Stone was Stone, then put the call through.

"Good morning, Stone."

"Good morning, Eduardo. I hope you are well."

"Better than I have any right to be," the

old man replied.

"I understand you have sent me a new client."

"That is so. Hillary is the widow of my good friend Thomas Foote, and she has told me that she is uncomfortable with being represented by the firm that handled Tom's affairs. Naturally, I thought of you and Woodman & Weld. I think your experience in handling your own late wife's estate will stand you in good stead with Hillary's case."

"As always, I'm grateful for your good thoughts, Eduardo."

"I hope that when you meet with her you'll like her — and her new husband, Jack Coulter, who I found to be bright and very good company at dinner last evening. I believe Jack's intentions are only for his wife's welfare. He seems to wish nothing of hers for himself."

"He sounds like a good fellow. I'm seeing them in just a few minutes, so perhaps I'd better go."

"May I call you for dinner one night soon?"

"Of course. By the way, Kate Lee will be speaking to the press on television today. I think you would find it interesting to watch. We can talk more about that when we meet."

"I shall look forward to it. Goodbye, Stone."

"Goodbye, Eduardo."

Stone hung up and watched as Joan wheeled in a little folding cart, holding three legal boxes. "What's that?"

"Mrs. Coulter has sent these over."

"I hope she doesn't expect me to read them before her arrival."

"No, I don't think so. And I hear someone at the front door."

"That would be Mike Freeman and his merry men."

He shook Mike's hand and excused himself for a moment. He went to the wine cellar, unlocked it, and rolled out the first suitcase, then returned for the second. "There you are, Mike. Mr. Crockwell is expecting your men. Have them tell him the load is ten percent lighter than when he last saw it."

When the men had gone, Stone poured Mike some coffee and gave him the white envelope. "I was asked to see that this reached the appropriate hands as soon as possible. Those would be yours, then his."

Mike opened the envelope and looked at the pardon. "How on earth did you do this?"

"I asked, God help me, and it was delivered in secret and sealed from the eyes of all. You may tell the gentleman that his name and any record have been expunged from all law enforcement and intelligence files, at his benefactor's order. He is, today, a new man. Tell him to wear it well and that I am grateful to him for my son's life and mine."

"I'll do that," Mike said. "I'm flying to L.A. this afternoon, and I'll deliver it personally." He drank the last of his coffee. "Joan tells me you have an eleven o'clock, so I'll run. Dinner?"

"Tomorrow?"

"Done." Mike left.

Joan buzzed him. "Mr. and Mrs. Coulter are here."

"Please send them in."

She came in first, and Stone saw an attractive, stylish woman in her late forties, then he saw her husband, who was very tall, slim, and wore a mustache and thick, salt-and-pepper hair, and a very good suit. He didn't know the man, and when he spoke that didn't help either. But why was he familiar?

"Mr. Barrington, I am Jack Coulter, and this is my wife, Hillary, until last week, Hillary Foote."

"How do you do, Mr. Barrington," she said.

They arranged themselves in the chairs provided, and Stone took one, too. "Please tell me how I may help you," he said.

Coulter spoke up. "We dined last evening with Eduardo Bianci, who, I understand, is your old friend, as well as Hillary's. Hillary feels the need for new representation."

"Yes, Eduardo called this morning, and I have just received the records of your old representation." Stone nodded at the legal boxes.

"That is everything I have in the way of records, Mr. Barrington," Hillary said, "and they go back some years before my late husband's death. I hope you will find the time to go through them, and afterward, that we may meet again to discuss my needs."

"Of course, Mrs. Coulter."

"Hillary, please."

"Hillary, I and Woodman & Weld will be very happy to represent you and your husband. If you will write a letter to the head of your old firm, announcing your having obtained new representation, and asking him to turn over his firm's records of your account to me, that would be very helpful. When I have received everything, I and my associates will go through everything, then send you a letter outlining our firm's services and fees, and if you will be so kind, sign a copy and return it to me. When we have done that, I will phone you and arrange another meeting."

"You are very brisk, Mr. Barrington, and I appreciate that. By the way, I knew your late wife, Arrington. We were quite good friends, to the extent that people who live on different coasts can be good friends."

"I'm sorry I didn't know you when she was still alive," Stone said. "One evening soon, perhaps you and Jack will come to dinner and we can get to know each other better."

Hillary stood, and Stone and Jack stood with her.

As he walked them to the door he took Jack's elbow. "Jack, have we met before?"

"Yes, but only briefly," Jack replied. "When I next see you I'll tell you more."

"I'll look forward to it." Stone waved them out.

Joan came into his office. "Do you know who that is?"

"Which one?"

"The woman. She's Hillary Foote! Very wealthy, very high-society."

"I guess I don't read those magazines," Stone said. "Tell me, was her husband familiar to you?"

"No, not at all."

"He said we'd met briefly, but I can't place him." Stone pointed to the legal boxes. "Bring the first one over to my desk, and let's start going through them and separating the wheat from the chaff."

She did so, and Stone began to learn about Hillary Foote Coulter. Later, he would make a point of learning about her husband.

ABOUT THE AUTHOR

Stuart Woods is the author of more than fifty novels, including the *New York Times*-bestselling Stone Barrington and Holly Barker series. He is a native of Georgia and began his writing career in the advertising industry. *Chiefs,* his debut in 1981, won the Edgar Award. An avid sailor and pilot, Woods lives in New York City, Florida, and Maine.

The employees of Thorndike Press hope you have enjoyed this Large Print book. All our Thorndike, Wheeler, and Kennebec Large Print titles are designed for easy reading, and all our books are made to last. Other Thorndike Press Large Print books are available at your library, through selected bookstores, or directly from us.

For information about titles, please call:
(800) 223-1244

or visit our Web site at:
http://gale.cengage.com/thorndike

To share your comments, please write:

Publisher
Thorndike Press
10 Water St., Suite 310
Waterville, ME 04901